STREETS
ON FIRE

STREETS
ON FIRE

A JACK LIFFEY MYSTERY

John Shannon

An Otto Penzler Book

CARROLL & GRAF PUBLISHERS
NEW YORK

STREETS ON FIRE

Carroll & Graf Publishers
An Imprint of Avalon Publishing Group Inc.
161 William Street, 16th Floor
New York, NY 10038

First Carroll & Graf edition 2002

Library of Congress Cataloging-in-Publication Data is available.

ISBN: 0-7867-1018-7

Printed in the United States of America
Distributed by Publishers Group West

For the members of the Suicide Club.

All that tight, crazy feeling of race as thick in the street as gas fumes. Every time I stepped outside I saw a challenge I had to accept or ignore. I had to make one decision a thousand times: *Is it now? Is now the time?*

—Chester Himes

one

Seven Degrees of Racism

Ab Ibrahim leaned out the window of his black Carrera for a better look. The two boys were about twelve. Their fingers were interlaced atop their heads, elbows jutting, like POWs in one of those grainy photographs from Europe from way back in the black-and-white war. A big white cop had one boy's face mashed against the graffiti-covered concrete block wall.

Ab—for Abdullah—Ibrahim double-parked beside what his white classmates in west Chicago had grown up calling a beater and his few black friends called a hoopty: a rusted and banged-up old Oldsmobile. He unfolded his tall frame out of the Porsche.

He could hear the boy whimpering a little.

"What's the problem here?" Ab Ibrahim asked.

"Who are you, with the mouth?" a second cop challenged, turning and resting a palm menacingly on the butt of his holstered pistol. He was skinny and wiry, and his hooded eyes came to rest on Ab Ibrahim with predatory languor.

This cracker five-oh doesn't know who I am, Ab Ibrahim thought with surprise. "I might be the vice mayor for all you know."

"Fuckin'-A roger that. We already had us a *brother* mayor. One is just skippy plenty. You best drive on, *sir*."

"Or I might be the nigger from your nightmares," he added, in an even tone of voice.

"You tryin' a head up with me?"

Ab Ibrahim was perfectly aware that it was not a good idea for an African American to challenge a white cop at random in Los Angeles—or anywhere else in the country, for that matter. You always had a 10 or 20 percent chance of things going nuclear, but sometimes life just threw you a knuckleball.

"*Please* move along, sir."

He was an expert on knuckleballs, if anyone was, and no twelve-year-old deserved to be treated this way. He liked to see himself sometimes as the soul and defender of South Central, unlike so many other black stars who bought white shoes for golf and moved to Bel Air with the movie Jews or took up residence in Baldwin Hills with the black bankers and doctors.

"*Now*, sir."

Knuckleballs. He wished he had a baseball in his hand right then, so he could try his knuckler out on the wall just a little right of the cracker cop's forehead, maybe two inches. Last year—his first full one out of the minors—he had won twenty-three games for the Dodgers with a knuckleball so fierce and unpredictable he loved watching Boogie Jeeter blanch every time the catcher had to break down and offer him the crooked-finger sign that let him throw it. His grandfather had taught him the knuckler: Cornbread Wilson, who'd won thirty games with it for the Pittsburgh Crawfords in the old Negro leagues.

"It's Ab!" one of the kids cried. "Help us, bwah. We dint do *nothin'*."

The crackers still didn't get it. The big one caught Ab Ibrahim's eye and mashed the boy's face a little more, just as a taunt. "Do us a favor, Slick, and shuffle on out of here. Everything is under control."

"That's what you'd like to think." He had a temper and it was starting to fray. "Po-lice brutality got an odor to it."

"What odor would that be now?"

"Maybe like bad sex on a little bitty dick."

"Well, try this odor, Slick." The wiry cop yanked a little tube out of his belt and started hissing it in Abdullah Ibrahim's face.

Ab screamed; then he found himself wrestled flat onto his burning face on the sidewalk, with a strong crooked arm levering up on his neck and a nasty voice *heh-heh*-ing in his ear.

"How you like that odor, Mr. Buttinski?"

The arm squeezed its choke hold another inch, and the tall black man wearing the expensive beige suit slipped into unconsciousness. The boys peered around, dumbstruck.

One of the boys started to cry, but the other struck a pose of high disdain. "You just got busy on the great Abdullah Ibrahim, *fool*. Booyah! I hope they eff yo' dead mama when this be on the TV."

The two cops locked eyes and tried not to look at the unconscious man. Already they could hear the plaintive siren of their backup, the patrol sergeant, heading their way from the 77th Street Division headquarters.

Tall young men were playing some form of netless basketball in the street, arching the ball high through an invisible hoop, and they yielded languidly to his car, ceding just a few more inches than he needed. Beyond them, Brighton Street south of 60th was lined with extremely tall fan palms, like a photo stretched out of proportion. The trees all nodded east, away from the prevailing sea breeze, but the fronds weren't even stirring now in the August heat inversion. Almost 100 degrees, and it wasn't even noon yet.

Jack Liffey wiped an arm across his sweaty forehead and wondered what this part of town would be called. To most Anglos it was an African-American area and therefore Watts, but that showed how little most Anglos knew about the heart of their own city. The 1965 riots had made the name Watts a synonym for *ghetto* a generation ago, but Watts was really only a tiny district ten miles farther to the southwest and across the Harbor Freeway. Watts wasn't even very black anymore. The relentless wave of immigrant Latinos spreading out of east and central LA had swept over Watts long ago, leaving it mostly Spanish-speaking. Even here on Brighton the

Latinos were buying in; he could see a few of the lovely old craftsman bungalows sprayed with pink stucco and their porches restruc-
tured with homemade arches.

It was a shame, he thought, because he liked craftsman architecture,
but everybody had a right to make their homes more homey. If it were
the French moving in, there'd be mansard roofs and little carriage
lamps.

He found the address, and it was a well-kept craftsman with the
porch off-center and a little draped napkin of manicured lawn down
a shallow slope. A light-skinned girl sat on a plastic tractor too
small for her. She was maybe eleven, with cornrowed and beaded
hair, and she looked dreamily off at the powder blue sky.

As he parked and got out, the girl watched him without any of the
suspicion he expected. He guessed that a white face down here
would usually mean cop or caseworker.

"Lemme tell you, mister, they was this big revolt of the rhinestone
animals," she began without prologue.

"Go for it," he said.

"They was all ready to go on they picnic one day, the donkey and
the elephant and the cocky spaniel too, and the mama just up and
say no, they got to stay home and clean up they room." She rattled
on for a while as he grinned at her, pinned in place by her insistent
garrulousness. This is one lonely child, he thought.

Finally he caught her in a breather. "Is your name Davis?"

"Ornetta Boyce," she said. "Ban Davis live here, though."

"I'll catch the rest of the story in a bit. I've got to talk to him."

She didn't seem disappointed. She leapt off the tractor and ran
into the house, calling out.

Normally he wouldn't be taking a job in the black community
where he was at such a disadvantage, but he'd been referred by a
friend, a black detective who'd decided he couldn't take the job himself. It was the first job he'd ever had where he knew pretty much all
the details in advance. All you had to do was mix sex, race, and
crime, and you'd make the front page in LA for weeks.

It had happened two months back. Amilcar Davis and Sherry
Webber had been juniors at Pomona College out in Claremont when

they'd disappeared together on prom night, with Amilcar's classic 1958 Impala eventually turning up five miles from campus in one of the last surviving San Gabriel Valley orange groves. An interracial couple was ordinary enough these days, but these two had been extra prickly about it, running afoul of enough people to send several police jurisdictions rummaging up a dozen blind alleys.

An old black man leaning on a walking stick appeared on the porch to invite him in. He had a magnificent white beard like an Old Testament prophet and his bushy Afro, shorter than his beard, was going white too. He looked great in it, but blacks tended to look great in anything, Jack Liffey thought, even yellow trousers and violet shirts. He wondered why that was.

"You're Mr. Liffey?" There was no complicated handshake. He seemed too old to be the missing boy's father, but Jack Liffey thought the papers had said he was. "Come in, please."

There was an educated southern drawl to his voice. The front room was a shock, like falling through into an alternate universe. It was all clean blond Danish modern furniture, the stuff that had been the cat's pajamas in the fifties. There was also an outsized African mask on the wall that was striking enough to make Picasso jealous.

"Wow," Jack Liffey said involuntarily, as he locked eyes with the mask. It took a few minutes for the old man to struggle across the threshold and catch up with him. "Is it real?"

The man's eyes went to the mask, as if seeing it fresh. "We got that in Guinea a long time ago, but I'm afraid *real* is too metaphysical for me."

Jack Liffey laughed, letting his eyes drift over the big startled rectangular ebony mouth and the too-tall wood nose. He wondered what religious or social function the mask had been designed to fulfill.

"I was the guest of an anthropologist out there," the man explained. "You know what he called these things? *Bois*." His voice took on a dismissive sarcasm. "Wood. It's all made for overseas sale and buried in the dirt for a few months to age it."

"It's still beautiful."

The girl squealed happily somewhere in the house. Beside the mask there were framed prints that he recognized as Danny Lyon photographs of the early days of the Student Nonviolent Coordinating Committee: brave black girls singing in a jail cell, a haggard white woman screaming in the face of an interracial picket line, young blacks crowding into a lunch counter. One was signed and dated: *For Ban, Mississippi, 1963.*

"Danny Lyon," Jack Liffey said appreciatively.

Bancroft Davis placed one very dark wrinkled finger under a determined young face at the lunch counter. This man looked a little older than the others, with a pipe in his fist and the beginnings of a mustache. "Me. This was a SNCC sit-in at the Toddle Inn in Wavecrest, Mississippi. Not the first time I went to jail, not the last."

"I'm impressed. I was a sophomore in college, but I wasn't brave enough to go to Mississippi Summer."

"I wasn't brave enough either," Bancroft Davis said. "I was a sharecropper's boy, already thirty years old and trying hard to emulate all those confident college boys down from the North like Bob Moses, scared out of my wits. You do what you have to, and later you wonder how in the Lord's name you did it."

A woman who looked even older than the man wheeled herself into the living room in a sparkling chrome wheelchair.

"My wife, Genesee Thigpen. This is the man Ivan Monk sent: Jack Liffey."

"Pleased to meet you." Her grip was strong, despite a stringy weak look to her arms. "You're studying my husband's trophy gallery."

"The newspapers said he'd been a CORE leader here in LA, but they didn't say anything about SNCC."

A gentle smile passed between them. "They probably didn't mention the Communist Party either," she said. "That was my bailiwick. Ban and I met at Ann Arbor. We had just formed the Du Bois Club and I was secretary. I arranged a speaking visit for this big rough denim-wearing hero from the civil rights war who blew into town like a typhoon."

"Denim-wearing indeed. I figure Levi Strauss still owes us a big commission. Please sit down, Mr. Liffey."

Jack Liffey settled into a black leather Eames chair and decided not to fight the "mister" at this point.

"When we went out on the campus speaking tour that fall, the college students we saw all wore slacks and tweed sport coats. Have you ever looked at photographs of the Free Speech Movement at Berkeley, Mr. Liffey? That was 1964, and they all look like Minnesota Lutherans on the way to Sunday meeting in their sport coats and skinny ties. We wore jeans down South so we wouldn't stand out, and we continued to wear them in the North as a badge of our struggle. Within two years every student in America was wearing jeans and boots—one of the big unheralded results of the civil rights movement."

It took him a long time to bend and sit on the sofa, and then he rested both palms on his walking stick and looked up with a grave enough-chitchat expression.

"Ivan Monk told us he was committed to another job that he could not get away from, and that you would be better for this investigation in any case. You're good at finding missing kids, he said. And you'll be better off where the trail begins out in Claremont. Amilcar always said the colleges there have only about a dozen black students, most of them exchange students from Africa."

"It's probably a little better than that," Jack Liffey said. "There's six colleges in town. I already know the TV news version of their disappearance. What don't I know?"

"Did the TV mention they'd had a run-in at a blues club with a motorcycle gang from Fontana?"

"Endlessly. Interracial couple harassed by skinhead bikers. The TV fed on that for a week, but it didn't seem to go anywhere. The fact that you're hiring a detective probably means you don't think the police did their job very enthusiastically."

"On the contrary, Mr. Liffey," Genesee Thigpen put in. "There's a man in Claremont, Lieutenant Calderón, who kept us well informed. We know they tried, even the FBI tried for a few weeks, but the locals don't have the resources or persistence of a big-city police force."

"It's been two months now. What do you think happened?"

"I don't think they just eloped," the woman said, with a hard edge. "That's what some of the police concluded. From the beginning, everybody except Calderón publicly discounted any thought that their disappearance had anything to do with race."

"Mr. Liffey," the man said, "at Claremont you will meet people who almost universally *think* they are not racist. It's not quite the same thing as not *being* racist."

"Yes, sir, I believe I know that."

The little girl came barreling through the room with a whoop and hurled herself onto the old woman, who rocked back and looked like she'd have a hard time looking after an energetic child.

"What is it, Ornetta?"

"I just wanna be with you."

Genesee Thigpen brushed a soothing hand over the girl's head and shoulders, and the child quieted.

"I'm not free of it myself," Jack Liffey said. They all knew what *it* was, except perhaps the girl.

They went quiet for a moment. It wasn't a topic anyone in America dealt with very well, and he figured he'd better meet it head on.

"Let me tell you one reason I know my own failings, before you decide whether to hire me. Several years ago I was working in aerospace out in El Segundo, and I was a bit more interested in science than I am now. One evening I was watching a Nova program on particle physics. I was talking to my daughter at the same time, so the TV only had part of my attention. Then all of a sudden my eye caught a black face talking about neutrinos, and I had to look immediately at the type at the bottom of the screen—you know, telling who he was. You see what I mean? I'd just sat through a dozen talking heads without giving who they were a second thought because they were white or Asian. But a black face? Unconsciously I had to check his credentials right off."

Bancroft Davis smiled. "Mr. Liffey, there are a lot of people around here who'd say nothing in this country has changed, whites are all the same no matter what they tell you, and conditions haven't gotten a bit better since slavery. Some of the militant kids say things like that. I'd like to take those kids on a tour of Mississippi back in 1947. I believe there are seven identifiable degrees of racism, and being snubbed is always better than being lynched. According to Ivan, you're not so bad, and that's good enough for us right now. You're hired if you want the job."

They talked awhile longer, covering the background. Their son had maintained his contacts in the local community and he'd come home every summer. He'd been an A-minus student, studying American history with his eye on Stanford Law or Berkeley's Boalt Hall. The girlfriend's parents had been sweet, kindly people up in Simi Valley, only a little uneasy that their daughter had a black boyfriend.

"Can I ask an uncomfortable question?" Jack Liffey said, as the man was winding down.

"If you can't, you're not much of a detective."

He smiled. "Touché. You both seem pretty old to be the parents of a twenty-year-old."

The little girl perked up.

"Amilcar was adopted, Mr. Liffey," Genesee Thigpen said, "as was his older sister, Ornetta's mother. We put off children because of our political work, and then I found out it was too late for me. Also, since we seem to be sharing, we're married but I kept my family name on political principle. I didn't leave the Party until after Poland, and I was well-known under the name Thigpen. Why did I wait so long to leave? I don't know: inertia? hope? I got tired of the road to socialism always turning out to be lined with Russian tanks. Oh, yes—Bancroft never joined. He was always too independent-minded and skeptical. And that's all our skeletons."

"I can't think of anyone I'd rather share skeletons with," Jack Liffey said. "Ornetta, please come sit on the porch and tell me the rest of your story about the rhinestone animals."

She skipped out the door as he said good-bye to the elders, and then he got to hear a remarkably peculiar and inventive tale about imaginary animals fighting back against oppressive human masters who expected them to do chores they hated. He kept thinking of his fourteen-year-old daughter, Maeve, and how she would like this bright little girl.

As he walked down to the car, he heard sirens in the distance, several of them. They sounded more like fire trucks than police cars or ambulances. There must have been quite a fire somewhere, but he couldn't see any smoke against the bright cloudless sky. Maybe it was just the mounting heat that made him think of fire. He waved back to the little girl, who gave an oddly foreign-looking wave in reply, holding her arm straight out and closing her fingers against her palm.

He wished he'd left the car window down. Baking heat tumbled out the door when he opened it and he swung it a few times to whiff some fresh air inside. He couldn't roll down the far-side windows because the whole right side of the car had been crushed in a partial rollover and the windows were now plastic and duct tape. One of these days he'd get the money to fix it up or replace the whole car, but the truth was he'd gotten used to it that way. My God, he thought, working out the dates, the old AMC Concord had been like that almost two years. There was a security in letting it go to seed. It was such a ghastly junker no one in his right mind would try to steal it.

On his way home along Slauson, sunlight seemed to bleach every corner of the universe to a painful brilliance. Just at Crenshaw, he saw a black man in a spiffy polo shirt standing alongside the road juggling what looked like hand tools. He slowed the car to check it out and saw the tools pass behind the man's back one by one and then heave up into the air: a big roofing hammer, a battery-powered drill that he whizzed every time it hit his hand, an awkward carpenter's square, and a small chain saw. He could tell by the angry buzz in the air that the chain saw was actually operating. Worth two points: He and Maeve had a running contest of pointing out LA oddities to each other.

A car honked behind and he drove on. When life became too strange, it made you uneasy; he yearned for a world he could ignore more often. So much raggedness made him feel old and tired.

"Young lady."

Maeve Liffey didn't like the sound of that as she turned back in the living room, carrying the old manual camera she and Dru had been using to learn about f-stops and shutter speeds. The tone surprised her. Brad wasn't a complete jerk-off, and he didn't usually try to discipline her. He had only been married to her mother for nine months, and he was still a bit uneasy in his step-dad role.

"Yes, Brad." He didn't really like being called Brad, but he could hardly insist on Dad.

"The back gate was open and the twins could have got out." The twins were his three-year-old boys, Bert and Bart; she sometimes figured he remarried only to get free babysitting.

"I'm sorry. It must have been my friend Dru, when she left. I asked her to shut it."

"That's as it may be, but I made a special point of asking *you*."

"I'm *sorry*. Really. I'll double-check from now on."

"They might have wandered away and been hurt. I'm afraid I'm going to have to ground you for the rest of the week."

Blood rushed to her face. She could feel it, but she tried to establish control, the way her dad had shown her. Three . . . two . . . one . . . *reconsider*. "Could we wait and talk about it when Mom comes back? I think this is threatening to get out of proportion."

"Young lady, are you questioning me?"

"Am I a *serf* in this house now?" It just burst out of her unbidden. "Have I no right to speak up for myself?"

He was stewing. She could see emotions seething right behind his face, and his hands were trembly. It could probably have gone either way. She felt a terrible fear rise in her, as if she had torn something that could not be mended, but she didn't see where there had been any choice.

"I'm sorry," she said quickly. "I know you worry about your boys."

But it was too late. His arm came out of left field, an astonishing act, like an object suddenly levitating in front of her. Her cheek stung and her head snapped back. Already tears were prickling behind her eyes.

"Go to your room!" He looked frightened, too, but he did not know how to step back across the brink.

Eat shit and die, she thought. You'll never *ever* be my dad. She had never been hit before, not once. And she had a dire premonition that her mother would take his side in this, even though she wouldn't really be comfortable doing it.

When the king is unjust, she remembered reading somewhere, *it affects the whole kingdom.*

A box fan was roaring away, exhausting the hot air out his front door, and his girlfriend's nephew Rogelio was dangled over the fender of a 1972 Chevelle SS in the drive, muttering at his friend Solomon and at the big carburetor.

"Trouble?"

"Man, don't never use a four-barrel. You know? Hey, Jack."

Rogelio had a dependent hangdog manner that made it hard not to tease him, but Jack Liffey liked him a lot. The young man was kind to a fault; Jack knew he'd had the decency to turn down the mild sexual experimentation Maeve had offered him a year ago. Maeve was a precocious *almost fifteen,* in her words.

"I always prefer a supercharger for an AMC car," Jack Liffey said.

Solomon cackled a little and held out a palm for a greeting slap. Jack Liffey obliged.

"Where do you get high octane for that thing?" Jack Liffey asked.

"Every time you get gas, you got to buy these cans of booster to high it up. That's not the problem here, though."

"Mar in?"

"Yeah." As if just remembering something, Rogelio tried to straighten up and banged his head on the raised hood. "Ooh, *hurt.* When you see her, don't get too disturbed. She fell down moving boxes or something at church and hit her face. She got a bad shiner."

"Were you with her?"

"Naw, Catholic's still good enough for me."

"Thanks."

Marlena had taken to going to a big fundamentalist temple in Hawthorne called the Church of the Open Barn Door. It didn't make him very happy, but it seemed to soothe something needy in her. He found her hanging laundry on the lines out back over the scruffy lawn, and the tight black skirt stretched over her ample rump set his libido thrumming right away.

She cupped a hand over the side of her face when she turned. "Oh, Jackie, I done a stupid thing."

"Rocky warned me."

"I was moving some rummage boxes down in the basement of the church and slipped on a rotten old grape down there. My face hit a old blender in the box."

She opened her palm like a door to show a mouse under her eye the size of a plum. It all seemed too pat. She had been too quick to volunteer details.

He hugged her, and there was something stiff in her response. He wondered if there was trouble at the church. "Who's minding your shop?"

"Anna. Maeve was supposed to, but she didn't make it. Remember? Maeve was gonna do Mondays for the summer. But Anna needs the work."

He didn't remember any plans like that at all, and he was surprised one of them hadn't told him. Maeve got on well with Marlena, though she lived most of the time with his ex-wife, Kathy, and her new husband. The shop was Marlena's Mailboxes-R-Us franchise, which had been directly beneath the office he had once kept in a minimall. His office now was a letter drop at her shop, a retrenchment to get him through a long dry spell in his finances.

They were interrupted for a moment when his dog sidled up and growled for attention. Loco must have spooked her horrible little chihuahua into a back bedroom. Loco was a scruffy medium-size whitish dog with flat yellow eyes, at least half coyote, and generally did his best to shun anything that could be construed as pet behavior. Lately Loco had taken to being more affectionate, so Jack Liffey bent over to hug the dog for a moment. He'd better not pass up any devotion he could get.

"Hey, boy, how's tricks?"

The dog gave another little growl and then broke free and wandered away.

"Be sure you don't overdo it. I might get to wanting my slippers fetched."

Marlena chuckled. Loco glanced back once disdainfully, like a being who'd been marooned on an inferior planet.

Jack Liffey thought about it and decided his own species was best, after all. He stood up and kissed Marlena's cheek softly. "Um, you tender here?"

"No. Feels good."

"How about here?"

"Ooooh. Try here, Jackie." She directed his hand, and before long they were in the bedroom, trying a lot of places.

two

It's Not Our Way

The driver of the van had a marine buzz cut and a white line across the edge of one lip that suggested one of the dueling scars Prussians had once given themselves in order to look fierce and brutish. It sure did the job for him. He was big, too, wide through the shoulders like somebody who had been built to fill up a doorway. When he smiled, though, a lot of the ferocity evaporated to leave an earthy ruggedness, the look of a guy you'd like to see in charge of the Scout troop when the blizzard hit.

The man with the salt-and-pepper beard beside him drummed a little nervous tattoo on the dash. "K, tell me again what in Satan's crappy name we're doing here."

"We're doing just what I said."

"Uh-huh, yeah. But, you know, we're super-de-duper out of place."

"No kidding."

It was well after midnight and they waited for some signal, known only to the driver, parked smack in the middle of the black community. A third man crouched in the back of the van with the wood beams and kerosene. "I've never done this before," the bearded man offered.

"Not many people in California have," the big man with the scar said. "That's part of the point. After we do it, who would you look for? Would you come looking for us?"

"Nobody's looking *now*, man."

"They will. Look, here's the theory. My uncle used to play bridge using the Chico Marx system. He never consulted his partner at all, just called out crazy bids—three hearts, one no-trump, five spades, whatever—and never let on. He said it gave his team an edge. One hundred percent of the other team was confused, but only fifty percent of his team was."

"You told us all that before, K," the bearded man said with a hint of annoyance. "Very funny and all, but I mean, really, what are we doing?"

"Okay. Really. I mean, cross my heart, right? *Really*. Sorry I didn't use little words. Here it is: We're the Green Berets of the fed-up honest people of this country. We know that multiculturalism as an idea and a social experiment has up and died. It sounded nice, it made some people feel real good inside, but it just didn't work out. People want to live with their own kind. We're not nutcases, we're just facing the facts ahead of the crowd. And one of the facts we get to face tonight is we got to muddy the waters a bit now because we— that's *you*, fuckhead—screwed up big-time."

"Is this all Christian?" the man in back asked.

"We're about to make a big wood cross. Can you think of anything more Christian than that?"

Jack Liffey never failed to get a kick out of the giant brown doughnut. It was a good twenty feet in diameter and crested the little drive-up building at Vernon and 11th like the beacon of some high-fat religion stuck in the heart of the black west side.

"Hi, Josette. Ivan in?"

She looked up from a flat tray of sugary crullers. Ivan Monk had bought the doughnut shop with his Merchant Marine savings to tide himself over during slack times in the private eye business. Jack Liffey wished he had something similar as fallback. Josette Williams,

Ivan Monk's only full-time employee, looked a lot thinner than he remembered, and a bit abstracted.

"Jack. He workin' in back. You gettin' any?"

"Regular as clockwork." He came back and leaned on the counter
to take a good look at her. "What's the matter, Jo?"

She winced. "I been had a pretty bad time, thank you for axing.
I got to using the Big Bad Boy for a time, but I went cold. They got
me on the methadone."

"I thought crack was the thing now."

"You out in left field. H is back for sure, but not for this girl. I
know it end up losing me my Jimmy."

"I'm glad you're clean. If Mar and I can help you any, let me
know."

"Thank you kindly, Jack. Maybe you could take Jimmy to the
basketball sometime."

Ivan was down a corridor behind a swing door in an inner office.
He was on the telephone and beckoned Jack Liffey in. Ivan was the
size of a pro linebacker and always looked like he wanted to tear
your arm off, but he had a sweet side. You just had to be around long
enough for it to show itself.

He had a sheaf of papers he was studying on his desk. "I want you
to change that same stuff on page fifty-five, too. I'm not like that.
You see, down ten lines, it say, 'You just a no-good yellow mother-
fuckin' dog.' That's *lame*, man." He made about a dozen faces, as if
an idea was working its way painfully down a constricted pipe.
"Okay, then you get back to *me*, Gary."

He put the phone down.

"Hey, Jack. What it is? Guy there is writing up my life. Him and
me working on a screenplay about bein' a detective in South LA and
I got to make sure he get it right."

"Is that what kept you from taking the Amilcar Davis case?"

He shook his head. "I wouldn't go near that one. Nothing but
grief in it. I say to myself, give it to that Jack Liffey. He *likes* grief."

"Gee, thanks, Ive. I'll do *you* a favor sometime. What is it worries you about the case?"

"Lemme think. Nazis on Harleys. A white girlfriend from Simi Valley. A dad who thinks he invented civil rights. A mom who liked Joseph Stalin. And Claremont, a place with nothing but uptight white people locked down in Victorian houses. A salt-and-pepper couple gone missing, two months stale. Cops who aren't gonna like a guy looks like me showing up in Wonderbread City asking questions. Would you like some more reasons? Trust me, it's not going anywhere. It's easy money, if the old dude will pay up, but I don't need the bread right now, not for marking time and upping my blood pressure. And I sure don't need the aggravation of putting my face around in *Claremont*."

"So you're pretty sure it's hopeless, even for Mr. Wonderbread?"

"You right, and you know you right." He made that series of faces again. Maybe it was his way of changing his mind. "You *might* find out something out there in Snow Whiteville I couldn't. I been wrong before—once."

"Thanks for the referral."

"You done the same for me a couple times."

"And happy to. By the way, you know what's going down over to the east a bit from here? The cops have a lot of barricades up on Vernon."

Ivan Monk stared at him as if he'd just asked how to spell his own name. "I wondered what you were doing over here today. You didn't read the paper this morning, I bet."

"Uh-uh."

"A couple not-so-bright cops roughed up Ab-Ib yesterday. Some folks took it in they mind to get a little payback and torch the police substation on Vernon. It's just a little bitty storefront and will not be mourned, but I have it on good repute that a couple other places burned yesterday too, and it's summer heat so a lot of bangers got nothing better to do these days but get busy."

"Ab-Ib some kind of sports star?"

Ivan Monk didn't deign to answer. He knew Jack Liffey didn't take to sports much, but there were things you just knew if you lived in a town.

"I think I'd better start on the Claremont end of things."

"That would be smart. Take care of bidness far far away from the land of the bad boys."

"This isn't going to turn into another 'ninety-two, is it?"

Ivan Monk shrugged. "Who can say? I doubt it. But I'm thinking of getting out the plywood say BLACK OWNED."

"Uh-oh."

Lieutenant Calderón had agreed to meet him at the police impound yard up on Foothill, but Jack Liffey was an hour early and he settled for driving around the shady streets of Claremont to look the town over. He had been out here on a Sunday drive once in the 1960s to visit some ill-defined relative of his father's, but the downtown was unrecognizable now. What he remembered as a couple of coffee shops, a little variety store named Bob's or something like that, and a family supermarket was now a couple dozen square blocks of pasta bistros, jazz clubs, coffee bars, and chichi boutiques.

How had the world come to this? There were no more people in Claremont now, or in the six little colleges that clustered there. It must just be a lot more money about, he decided. He remembered finding an old *Life* magazine from the 1950s under his dresser a few years back and thumbing through it idly to see glossy display ads for a can of peas, a ballpoint pen, and DEMAND CONCRETE HIGHWAYS— THEY LAST. We weren't really a consumer society yet, he had concluded, startled by the commonplace nature of what was being offered. This deep need for all the material goodies must have sneaked up on the country while he was busy over in Vietnam.

The first campus he ran into, Pomona College, was just a block east of the village shops. It was a daydream of a social class that was utterly beyond his ken, all Corinthian pillars, ivy, long arcades, and big green quads. Five more private colleges inhabited the north and east sides of the town, sharing a big library and other facilities in the middle. The Oxford of California they liked to call it. He'd bet nobody had ever called Oxford the Claremont of England.

It was summer and there weren't many kids around. Still, something was going on out on a big grassy no-man's-land that seemed to separate a couple of the colleges. Yellow crime-scene tape from tree to post to tree cordoned off the middle of the quad, where there was a complicated machine the size of a Greyhound bus, bristling with big cams and gears and belts. Maybe thirty young people stood outside the tape, well back from the machine. Jack Liffey parked and ambled closer across the springy crabgrass.

The leader seemed to be a man who was older and hairier than the rest, wearing a sheepskin vest and standing in front of a portable console of buttons and knobs. There was a video camera on a tripod, and everyone else seemed to have a still camera.

"Flag up!" someone cried, and sure enough a girl on the far side of the quad raised a red flag.

"Fire in the hole!" somebody else called, which gave Jack Liffey a real chill; it was the traditional warning for blasting. In his very limited experience—a few days caught up in Tet in Saigon—it meant a grenade going down into a basement.

"Roll tape!" the leader called out. "Phase two self-immolation." He stabbed at a button on his console and all eyes went to the machine. Belts ground up, wheels spun, a mirrored ball sent sun sparkles everywhere. Jack Liffey wasn't quite sure, but he thought he heard a deep groaning emanate from the machine.

"There it goes there it goes!" somebody called excitedly, as a puff of dark smoke spurted out the side. A big cogwheel spun up into the air, a double-jointed mechanical arm reached out and then flung off its own forearm, and a section of the machine began to bob insanely, like a pigeon strutting along a windowsill.

Cameras ticked and flashed all around him as the near half of the framework tilted and then collapsed on itself.

"All *right*!"

A titter of laughter and then applause spread through the group. The older man pushed another button. "Cut! Okay, let's put it back together." He had a pronounced Eastern European accent.

A few young people offered him hand slaps, and then they stepped over the tape to flood toward the remains of the machine. Jack Liffey drifted over to a young woman in a yellow tank top who seemed to be in charge of the video camera.

"Art project?" he asked.

"Uh-huh. We can only test it in small bites until the big performance in September."

"You like destruction?"

She shrugged. "It's a job. Most of them are volunteers, but I'm paid for the summer. Harvat can get big corporate grants for anything he wants. Like Christo."

Christo was the man who wrapped buildings and mountains and had littered Tejon Pass north of LA with several hundred giant blue umbrellas a few years back. There didn't seem any point mentioning the homeless people downtown who were going hungry, and he didn't really suppose any more people would be fed if the avant-garde gave up their art happenings.

"It *is* social criticism," she added defensively.

"Of what?"

"I'm not sure. The object of social criticism is getting a lot harder to identify these days."

"We have met the enemy and he is us," Jack Liffey said.

"Derrida?"

He shook his head. "Pogo."

She hid out in the garage, tears still streaming down her cheeks. Something about the slap had made her feel terribly weepy. She knew it was way out of proportion, but she felt a dreadful guilt inside. Any physical blow was like a murder to her, and somewhere deep in her psyche she felt you had to have done something really bad to merit a slap.

Well, the hell with Bradley Bartlett, Maeve tried out. *He's nothing to me.* But that didn't really help much. Part of her knew it wasn't really a simple question. In a funny way, what was happening inside her had a lot less to do with her stepfather than with herself, her protected life. Life was finally tossing her a few hard pitches. She had to learn to deal with things. Was it possible to have parents who were too kind and loving? Maybe you were better served getting used to a little cruelty early on. Still, she longed to hug her father and be hugged back.

After a while she calmed down, but she didn't really feel like going back into the house. There was too much in there that she'd have to deal with. It was hot and steamy in the garage, but she felt that was a kind of penance she was paying for being disrespectful.

The corner of a cardboard carton was poking her in the back where she sat, and she squirmed around to straighten it out and then got interested and peeked inside. It was one of her mom's storage boxes from the big house. *The big house*, from when they'd all still lived together, she thought with a pang. How she missed that happy, secure time.

They were slim, colorful books, her mother's childhood books, and she tugged the box out into the light that washed in from the frosted side window of the garage. Mostly they were Nancy Drew mysteries. *The Mystery at Lilac Inn. The Ghost of Blackwood Hall. The Clue of the Velvet Mask. The Crooked Banister.* She plucked one out at random and settled back with it. She'd never read a Nancy Drew.

A few minutes later she was making a face, as if she smelled something bad. The prose was weirdly old-fashioned and terribly earnest, she could feel that much. Still, there was something about the book that swept her up, the pluck, the good cheer, the energy of Nancy Drew, and a whole universe there in River Heights that was susceptible to the good-hearted ministrations of a young girl.

But, oh, dear, she thought, unconsciously echoing Nancy's diction. Right away she found out that the plot turned on a missing will, and the book was titled *The Secret of the Old Clock.*

Duh, she thought, like Homer Simpson, I wonder where the missing will could be hidden?

He was still early to the impound lot, but it appeared Calderón had beat him there and the gate was open. He decided to leave his Concord outside. He wasn't sure he'd ever get it out if it found its spiritual home. The place was full of dusty junkers, parked only inches apart, with grease-pencil scribbles on the windshields. A lot of them were visibly wrecked.

Off to the side was a black 1958 Chevrolet Impala with a lot of chrome, heat off the black metal shimmering the air above it. Calderón was dark and portly, like a campesino, and had the regulation short police mustache. Unlike big-city lieutenants, he wore a uniform.

"Mr. Liffey?"

"Jack. Lieutenant Calderón?"

"José." They shook hands. Another polite cop, he thought. The last few police officers he'd met had all been helpful and mannerly. It was enough to shake your worldview. The man pointed at the Impala.

"This is it. You help me push, we can look inside."

The brake wasn't set, and together they shouldered the big, dusty car out into the central lane. Calderón grunted as he thrust, probably providing more than his share of the manpower. Jack Liffey saw right away that a side window in back had been smashed.

"The car wasn't reported for a week where it sat back in the orange trees, so we assumed the window was vandals, but who knows?"

Because Calderón was small, dark, and portly, Jack Liffey caught himself selling the man short—probably not very worldly, maybe not very clever. Migrant-worker background, up from the ranks, no college. Shit, he thought. It was like reading the caption on TV to see the black man's credentials. Latinos could only be smart if they looked tall and light-skinned, with lots of Spanish blood, and wore big glasses. He hoped his degree of racism didn't show.

"I'm not going to find anything you didn't, am I?"

"Nope. But you can say you tried."

"That's not the point. I'm not in this to make money off Mr. Davis."

"I'm glad. He seemed like a fine gentleman."

It would be too hot to stay inside the black car for long. He poked under the seats and looked in the empty glove compartment. There was a good-luck sticker with a pair of dice showing seven on the dash. Pomona College and Scripps College decals on the rear window, and a couple of Greek letters on the wind wing.

"What's the sigma and omega for?"

"His fraternity at Pomona. You won't have heard of it because they're all locals. They're not even live-in, just social clubs. We found out Amilcar dropped out of his after a year."

"Ah," Jack Liffey said.

"They claim he was just too busy with schoolwork."

"Instead of too black?"

"Presumably they noticed that when they bid him."

He had a wary irony playing around his eyes, and Jack Liffey smiled. "I hear Amilcar could have a chip on his shoulder. No one in town here ever called you names?"

"You mean like wetback?"

"Whatever."

"My folks *were* wetbacks. They swam the Rio Grande to Texas at a place called Las Esperanzas. I'm proud of it."

"Of course, but it still isn't pleasant to be called names."

He pursed his lips. "I've probably been called greaser or bean or taco head or other things ten thousand times in my life. Each time it has a weight, you know. But what I find is if you spread the weight out as evenly as you can, maybe one or two insults a day, you stay on a pretty even keel. It's only when they bunch up on you, all that weight tends to—" He made a gesture with his hand flat in front of him, like a raft going over on one side. "Then you lose it."

"There can't be a lot of Latinos in the Claremont Police Department."

"There can't be a lot of Latinos in Claremont period. But I get to arrest gringos every day. That makes it all worthwhile."

The wry look was back and Jack Liffey smiled. He could see he was going to like José Calderón. "Do you have any hunches on the disappearance that you haven't had the time to follow up?"

"You want me to do *all* your work for you?"

"Why not? I'm not very bright, and it'll save Mr. Davis some money." Sweat was rolling down his neck. He got out of the car.

"Okay, first I'd sit down and read the case file again. Then I'd talk to David Phelps. He was the roommate. He's from here, so he'll be around this summer. Then I'd look into the bikers that got on Amilcar's case outside a Fontana blues club, him having a white girlfriend with him. The FBI talked to them because they had some overlap with the Fourth Reich skinheads, but the suits didn't seem very interested. Then I'd go down to Amilcar's home, your neck of the woods, and talk to Umoja. The boy seems to have retained a paid-up membership."

"Whoa. One at a time."

"Help me put this back." They set their hands on the dusty hood to heave the Impala back into its slot.

"You going to give this to his dad?" Jack Liffey meant the car.

"He hasn't asked for it. I think we're going to want it out of here pretty soon. We're not even sure it's a crime scene."

"Tell me about the bikers."

He slapped dust off his palms. "They're called the Bone Losers." He chuckled. "It was apparently a misspelling for Born Losers, way back when, but it took, and they made a broken legbone their logo. There's the Hell's Angels, Gypsy Jokers, and Satan's Slaves up at the top of the charts, and then way down in single-A ball there's groups like Bone Losers. They're fifteen miles east, in Fontana, and you're welcome to them."

"Umoja?"

"As far as I know, it's a black nationalist outfit in LA. It's about cultural stuff: roots, teaching Swahili, and promoting pan-African unity. You haven't heard of them?"

"Just wanted to know your take on them."

"Come with me," Calderón said. He led Jack Liffey to his plain-wrap, a white Crown Victoria, and he fished a fat manila envelope out through his open window. "This is a Xerox of the case file."

"You really are a godsend. I've never met such a helpful police officer."

"Mr. Davis asked."

Jack Liffey stared thoughtfully at the thick envelope. "Do you have a personal theory?"

"I used to, but theories can get in the way of police work. Sometimes it's best when you're hunting for the truth to have your mind free."

"Free's not bad, but I try to do my hunting on credit," Jack Liffey said.

He hadn't seen any pillars of smoke over South Central so he figured it was okay, but he started getting nervous when he noticed three black-and-whites at the corner of Brighton. Two cops stood watchfully at the corner, but most were just moon faces in the front windows of their sedans, swiveling to follow his progress around the corner and down past 60th. There was another cop car a block short of the Davis house, but that wasn't what caught his attention. Six young black men stood at parade rest along the sidewalk in front of the house, carrying a motley assortment of shotguns and rifles. There was also a hole and a big scorch right in the middle of Bancroft Davis's lawn, near where the little girl Ornetta had been sitting on her tractor.

Jack Liffey parked across the road, and they all got interested fast. Colors were up, blue bandannas knotted on their heads or dangling from a pocket. Crips. As far as he knew, it was legal to carry a long gun in the city, as long as it was unloaded; he didn't think too many of the cops would want to come up and inspect the breeches. He didn't want to, either.

He took a deep breath and crossed the road and was met by a tall, hard-eyed young man with half a dozen earrings and a coal-black teardrop shape tattooed under his right eye.

"What you want here?" He carried a big pump Winchester shotgun, the kind the cops kept strapped to the dashboard. It was pointed diagonally at the sky, but not so far that it couldn't get around in a hurry.

"I need to see Mr. Davis."

"You got bidness?"

"I got business."

There was a long pause. "Who the *fuck* you crackin' off to, Arnold? You a fifth wheel in this 'hood."

The gangbanger got Jack Liffey's back up, even though there was nothing to be gained by antagonizing him. He remembered a rule of life he'd heard once, probably from his pragmatic friend Art Castro: *Never kick a bear unless you can kill it.* It made a lot of sense, but it wasn't a rule he'd ever followed assiduously. His rule had more to do with not giving up the square foot of turf you occupied in life or you'd never get it back.

"I am employed by Bancroft Davis—friend."

"I ain't your *friend*." But he'd gone uneasy. There was a shrill whistle, and the man with the tear glanced to catch some signal from another young man on the porch. He gave Jack Liffey a long look, sucked at his teeth a bit, spat at his feet, and stepped aside.

As Jack Liffey crossed the lawn, he looked at the hole dug in the center of the big scorch and noticed that the area smelled of char and gasoline. Bancroft Davis held the front door open for him. "You're braver than I thought. Or crazier."

"Just crazier. What's going on?"

"While the police were preoccupied last night with a number of disturbances, somebody sneaked up and burned a cross on me."

"No!"

"Big as life. About two A.M."

He followed Jack Liffey slowly into the living room, leaning heavily on his walking stick. Neither the little girl nor his wife were in evidence.

"Come on out back. It's too hot."

It *was* too hot, sweltering and close in the tiny house, ten degrees hotter than outside, though all the sash windows were open.

"Somebody burned a cross in the heart of the black community? That's like those kids out there moving to Coeur d'Alene, Idaho, to start a Crip franchise."

"Uh-huh."

There was a patio of cracked cement with a fine arbor of grape leaves overhead. The rest of the yard was a vegetable garden with tidy lanes and one small square of grass.

"Speaking of those kids. . . ."

"That was BigLenin you were trying to commit suicide with. The name amuses my wife."

"I should think so."

Bancroft Davis lowered himself painfully into a plastic bucket chair. "They're the Rolling 60s Gangsta Crips. This is their 'hood, insofar as that has any meaning these days, and they seem to have adopted me. Genesee says it shows a rudimentary class consciousness."

"Or a predatory mammal's sense of territory. Who do you think burned the cross?"

He shook his head slowly, then shrugged.

"You know," Jack Liffey said, "the whole point of intimidation is we're supposed to know who's doing the intimidating. It doesn't make any sense otherwise."

The old man nodded, probably to indicate the bangers outside. "They think it was *their* enemies, either Eighteenth Street or Mara Salvatrucha. They're big Latino gangs that are encroaching. Mara is Salvadoran and Central American, reputedly started by ex-guerrillas."

"Latinos don't burn crosses. They wouldn't even know what it means."

"Maybe. There's always a few Nazis in the police, or some loose cannons from the white hinterlands. I never could keep track of enemies. All in all, I think you waste your time trying. You just have to do what you have to do without regard to what some warped mind will think of it."

Jack Liffey noticed the alley at the back of the yard, beyond a chain-link fence. It was filled with unspeakable drifts of rubbish, two feet deep. Apparently the city made no effort to clean it out.

"Have you done anything recently to attract bigots?"

"Breathing their air is enough for some of them. But no. My name doesn't come up much anymore. I *was* interviewed on radio about my son's disappearance, though, and Genesee still goes to events, so we're not invisible in this town."

An old German shepherd on a chain finally came awake and sauntered over soundlessly.

"He's pretty quiet."

"She woke me last night, but she couldn't get out front to get at them."

They talked for a while about cross burnings Bancroft had seen in the South, but there was no more useful information forthcoming.

"I hear your son is a member of Umoja," Jack Liffey tried. He was careful not to use the past tense.

The old man thought this over for a moment. "Well, not a *member.* Mr. Liffey, I spent my life fighting for civil rights and integration, and Genesee fought for proletarian internationalism, which she would tell you is an even more inclusive form of integration. Umoja does not believe in having any truck with whites, in any way, shape, or form, and they certainly do not read the writings of German Jews or Hindu pacifists. Cultural nationalism, separatism, call it what you will—it's an understandable response to a lot of unspeakable racial antagonism in this country, but it's not our family's way. And it wasn't Amilcar's.

"That said, Amilcar was a good friend of Kidogo Kukwenda. They went to Manual Arts together, played basketball together, and graduated together, when Kidogo was still Clyde Waters. He's a leader of Umoja's youth wing these days, and he and Ami stayed friends."

"Mr. Davis, I have to ask this. Knowing you and your wife feel the way you do, would Amilcar have told you if he joined up?"

He sighed. "I'd like to think so. He told me he tried crack once. It scared the bejeezus out of him. Anyway, Amilcar has a white girlfriend. That's just about the ultimate no-no for Umoja, and Ami wouldn't have put her at risk of insult. He's a thoughtful young man, respectful of women."

"Do you think Kidogo would talk to me?"

"He will if I ask him to."

For two days now, Jack Liffey had been thinking he wanted nothing more than to sit at this man's feet and ask him to talk about his life, to ask about SNCC and Freedom Summer and the leadership struggles inside the Movement and what Martin Luther King had been like and what he felt about the future of race relations in America, but the timing was obviously wrong, with his son still missing. Still, he couldn't resist entirely.

"How did you happen to come out to California?"

"Like everyone else who came here, I wanted a better life for my family."

"Is it?"

He frowned and sighed. "I think the greatest mistake the African-American people ever made was flooding out of the South for the promise of industrial jobs in the Rust Belt and the West. Look what they did to us. They needed us, particularly during the war. They clustered us and used us for a generation and then they closed all the plants or moved them overseas, and now we're trapped here, discarded, no jobs, away from our roots, with no future."

"You think it was a conspiracy?"

"No, Mr. Liffey, I don't. But it happened. And nobody gives a damn to help fix it."

three

Separating from the Main Craft

She came marching up the road in the early evening, carrying the tiny suitcase like a plucky female Tom Sawyer, and his heart skipped a beat as it always did.

"Punkin, what's up?" Jack Liffey tried to keep it light, sensing that the unannounced visit meant something bad had happened. He took his feet down from the porch railing and tucked the case file back into its envelope.

"I came to stay a bit, if it's all right."

"Is it all right with your mom? The court says I must defer."

"Mom thinks it's a good idea."

He let it go for the moment. "Come on up. How did you get here?"

"I took the bus up PCH and then Lincoln."

"Aw, honey, you've been walking a half hour from Lincoln. You should have called."

"It's okay. It keeps me svelte."

He smiled. "I thought you did that by vomiting."

"Daddy!" He hugged her and felt a little tremble, as well as a kind of clinging he didn't usually get. He also did his best not to notice her large breasts pressing against him. She wasn't a girl starting to grow a woman's features any longer; she had crossed over to having a woman's body now, and she was only a few inches shorter than he was. It was hard to define exactly what it was that took her appearance across that borderline to womanhood, but despite it, whatever it was, there was still a gawky girl inside the body.

"Let's fix up the trundle bed in the side room. Mar, we got a bed-and-breakfast client!"

Marlena bustled out of the kitchen, stripping off a frilly apron that said KISS ME—I'M POLISH, and Maeve gave her a big hug.

"I'll be right back, hon," Jack Liffey said. He passed through the kitchen and the utility room, picking up the cordless phone on the way. He went down the back stoop and all the way to the low block wall at the tidy alley before dialing. Mar Vista was just enough up-market from Bancroft Davis's neighborhood that the city still cleaned out the alleys once in a while.

"Kathy, this is Jack. What's up?"

"Is Maeve there?"

"Uh-huh."

"With her suitcase?"

"Uh-huh."

"I figured, when she wasn't at her friend Dru's. Maybe it's best for a few days. Is it all right with you?"

"Hold on, Kath. It's okay at my end, but what is this about?"

There was a long pause with a lot of electronic whooshing on the line.

"Hello."

He heard a sigh. "Things are a little tense, that's all. Can we give it some space to work itself out?"

"Kath, she's practically in tears. What happened?"

"She had a disagreement with Bradley."

"Define *disagreement*."

"Well, you're going to find out sooner or later. You've got to understand, Maeve has gotten very sassy recently. She hasn't really adjusted to him yet, and I think her hormones are catching up to her. She doesn't pay attention. What happened is, she left the back gate open and the twins might have wandered out into traffic, so he was pretty upset."

"Did . . . he . . . hit . . . her?" Each word was a separate achievement in enunciation.

"He feels terrible about it, Jack. Really. He's been apologizing nonstop since I got home. He just lost it for a second when she sassed him. It was just a little slap. He didn't really *hit* her."

Jack Liffey's vision went red, and he felt his heart start to thunder. "You tell him this for me, Kathleen. If he ever . . . *ever* touches Maeve again, I'll break his arm in three places."

"It wasn't like that—"

"*Listen* to me. I know you don't respect what I do. I just fell into it myself. I didn't plan to make it my life's work, but I *like* it now that I'm doing it. I rescue kids, I save kids from things, I find kids. There is no excuse on earth for hurting a child."

"We feel the same way, Jack. Honestly we do. He's already a little afraid of you, and he feels really terrible about it. It won't happen again."

"I have your word then," he declared, not a hint of a question. He stabbed the button to ring off and breathed deeply in the motionless hot air off the alley. This was one of the things he had always dreaded—not being able to be there to protect her. But he knew it was inevitable, whatever happened. She was already separating from the main craft, a little lunar landing module readying herself to go her own way, and a good parent had to trust the years of training and encourage the separation.

"Want half of this?" Maeve glowered at the Tab in her hand as if it were bottled rat. For some reason Marlena loved Tab and wouldn't buy Diet Coke.

"It's pretty bad, isn't it? I'd love half."

She frothed it over the ice in his glass, kissed his bald spot, and sprawled back on the second lawn chair on the front porch. The TV muttered away indoors with one of Marlena's favorite doctor shows. This, he thought, was as close to heavenly peace as anyone deserved.

They had already agreed not to speak any further for now about what had happened at her mother's in Redondo Beach.

"What are you working on these days?" she asked. "Some runaway cultist from the Valley?"

"Sexier than that. Have you read about the college kids who disappeared from Claremont?"

She pursed her lips thoughtfully.

"He's black, she's white, and they were threatened by bikers."

"Oh, *yeah*. That's famous, Dad! You're going to be a famous detective."

"Yeah, like the Hardy Boys."

"Or Nancy Drew," she put in with a grin.

"Uh-huh. Same guy invented them, you know, and the Rover Boys too, *and* the Tom Swift books, but that was long before both of our times. He must have been a real terror with his quill pen."

"Mom read Nancy Drew. I was just looking at them in an old box."

A motorcycle ratcheted painfully up the street, with a hundred-gallon Stetson, big enough for Gulliver, covering the whole top of the bike. Eyeholes had been cut into the crown of the hat. They both watched the big two-wheeled hat disappear noisily around the corner. There were some things in life you would probably never figure out, he thought.

"One point each," she said. For years they had played this game, and one point was a fairly tame reward. They'd once gone all the way to four for the Normandy Landing Restaurant. You entered up an artificial beach with a blown-apart landing craft and fake dead bodies and then, for no discernible reason, emerged into a room where every square inch of wall space was covered with glued-on Pez dispensers, plastic dolls, colored trinkets, Christmas lights, and varnished bread rolls. It was the cages of talking parrots greeting you near the door with insults in French that put it all over the top.

"What books did you read when you were young?" Maeve asked.

"Would you like me to lie and tell you I filled my evenings with *Moby Dick* or would you like the truth?"

She laughed. "You can't lie. You've wrapped yourself in the most rigid ethical code of anyone I know—except that little problem you get sometimes, keeping your pants zipped."

He winced. "I've been zipped up for a while now, punkin."

"Marlena must be good in bed then," she whispered, with a feral grin.

He didn't know what to reply. This sauciness of hers was a whole new tack. "I think maybe we could talk about something less personal—like hemorrhoids, for instance."

She giggled. "Daddy, you're embarrassed! It's okay, you know. These days we learn all sorts of things younger than you did. Redondo High has a whole class on techniques of oral sex."

He blinked and swallowed and then decided he'd better laugh, so he did. "I award one point to you, just for being you, Miss Bizarro."

He broke down and owned up to his teenage reading habits, which seemed preferable to talking about his sex life. Until his sixteenth birthday, he had read nothing but science fiction, working his way doggedly through the entire case of interplanetary romances at the San Pedro Public Library, book after book. And they were almost entirely without redeeming value, he admitted, except that they did encourage you to look at the world in fresh ways. She, on the other hand, was reading Charlotte Brontë and Dickens. She didn't say a word about Nancy Drew.

"You folks okay out there?" Marlena called.

"We're fine, Mar," Jack Liffey replied.

"Are you going up to Claremont again on your case?"

"Sure."

"You know, my cousin Mary Beth lives up there," Maeve said. He must have looked blank. "Tom Leary's daughter. You remember."

The Learys. They were the people his dad had hauled him up to visit about 1963, some very distant cousins, he guessed. He was astonished Maeve had found them and stayed in touch.

"I could call Mary Beth in the morning," she suggested. "I think it would be good for me to get out of the city for a few days."

He watched her carefully. Some other agenda was simmering away beneath the surface, but for the life of him he couldn't figure out what it might be.

"I'll check with your mom."

"Your all-purpose hedge," she accused.

She waited until long past lights-out and then tiptoed out her door. She hesitated at the hallway for a moment to listen for exciting noises from her dad and Marlena down the hall, but there weren't any. She wouldn't *actually* eavesdrop, but if she happened to hear some panting or something else juicy she was willing to let it work on her imagination.

Then she went to his little post-office desk in the alcove, and sure enough there was the fat case file he'd been reading, back in its manila envelope. She carried it into her room, placed a rolled-up towel at the base of the door to block the light from leaking out, and turned on the old gooseneck lamp on the bed table.

Sitting cross-legged on the trundle bed, she set out the contents in tidy piles around her, making sure to keep everything in order. She looked at the 8-by-10 photos first, an astonishingly handsome young black man with a big square jaw and a neutral expression. Sherry Webber had a toothy smile and long ironed blond hair that made her look like a throwback to the Joan Baez era.

There was the initial police missing persons report; a thick pad of stapled investigative reports written in a kind of impenetrable English with a lot of passive verbs; a number of statements that seemed to have been taken from students at Pomona College and Scripps; a forensics report on a 1958 Chevrolet Impala; a long list of the contents of two dormitory bedrooms; a summary of an FBI investigation into some biker club in Fontana called Bone Losers, but not the report on the bikers itself; and another FBI summary about something called Umoja.

She started at the top, reading where it seemed important but skimming a lot. She had taken Mrs. Beard's speed-reading class, and though she loved words and resented the very concept, she did find the skill useful.

Cowabunga! she thought an hour later. She started taking notes on her own pad.

* * *

AB-IB THREATENS
LAPD LAWSUIT

That explained the uproar in the African-American community that he kept running into, Jack Liffey thought. The police review board was up in arms, the chief had apologized profusely, and the two officers involved had been suspended pending an investigation. But the great pitcher Abdullah Ibrahim was not to be mollified. He said it was only because he was famous that this incident had come to light at all, and he wondered how many more illegal choke holds were still being used throughout the city. Frequent references were made to a previous police chief who had notoriously insisted that choke holds only affected African Americans, not "normal" people.

Jack Liffey flipped through the paper, but there was nothing about a cross burning on Brighton Street. There seemed a conspiracy of silence around the other incidents, too: the burned-out police substation Ivan Monk had mentioned and the fires he had hinted about. Jack Liffey knew the newspaper had a policy of minimizing riotlike incidents since the big one in 1992. He wondered if somebody in authority really believed it was gangbangers reading the *LA Times* who spread the impulse to riot; that was a little like hiding the thermometer when it got hot. But it was a lot easier to edit the news than address the underlying social problems.

"You're up late, punkin."

She yawned and stretched. "I must have needed the sleep. Are you going soon?"

"Take your shower. There's no rush. Kathleen said it was okay for you to stay with Mary Beth for a couple of days."

"Oh, great. Thanks."

"It's a lot hotter out there in what they call the Inland Empire, so dress warm."

She wrinkled up her eyes. "Shouldn't it be, dress cool?"

"Ouch. Probably. That's what comes of reading science fiction instead of Charlotte Brontë."

"I happen to know you have a master's degree in English Literature, Daddy," she insisted.

"And look how I'm using it."

four

Attempting to Complicate the Cultural Space

For probably the twentieth time in his life at the exact same spot in the East LA freeway tangle, Jack Liffey got caught in an abrupt exit-only lane and almost found himself hurtling down the off-ramp. He accelerated his clunky Concord back on between a couple of eighteen-wheelers and was happy when neither of them blew an air horn at him.

"Man, it's getting hot," Macve said.

"Sorry, the air's on the fritz." That wasn't strictly true; he couldn't remember whether the air conditioner in his Concord had ever worked.

He did another hard lane change and finally settled into a lane that he was pretty sure continued on toward Claremont. The I-10 east of the LA River had been cobbled together out of three other routes, and you had to change lanes like a madman, hard north and then hard east, to stay on it. One inattentive moment and you were heading for Bakersfield or paying a surprise call on the decaying frame houses of Boyle Heights.

He saw the tops of these big old houses drift past. He knew a lot of them had been built in the mid nineteenth century by a spooky

Russian sect called the Molokans. Before long all the spare rooms had been rented out to Mexicans fleeing the downtown slum then known as Sonoratown. Then, by turns, these same uplands east of the river saw LA's first tiny black ghetto, its first artisan suburb on the Redcar line, and its first sizable Jewish community. Finally, beginning in the 1930s, the big aging houses had been chopped into apartments and filled to overflowing with Mexican Americans retreating northward in the city before the press of the great Anglo migrations out of the Dustbowl and the Midwest. He had once been deeply into LA lore, but he was having trouble now finding a purpose for it all. He did know this: Close your eyes for half a generation and your community sneaked away somewhere else.

"Sometime we ought to do a mural tour," Maeve said. Boyle Heights had been the heart of the great mural revival of the 1970s, and there were scores of them scattered around on minimarts and park walls.

"Love to. You feeling any better about what happened, hon?"

"No."

"You probably won't until you talk to Bradley again and clear the air. That's the way it usually goes."

He could sense her staring at him. "Were you that controlled and forgiving when Mom told you what happened?" she asked.

He sensed an intensity in her and realized this was no casual question. "What you want to know is didn't I suggest that I might break every bone in his *bleep* body? Yes, I did."

"Dad, I know you love me. You don't have to prove it by going apeshit."

"It's just what I felt."

"It's patronizing, though. Really. And, for you, it's not just that I'm young, is it? It's that I'm a *girl*. I've got to fight my own battles some, you know."

He stole a peek. "Maybe if I'd seen you more often recently, I wouldn't be so surprised by this brand-new all-grown-up Maeve." He bobbed his head back and forth a little, as if considering something. "So I've got to let go a bit, huh?"

"That's the ticket. Let me goof up. Let me pick up my own broken china."

"Pay your own college fees?" he tried out brightly.

"Dad!" But he heard her giggle and then suppress it. "You're impossible. I might even want to kiss a boy, you know?"

That shut him up for a moment. He knew "dating" was coming soon, and he just hoped he'd like the boy when it arrived. Please, please, not some dull sports-obsessed surfer with that horrible know-nothing suburban mush-mouth enunciation and a pointless grudge against everything. *Uh, shr, dude man, tha's gnarly, fr shr.* In his experience, there was simply no accounting for the men that women fell for.

"Or you might want to kiss a girl," he said.

"Or kiss a girl," she agreed.

"It wouldn't kill me," he said, "whatever you choose."

"I haven't tried girls, but thanks."

"Speaking of girls, how did you happen to stay friends with Mary Beth?" That seemed safe. "The only time I remember going out to Claremont to see Uncle Tom was when *I* was a kid."

"Don't you remember we met them at the fair in Pomona a few years ago?"

"Oh," he said. That explained it. That particular family excursion had come at an extremely low point in his life, after the big layoff, when he'd been tending a friendship with demon rum. He only vaguely remembered the county fair—heat, dust, cotton candy stuck to his shirt, and some strange agrarian event with teenagers in white shirts kneeling beside sheep with their eyes locked on a stern old man and their hands apparently up the sheep's asses. It must have been the scotch.

"We wrote each other for a while, and Mom has taken me out there a couple times. Mary Beth and I are good friends."

Maeve wasn't sure exactly why she was lying so hard, but she had to lay the groundwork for the visit without making her dad suspicious. On the phone Mary Beth had been astonished to hear from her. They had exchanged a grand total of one postcard after the fair, and that was three years past, and there had been exactly zero visits. She caught hold of herself and stopped explaining, figuring Nancy Drew would call it quits about then.

"Tom was *my* uncle," Jack Liffey said. "How does he have a daughter your age?"

"His wife died, remember? He married again, a younger woman."

"Okay."

She could see he didn't remember. Her dad had never been very good at relatives, or birthdays, or the names of her friends. He remembered movies, but he never remembered if he'd seen them with her, unless they'd been obvious kid movies. Whereas she remembered who she went with to every single movie, where they sat, what movie house it was, and what they'd done afterward. Her dad's mental filing cabinet just seemed to index movies under: *title—seen it—liked it/hated it.* A guy thing, she figured. Women filed everything under people and guys under things. There was no question which was superior, more humanist, but it was probably in the genes.

"Yoo-hoo, wake up, Dad. Indian Hill Boulevard means Claremont."

He was surprised that Maeve had chosen Mary Beth as a friend. From what he'd been able to gather, dropping her off and having a quick coffee with the family, Mary Beth was a chubby, brooding, not-very-bright girl a year younger than Maeve. There was no accounting for tastes, he thought, and to be charitable, maybe there were things in the girl he didn't see. After all, at one point in the fifties he'd probably seemed a pretty somber and antisocial kid himself. He hadn't been very happy as a boy. He wondered why the human species had to go through so much trouble and pain growing up. Puppies got it right almost every time.

Amilcar's former roommate, David Phelps, was in the phone book, and his apartment turned out to be upstairs in a cheap complex edging toward the larger town of Pomona, the kind of building with a balconied runway past all the doors. Heat radiated off every surface, and a lot of the windows had aluminum foil on them.

"David Phelps?"

"Who wants to know?"

"Would it matter?"

He had a big ring in the septum of his nose, spiky hair, and a tattoo on the side of his neck that only the highest of turtlenecks would cover: It read AVENGE BAUDELAIRE.

"It might."

"I've been hired to find Amilcar Davis, by his parents. My name is Jack Liffey."

The young man seemed to relax. "Sure. Come in."

Jack Liffey could see the place would take him awhile to assimilate. There were books stacked all over the room, and the walls were a solid pastiche of posters, photographs, bits of butcher paper with scribbling on them, and what looked like finger paintings.

"Beer?"

"No, thanks. But cold water would be nice." It was over 100 outside, and hotter in the baking air inside.

"Can do."

"You have anything to do with that self-destructing art machine out in the quad?" Jack Liffey called toward the kitchen.

"Harvat's thing? Not a chance. That dude is the very oldest hat of the middling new hats. Jean Tinguely did all that decades ago. What a bore."

While the young man was banging through cupboards, Jack Liffey examined some of the wall sayings.

THE PRACTICAL IS THE LONGEST DISTANCE BETWEEN TWO POINTS.

EVIL BE THOU MY GOOD: AN UNSATISFACTORY ALTERNATIVE BECAUSE EVERY INVERSION RETAINS THE STRUCTURE OF THE MORAL AXIS.

There was a *Life* photo Jack Liffey remembered from the late fifties of fraternity boys cramming themselves into a phone booth, and under it:

YOU CONSTRUCT ELABORATE RITUALS TO ALLOW YOU TO TOUCH THE BODIES OF OTHER MEN.

All by itself was a neatly lettered

WE ARE ATTEMPTING TO COMPLICATE THE CULTURAL SPACE TO
RENDER CRITICISM AS DIFFICULT AS POSSIBLE.

He was back, holding out a glass. "That's the last ice cube. This
heat has overdetermined my old fridge."

Jack Liffey glanced at the tiny cube. "It deconstructs as I watch."

The young man smiled at that, but he didn't bite. "Sit, please. I'm
glad somebody is looking for Ami."

"Did you two get along?"

The young man thought about it for a moment as they sat in noisy
burgundy-colored bean bags. His spiked-up hair bobbed whenever
he moved. "Yes, like brothers. The college put us together our freshman year, on the theory that grouping all the unusual students would
insulate the rest."

"You're unusual?"

He smiled. "When they asked for hobbies, Mr. Liffey, I said, 'Being very gay.' I could have said being subversive, too, but gay was
fine for drawing their radar."

"I'm Jack."

"Ami and I got along fine, once I got over my own prejudice. Not
about blacks per se. But I've had this sense for a long time that the
African-American community has special trouble accepting gays. You
know, there's all that working-class macho to deal with, and the street
culture, and then they're already oppressed once, automatically."

"How did Amilcar deal with your being gay?"

"Better than you."

"Did I say something?" Jack Liffey was a little taken aback.

"You reacted when you saw me."

"Whoa. Isn't it a little disingenuous to dress to shock and then be
surprised when people are shocked? That nose ring does make you
look like Ferdinand the Bull."

He laughed quite hard. "That's the spirit, Jackie. Okay: Ami
and I were *very* different. Maybe that's why we got along so well. I'm
doing cultural studies and he's history. He wants to be a lawyer"—

he gave a shiver—"probably a senator, and I want to be . . . opposi-
tional. I think we both learned a lot from each other and respected
each other. I grew up in Claremont, so you can imagine how little I
knew about the black community before I met Ami. We even double-
dated. He and Sherry got a kick out of being with me and Jeff. They
were good folks."

There was a buzz from the back of the apartment, and he jumped
up. "Oops, some art's cooking. I've got to turn it over. Be right back."

Jack Liffey watched him swish a bit as he left, probably just twit-
ting his guest. He got up and opened the door to get some air into
the hot, heavy room and then studied the wall again. He could feel
his shoulders sticking to damp geometric patches of his shirt.

There was a tall red flocked dog on the floor with a printed notice above it:

DISPLAYING A KITSCH ITEM AS HIGH ART IS NOT A CRITICAL COM-
MENT ON THE COMMODIFICATION OF ART BUT A MEANS OF REN-
DERING THE DISTANCE NECESSARY FOR THAT CRITICISM NULL
AND VOID.

He'd always disliked making fun of kitsch art, because it was
making fun of ordinary people and their tastes, but he couldn't quite
discern the attitude here.

There was a snapshot of a German-looking pub on an uphill cob-
bled street with the legend CAFÉ VOLTAIRE. Beside it was another of
Phelps's hand-lettered signs: DADA SMASHES THE WORLD, BUT THE
PIECES ARE FINE.

"Aha, Dada." He was back, bare-chested now. Jack Liffey was relieved there were no nipple rings. "That's its birthplace in Zurich. I
did a pilgrimage."

"I've always had a soft spot for avant-gardes, but not a very big
one," Jack Liffey said.

The young man shrugged. "Without them, you'd still be square-
dancing and listening to cowboys yodeling."

"Fair enough. Were you double-dating when Amilcar had his run-
in with the bikers in Fontana?"

"Oh, yes. I think the whole incident has been overblown, though. Those Bone Losers are just local morons. They didn't like seeing me and Jeff together any more than Ami and Sherry."

"What actually happened?"

"Some insults from one of the guys sitting on a Harley with swastikas all over his arms, but they didn't reckon on a thin black guy with a black belt. Ami got in his face and goaded him into swinging and then flattened him with one punch. The cops came and separated everybody and there was a lot of we'll-meet-you-later-in-some-dark-alley swaggering. I hear one of the bikers had connections to the Fourth Reich skinheads. Now *those* are guys who make your average biker look like a genius. If brains were shoes, they'd be naked all the way to their knees."

"Pogo," Jack Liffey said. The second reference to Pogo in two days.

"Actually, it was his pal Howland Owl. You know, when these foreskinheads decided to go after prominent blacks in LA they sent bomb threats." He laughed. "These guys were so out of touch, the only blacks they could think of were Rodney King and some forgotten rap singer. Imagine. Threatening to bomb poor Rodney King. These guys didn't have a clue. I don't think the Bone Losers even know where Claremont is."

"So you don't think they had a hand in the disappearance?"

"Nah. Life is never that obvious. I'd put my money on leprechauns first."

"What is your theory?"

That slowed him right down. "How's your water doing?"

"It's doing fine."

"Let's stand on the balcony. This place is an oven." They went outside. A half-dozen people were lying inert in the pool below or on chaises alongside it. Nothing in the world seemed to be moving in the oppressive air. "Okay, don't overdo this. The weekend before they disappeared, he and Sher went home to South Central. He came back pretty pissed off."

"How did his parents feel about Sherry?"

"Oh, man, they loved her; they have no trouble with interracial stuff. They're saints, I mean it. You must have met his dad, a sharecropper's kid who changed his life through the movement. He left SNCC when Stokely started his Black Power stuff and refused to work with whites. Ami's old man is the kind of guy makes you wonder whether there really is any need for irony in the world. He's holy."

Something was still unsaid. "So?"

"Amilcar came back pretty upset Sunday night. All he told me was, there's some folks worse than the Nazis."

"Do you think it was Umoja? Reverse racism?"

He shrugged. "I didn't know his old homies. He'd sure run into something."

"Did he have anything to do with drugs?"

David Phelps turned and glared at him. "Man, you've got the wrong idea. Everybody's got *something* to do with drugs, but if you think he was the big mule for the Crips out here in Claremont, you're crazy. He didn't touch anything beyond a little weed, like everybody else."

"I had to ask."

"He was more political than drugged up. Do you know who he was named for?"

"Amilcar Cabral? The African revolutionary. Probably his mom's idea."

"Uh-huh. From Guinea-Bissau. Luckily Cabral died young, so he didn't have to see his name tarnished by later events. Look just inside the door, it's a poster Ami gave me."

Jack Liffey stepped back into the blast of heat, and on a stub wall dividing the living room from a dining area there was a poster of a young African in guerrilla getup, with the legend:

TELL NO LIES. CLAIM NO EASY VICTORIES!
—AMILCAR CABRAL

"I don't know what happened, Jackie. I can't imagine somebody driving out here from LA to get Ami and Sherry, but something did happen in LA that weekend. That's all I know."

"Thanks for your help."

He gave the young man his card. Luckily, he still had a few of the old ones from before Marlena printed them up with the eyeball on them.

"If you do find him, man, give him a big kiss for me. But no tongue."

The children huddled up close on the rec-room sofa and he hugged one with each arm, immensely grateful that God had blessed him at his age. He had married late, choosing decent, quiet, loving, and ac- quiescent Kelly Wade, almost twenty years younger than he was. She had borne him the decent family he knew he needed to ride out a lot of bad memories of Vietnam and two bad marriages. The commer- cial was still on, so he opened his mouth and bellowed out:

> In the eyes of a ranger,
> The unsuspected stranger
> Had better know the truth of wrong from right,
> 'Cause the eyes of a ranger are upon you,
> Anything you do, he's gonna see.
> When you're in Texas, look behind you. . .

The kids perked up and joined in.

> 'Cause that's where the ranger's gonna be.

"Cool, Daddy."

And then there they were, Cordell Walker and his loyal pal Jimmy Trivette, walking into a Laundromat for some reason. It was a rerun but he couldn't remember the plot. Somehow he'd gone into lecture mode and couldn't stop himself.

"See how good they work together when they're decent and Chris- tian? It doesn't matter they're different races. One to one, it's like that. An African American and a normal American can be partners and respect each other. It's only in groups people start whining and go bad."

"Uh-huh, Daddy," Ginny said, but her eyes were on the set, where Chuck Norris was high-kicking an evil-looking Latino in the face.

"Perry." His wife stood in the doorway, and his irritation flashed for a moment.

"What is it? You know this is my favorite show."

"I'm sorry, dear. There's a phone call."

He picked up the cordless on the end table.

"Yeah?"

"K?"

"Uh-huh." He went very still inside, the TV flashing right out of existence, as still as he had gone on long-range reconnaissance patrols thirty years earlier, holding at the point of balance, ready to *move*.

"The old guy's hired somebody, a detective."

"Is he heading our way?"

"We don't know yet."

"Thanks. Keep me posted." He hung up and set the phone down thoughtfully.

"I'm really sorry, dear. He sounded insistent."

"It's okay," he said.

"I mean, you know I wouldn't cut in on—"

"It's *okay*, Kelly, *okay*."

"Daddy, he's *hurting* the Mescan."

"The Mexican must deserve it," he said absently. "Walker only hurts bad guys."

five

Can You See More Clearly from There?

"**L**isten to this! It's da bomb!"

Mary Beth squatted cross-legged on the other side of the old pink 45rpm record player with its fat spindle. The Leary home on the suburban edge of Claremont had central air, so at least they were comfortable hanging out in Mary Beth's bedroom.

On the turntable was "Mony Mony" by Tommy James and the Shondells. Mary Beth had been slamming through a stack of her dad's R & B 45s like "Silhouettes" and "96 Tears," playing about thirty seconds of each one before getting bored and whacking down another.

That restlessness made Maeve nervous too. It seemed to suggest that Mary Beth had never felt comfortable in her life, had never let herself settle into a rhythm. Unease was woven into the whole fabric of the girl's life, Maeve thought. She looked around. Her cousin had collected a number of things, just because she could afford them, without knowing or caring enough about any of them. There were rows of ignored dolls in national dress, bags of POGs, an elaborate Victorian dollhouse, even a trunk of Archie comic books—another hand-me-down from a father who had inherited the Chevy dealership in town from his own father.

Mary Beth's dad, too, seemed to spend his time on restless, barren projects, staring at his computer, moving his money around from investment to investment, or exercising in a halfhearted way with the expensive equipment in the backyard. Mary Beth's mother lolled on a chaise by the pool reading romance novels.

Out the full-length window, Tom Leary now held a set of light-looking barbells over his head, pumping away at great show-off speed for about thirty seconds. Then he stopped to rub his potbelly.

"I like this song," Maeve said.

"Yeah."

But it was gone, wrenched away to make room for "In the Still of the Night" by the Five Satins.

Maeve was beginning to wonder if she'd made a bad mistake. *Three days*, she'd told her dad. *Come get me Saturday.* Of course, it might have been worse. She might have been forced to listen to Mary Beth's new CDs. The girl's tastes seemed to run to Top 40 bubblegum like 'N Sync, while Smashing Pumpkins was about as mainstream as Maeve's listening ever got.

But then she got lucky. "I read a Nancy Drew the other day," she offered casually.

Mary Beth just lit up. She bounced and boiled with enthusiasm. "Yo, Maeve, you're gonna just *expire* when you see this!" She skittered across the room on her hands and knees like a startled spider and pulled open the doors of a walk-in closet to show off a free-standing bookcase. "I got Trixie Belden, the whole set!" she exclaimed. "And the Three Investigators. But this is best." She pointed to the two bottom shelves. Maeve crawled over with her and plucked *The Secret of the Old Clock* off the shelf.

" 'While I's done sowed all mah wild oats, I still sows a little rye now and den,' " Maeve read aloud.

"Can you believe this?" It was good to find something Mary Beth actually cared about, and she figured she'd better appear more knowledgeable than she was if she wanted to use Nancy Drew as a lever.

"In the fifties they censored out the guns and the liquor and even the *coffee*," Mary Beth said. "Look!" She flipped through another book to find a favorite passage.

"Have you ever thought you might want to be Nancy Drew?" Maeve essayed cautiously.

"I don't think I'm brave enough, but maybe I could be her best friend, Bess."

"Oh, really?"

Coming back in on I-10, the 10, as people in LA said, the traffic slowed maddeningly into a snarl around El Monte, and eventually a line of fizzing flares funneled everyone into the far left lane. A gigantic sparrow the size of an elephant, evidently meant as a movie prop or some kind of advertising display, had got stuck under an overpass on its flatbed truck, the top of the bird's papier-mâché head shredding a bit against the bridge. Several men stood around arguing and tugging on ropes, trying to extricate the bird. A family had piled out of a wrecked station wagon off to the side, and several kids were screaming at one another or bawling.

It was hotter than he ever remembered the city getting this time of year, and he had half a mind to take advantage of the stop-and-go to lean across the front seat and rip off the plastic that stood in for passenger-side windows. It was only August, and the worst wasn't usually until September.

Maybe the thing on the flatbed was meant to be a wren, he thought, as he inched up to it. It was hard to tell. He didn't know very many birds once he'd exhausted the obvious ones like seagulls and owls.

As he'd left Claremont, he'd stopped at a Chevron station to call Bancroft Davis and ask him to arrange a meeting with Umoja, and he'd rung up a pal named Mike Lewis, who lived in Pasadena. Mike had been home and willing to receive guests, allegedly hard at work on his next book. Mike was a social historian who'd been lionized after his first big book on LA, even got a MacArthur grant, but the next book had gone after the boosters and developers and they'd come back at him mercilessly, even yanking a university job he coveted.

Mike's house was a pretty little bungalow overlooking the Arroyo Seco. Across the street, a crew of workmen with a small crane were excavating what appeared to be a statue of the Virgin buried in the yard. The beat-up old Buick was gone from Mike's drive, in its place a workaday new Toyota Celica. Jack Liffey could see he hadn't gone extravagant with his three hundred grand from the MacArthur, but Mike had never cared much for machines or other possessions. As if to prove the point, he was visible in the kitchen window hammering away hunt-and-peck on an old upright L. C. Smith typewriter, the sleeves of some loose white gown flapping away like mad.

"It's me, Mike," Jack Liffey called through the open window. "I'll let myself in if there's no dog."

Mike Lewis beckoned. There was no dog, but in the front room there was a really stunning blonde in a white djellaba that matched Mike's. She sat cross-legged in front of a portable light table that was glowing up at her.

"Hi," he said. "Mike waved me in."

"That's okay. I'm decent."

Mike had slipped in under the civic radar to take jobs teaching urban studies part-time at an assortment of small local art colleges. He'd collected quite an ardent following among his students.

"You can say that again."

She smiled. "I'm China Cho." There was only the faintest suggestion of Asian features in her face. "Mike's my teacher."

"Jack Liffey. I guessed that." He'd guessed a bit more. Mike had been married four times, and number four had even been a friend of Jack's wife number one. Mike always had a woman around somewhere. All colleges were steeped in hormones, and art schools were probably at the top of the charts.

China Cho was arranging big 2-by-2 slides from a Rolleiflex or Hasselblad, so big he could make them out pretty well standing above the light board. They showed bare breasts with ornate tattoos. Some were dragons, butterflies, and flowers, one was a whole seascape of Japanesy waves, and another was a helix of barbed wire. One breast with a painful-looking nipple ring seemed to be inscribed in Arabic, round and round.

"I'm trying to come up with an organizing principle," she said, as she swapped slides around. "A breast tattoo taxonomy. Color or subject matter or quantity of design—which comes first?"

Or size of breast, he thought. "This your art project, or are you in the business?"

"The tattoo business?"

"I'm not sure what I meant."

"Call it body art. I'm in photography. I got interested in tattoos because I've got a pretty good one myself on my right breast. Would you like to see?"

"I think I'd better give it a miss."

She laughed, and it was hard to discern how serious she had been.

"Jack, come on in here!" Mike Lewis called.

"Nice to meet you," he said.

"Likewise, I'm sure."

Mike opened a tiny desktop fridge and tossed him a Vernor's ginger ale. "Rent plantations," he said, out of the blue.

"Pardon?"

"All those separate little cities on the east side, that's all they are. No industry, no commerce, no tax base, just thousands of rental units for Latinos. It's no wonder those cities fight each other to offer cheap land to auto malls and big-box stores just to get a little sales tax into the city. The whole structure is so irrational."

Jack Liffey nudged aside a book and sat on a kitchen chair. "If it were rational, what would you have to write about?"

"Unfair. Remember when we protested 'Nam? Our dads said we were just spoiled kids, and we replied, 'When a finger points at an evil, *you* just study the finger.'"

"I went, Mike. I was the evil."

"That was an abstraction—"

"Don't apologize. I shouldn't have gone, but I didn't do too much harm. I just made it possible for others to do harm." He decided the moral balance needed adjustment. "How does it feel being rich?"

Mike Lewis grinned. A big fan was pumping air in through the open window, and they heard the sudden groan of a diesel engine from outside. He glanced at the crane working on the statue of the Virgin across the road. "You mean the MacArthur? It gives me time to work. I love having undisturbed time. Normally I won't take grants, I don't even believe in them. Why on earth should social critics expect to be subsidized? But this one came unasked. Siobhann called to congratulate me, by the way."

She was the wife Jack Liffey had known, returned now to Ireland with their two kids. They talked about her and the kids for a few minutes as the desiccating heat went up another notch and they both sucked on the ginger-ale cans.

"Tell me about Umoja," Jack Liffey said, after he'd explained his new job, hunting down the missing boy and girl.

"Black nationalism," Mike Lewis said thoughtfully. He half rotated once, very slowly, in the desk chair. "They have to be situated in that historical current."

Jack Liffey feigned a groan. In fact, he had come because he wanted Mike's take on Umoja and its background, all of it. Still, he felt he had to pretend to demur a bit on so much abstraction. Mike would plow on, regardless.

It was Mike's thesis that black nationalism only really gathered force when white society turned its back on African Americans. In the 1920s, with the Klan on the attack—even electing governors in Colorado and Oklahoma—the black community turned to Father Divine and Marcus Garvey and Back to Africa.

"Nationalism went on the decline in the 1930s," he maintained. "The textbooks won't say it, but it was at least in part because the Communists built these huge national campaigns for black issues. Defending the Scottsboro lads. Bringing blacks into the CIO unions. Organizing poor black and white sharecroppers together in the South.

"Then, toward the end of the civil rights movement, things turned around again. I think leaders like Stokely and Malcolm saw that they'd got about as far as white society was prepared to let them. And really, Jim Crow in the South didn't matter that much anymore. Much of black America had migrated to the industrial North, and that's where the struggle was. They were the heart of the unions, trying to resist union busting for the next fifty years. They pretty much lost that one, too."

"So nationalism comes back again?" Jack Liffey said.

"Ask yourself why. Is anybody doing *one thing* for the inner-city poor?"

There was a crash outside and they both glanced out the broad window. Across the road a number of workmen peered down into the pit where the crane's cable disappeared.

"Oops, dropped the Virgin," Jack Liffey said. "I hope they get her out safely."

"They're not taking her out. They're burying her."

"Did she just die?"

"That house is owned by a rich guy who belongs to some Catholic sect that thinks the world is about to end. Something about Our Lady of some kind of rose and this old woman on Long Island who saw visions."

"I think I've heard of her. But still."

"The guy believes the Pakistanis, or maybe the Iranians, are about to nuke the Christian world. You know, the Islamic bomb."

Jack Liffey couldn't help chuckling. "So a big statue of the Virgin will survive. That's a comfort."

They glanced at each other. "You still wonder why blacks give up on us from time to time?" Mike Lewis said.

"Tell me about Umoja."

"Umoja, sure. They're a lot like Ron Karenga's group. They've got a storefront, they give breakfasts to poor kids, they wear dashikis, and they teach black kids pride. They give classes on African history and African languages. Off the record—they don't know very much about Africa, but they try hard. There's a lot of do-it-yourself ideology about Egypt as the root of civilization and some invented stuff about the 'African philosophy of life.' I can understand a people that was so badly used working up their pride, but some of the history they believe is pretty touch-and-go. The Egypt stuff is pure bunk. It's not all that many steps from 'an innate African worldview' to 'they've-all-got-rhythm,' you know?"

"I was in Africa for a couple weeks," Jack Liffey said. "I worked a fiddle to come home the long way from 'Nam. It was nice to go into a dance club and see that a whole cross-section of Africans couldn't dance for shit."

"You're Irish," Mike Lewis said, "and you quit drinking."

"I reconsider that every time I have to listen to you."

Her palms throbbed and ached where they pressed down on the low racing handlebars. Maeve didn't like racing bikes. Back home in Redondo, she rode her mom's old British bike that had nice ordinary handlebars and a comprehensible lever marked L-M-H on the handgrip. Here she had to settle for Mary Beth's brother's hyper-expensive Peugeot racing bike with low bars and so many levers she had no idea what gear she was in. Robert—they called him Bucky—was away in a summer catch-up session at some expensive eastern college for rich dummies. Mary Beth was riding her own mountain bike with straight handlebars that would have been a lot more to Maeve's liking.

A truck whooshed past them on Arrow Highway, rocking the two girls in its wake. Thank heaven she'd brought jeans, Maeve thought, or the sharp seat would have defeated her. They were both dressed in torn jeans and baggy T-shirts.

She thought again about poor Mary Beth's parents. Staying in the Leary home, Maeve realized she'd actually begun maturing in ways she hadn't been aware of. For the first time in her life she found herself observing a couple of grown-ups more or less for what they were. Mary Beth's parents weren't just another mom and dad, relatively interchangeable with all moms and dads. They were in fact jerks, a bit like some of the jerks her own age. They sat around their pool, drinking and arguing and wasting their lives, talking about nothing but shopping and TV and sneering mercilessly at the neighbors.

"Slow down, you've got the racer," Mary Beth complained.

"You mean Rocinante?"

"Huh."

"Don Quixote's horse."

"Erf, who's that?"

This unexpected growing up seemed to have done something to her feelings for Mary Beth, too. Ordinarily she wouldn't even have liked her very much, if she'd just met her and they weren't related. Mary Beth had almost no attention span and wasn't all that bright by the standards Maeve usually used. But she did have a big welcoming heart and she laughed at Maeve's jokes. Also, even though Mary Beth had seemed a bit of a scaredy-cat at first, she always seemed to pluck up her courage and give things a go. Maeve decided she liked her cousin despite her faults.

"It doesn't matter." Anyway, Don Quixote was a man, she thought. "I'll be Calamity Jane and you can be Annie Oakley."

To let Mary Beth catch her breath, Maeve slowed a bit as they approached a derelict motel called the Old 66 Wigwam with separate cabins shaped like tepees. The plaster was beginning to peel away from the framework of the tepees, and a few of the poles sticking up on top had fallen at funny angles. She would have to remember this for her dad. Two points at least.

"What are Calamity and Annie planning to do out here?" Mary Beth asked.

"We're going to hunt down enemy Indians and spy on them."

Maeve felt a little uncomfortable about using that description. She didn't really want to make Indians the bad guys, and she knew she should probably call them Native Americans in any case.

"Tribe has abandoned tepees, gone on warpath," Maeve offered as they both gawked at the motel for the last time and pedaled on.

"What tribe are we after?" Mary Beth asked gleefully, getting into the spirit of things.

"A band of Apaches called the Bone Losers."

His appointment with Umoja wasn't until four, so he stopped off briefly at the house to change his sweat-soaked shirt. There he found a note on the fridge.

I'm at the church this afternoon, Marlena had written.

The church. The definite article said a lot. She was spending more and more time at the Church of the Open Barn Door, down in the low-rent area of Hawthorne. Father Paul Something-or-other had started out preaching off the back of a truck in a used-car lot in the 1960s and ended up building a big domed stadium. Jack Liffey had met a few of the Open Doorites and done his best to like their cheerful, clean, and energetic working-class bearing. They were millenarians, but they made no real attempt to predict exactly when Jesus was going to be touching down again.

He strolled out into the backyard to offer Loco a hug and gave a groan when he saw a burrowed-out spot that was almost finished under the wire. It was hard to keep a half coyote down. Loco was staring sheepishly in another direction. He was ridiculously affectionate in response to a few pats, then frowned a bit as Jack Liffey piled some loose concrete blocks over the escape tunnel. Loco seemed to take it in stride, though, Jack Liffey thought.

Back inside, he swung open the fridge and eyed a few bottles of beer off to the side that looked pretty lonely. He hadn't had a drink in over four years. Though his marriage had gone under to it, he wasn't really an alcoholic; he'd given up cold turkey one day just to prove something to himself. He'd also given up drugs and tobacco and beef and even the hard-edge mystery stories he'd once loved. It was all a matter of making it damned clear to your ego, or maybe it was your id, that gratification was not in charge. But now he wondered if it might not be a good time to ease up a little.

He sighed and shut the fridge door. There was Marlena's note again. He wasn't sure what he thought about her spending so much time with the Open Doorites. They had her making contributions to some pretty dubious Central American missionaries, probably a front for the CIA and the local oligarchies. And then there was all that energy the Doorites exuded. Like most people who'd grown up in the suburbs, Jack Liffey was generally uncomfortable with people who believed things with that much enthusiasm.

For a brief time after coming back from 'Nam he'd fallen in with the Vietnam Veterans Against the War, and he'd seen a lot of fervor running out of control, not unlike religious fervor. He'd only had a Good Conduct medal to toss back over the fence toward the Federal Building, but he'd watched as a lot of pretty sharp guys ended up hypnotizing themselves into believing in some pretty weird radical stuff: dire conspiracies, imminent revolutions, and some fairly dubious street thugs as leaders.

It had all left him with a bad taste for enthusiasm. And it brought back one of the few words of wisdom from his father that he had ever taken to heart: *When you want to decide which square of the game board you're going to next, ask yourself, can you see more clearly from there?*

six

The Secret Language of Cars

It was the biggest truck parking lot she'd ever seen, the big square unhitched trailers lined up side by side like an endless wall paralleling the highway. Here and there, a rig was backing up to attach a trailer and pull it away.

"This must be where they breed," Maeve said.

"Or come to die," Mary Beth suggested. "Maybe it's like an elephant boneyard." She was getting into the spirit of things.

Across the narrow highway there was a long saloon with a neon sign, flashing even at noon: GIRLS GIRLS GIRLS. ALL NUDE. TRUCKERS WELCOME.

Maeve nodded to the sign. "I think breed's closer."

As they rested on their bikes, she studied the old-fashioned swing doors of the saloon. No one came or went, and she could hear faint music with a strong beat. Maeve was curious about these sex-tinged places. She knew the shuddery excitement of having a boy touch her body a little bit or peek at it, but she couldn't imagine anything but horror in strutting around with your clothes off in front of a bunch of hooting men—if that's actually what went on in there. Movies only hinted at it. She couldn't really believe places like that were real.

Mary Beth was studying the saloon too.

"You ever let a boy see you undressed?" Maeve asked.

"Sort of. Last year I played a game with this jerk from school, but when it got to the important stuff he cheated and wouldn't show me his."

"It's just skin," Maeve said. "Tell them to go buy *National Geographic.*"

Mary Beth laughed at the quip, but that wasn't exactly Maeve's attitude. Actually, she was pretty confused about the subject, all in all. One day she'd shown up in Mar Vista unannounced and walked in on her dad and Marlena with the radio going loud. They'd been on the bathroom rug and they had their mouths in places she couldn't quite believe, something she'd thought was pretty much theoretical, and they seemed to be having fun doing it. She thanked whatever stars there were that her dad hadn't felt compelled to have a little "talk" with her afterward.

They pushed on again in the bright sun, and before long they turned off the highway and pedaled into downtown Fontana to begin scouting the streets. It looked like a real disaster of a town, with about half the shops boarded up and nobody at all out on the streets. Even the shops that were open didn't seem to sell anything anybody would want: gingham doll supplies, bowling trophies, used bathtubs.

"Pardner, what happened to this place?" Maeve asked.

"They used to have a big steel mill, I mean a *giant* one. Kaiser Steel. It closed down a long time ago."

The girls stopped and rested against the curb, sweat pouring off them. They needed Cokes. "It's funny companies can do that, isn't it?" Maeve said. "People work someplace all their life, and the company just pulls up one day and goes somewhere where people have to work cheaper."

"I never thought about it."

"They did it to my dad. He had two weeks' warning that they were going to treat his life like Kleenex."

"What did he do?"

"Well, it sure changed him. I mean, it almost wrecked him for a while. I'll buy you a Coke."

"Thanks. Diet."

Now that she'd grown used to the changes in her father—as well as the wholesale changes the divorce had brought to her own life— the calamity of that period wasn't quite so devastating. But it had sure seemed so then. From an unquestioned sense of security in a stable family in a big house, she went to an almost constant churning and unease, two semi-families, and two smaller houses. She knew she'd never feel quite as trusting and peaceful again.

They found a dusty convenience store. Then they rode their bikes slowly up and down the dispiriting streets of the town, sipping their drinks, past Bud's Market and a closed hardware store and an empty place where a store had burned down to look like a gap in a denture.

Maeve declared she was a cavalry scout and she would have no trouble tracking the Indians, though she was really doing nothing more esoteric than keeping her eyes peeled for big motorcycles, which she couldn't seem to find anywhere. Finally, in desperation, she led her scouting party back to a dive called the Bar-66 where the main street hit the highway and plucked up her courage. There were no windows, and a rusty swamp cooler was buzzing away on the roof. At least there was no GIRLS-GIRLS-GIRLS sign. Somebody in there would probably know about the Bone Losers if anybody did.

Mary Beth absolutely refused to go in with her. "We'll get raped or something," she objected. So she hung back in the weeds by the big metal pole for the bar's sign and watched over their steeds.

Maeve pushed in through a set-back door that swung open with a little squawk into darkness. As her eyes were adjusting, she heard a clack of billiard balls and a scratchy jukebox softly playing country music. The first thing she made out was a waterfall beer sign; then, as her vision adjusted, antlers on a sad, molting deer head; and then a heavyset woman behind the bar, leaning forward wearily with her head down on the bar surface. Two young Latinos were pacing around a pool table to one side.

"Excuse me, ma'am," Maeve said to the woman. The woman looked up blearily and took a moment to focus. She wore a print dress and looked like a kindly Barbara Bush.

"You're too young to be in here, honey."

"I don't want to drink anything. I just want to ask directions."

The woman appeared to ruminate for a moment before deciding not to throw Maeve out.

"¡*Chingate*!" a pool player barked.

"¡*Pendejo*!"

"¡*Borrachito*!"

"*Usted dos*, try to be grown-ups!" the woman snapped at them.

"*Bruja*," one muttered, but they subsided and went back to their game.

"What is it, honey? Speak up."

Maeve winced as the Latinos broke a rack hard. They hadn't even noticed her. "My cousin told me to meet him in front of the place where the Bone Losers get together. Is this it?"

The woman eyed her for a moment, as if she could see right through the subterfuge. Maeve wondered if she was making her tale too complicated once again.

"No, this ain't it. They ain't one whit welcome here. And, little honey, you don't want to go messing with the Bones."

"That's just where I got to meet Stan."

Stan? Where had that come from?

"They got their own clubhouse up on Sierra, but I tell you, girl, you call up your Stan on the telephone right now and tell him to meet you at the county library, right in front of the biggest stack of storybooks you can find." The woman looked around, as if she'd misplaced a drink.

"I don't know his number. But thanks."

"Sweetie, them Bone Losers, some of 'em think a girl your age is just asking for it if she tells 'em the time of day and ain't wearing no Arab veils."

"Girls shouldn't have to hide in the attic just to prove they're not asking for sex," Maeve insisted.

"Some little girls don't rightly know what they're asking for these days, hon. They play with it a bit and end up pullin' a sorry train."

"I'm not playing with anything."

She tried to hurry out, but the two young Latinos were blocking her progress. She'd been wrong about them not seeing her.

"Hey, you want to play with us, *perra?*"

"We got lots of balls for you to play."

"Leave me alone."

"You got some nice *chupas*, girl." He cupped his hands and leered.

"We play any game you want, *funciete*."

"Get out of my way."

"So, go be stuck up, bee-yitch."

Out front she came to a halt in the bright sun with her heart pounding. She could feel her face flushing and sweat prickling out all at once. There hadn't been all that much animosity to the confrontation, but it was the first time anyone had ever called her the b-word to her face, and there was such freight to it that her knees trembled a little. She couldn't imagine any of the boys she knew referring so vulgarly to her breasts or using the b-word like that. She'd always known there were a lot of different little worlds out there, and some of them didn't overlap very much with hers. But coming face-to-face like this with one of these harsher provinces, she was beginning to wonder if she had what it took for her Nancy Drew mission.

"Hey, Maeve, what's going on?"

"A couple of guys in there started coming on to me, that's all."

They mounted their bikes. Mary Beth was still thinking it over. "How old were they?"

"Don't even go there."

"That's really acrylic. Some busters did that red-heat thing all around me at the mall last month. They'd get in front when I walked and wiggle their tongues, and I thought I'd just die. I wish I was braver but I don't know what to do. I want to just stick up my nose the way women do in the movies, but then my heart starts to trip."

"Yeah. I've seen my dad tough things out, but he says he's just as scared as anybody and it's all a trick. I think it must be a guy thing."

"Maybe it's being too stupid to see what's gonna happen."

Maeve decided Mary Beth didn't realize she'd just dropped a big insult on her father, so she let it go. She knew which way to direct the hunt now. They'd passed a Sierra Avenue at the edge of town. Her racing bike drew ahead easily, and Mary Beth pedaled hard to catch up.

"I went on a hike with my brother a couple years ago up Icehouse Canyon," Mary Beth started in. "We got to this place where you have to go along a cliff, and I got halfway along and then I just froze up solid. I couldn't budge an inch. I looked down and it was pretty far. It would have broken half my bones if I'd fallen. I thought they were gonna have to get the helicopters. Bucky kept begging me to be courageous but I couldn't unlock my hands from this little tree that held me up, and finally he had to come back and hold my hand and make me move."

Mary Beth made a dismissive sound.

"Not that he's such a wonderful big brother and all, but he knew Dad would blow times ten if I got hurt."

"I always wanted a big brother, but I ended up with two little step-brothers," Maeve offered.

"You like them?"

Maeve considered, but since they were both in a confiding frame of mind, she grimaced. "Not much. They've both got mean streaks for such little kids. They torture insects. And they keep trying to peek at me in the bathroom."

There wasn't much question which house it was as they headed out the ragged road on the farthest edge of the town. There were a half dozen big shiny motorcycles on the dirt in front where grass should have been, the kind of motorcycles with weird high handlebars and teardrop gas tanks with flames painted on them and seats like tractors. The old clapboard house hadn't been painted in a long time, and a lot of shingles were missing from the roof. Out here it was a long way from house to house, and the last one had had chickens and even a pig in back.

Seeing the pig, Maeve experienced a momentary sense of complete dislocation. Only that morning she and Mary Beth had sat out by a swimming pool with a maid bringing fresh-squeezed orange juice and smoked salmon on bagels; now, chickens and pigs. She smiled to herself. Plus *hogs*—she'd read that was what bikers called their Harleys, or at least they had at one time. You couldn't keep up on every subculture. Her dad tried, but he got the school slang hilariously wrong all the time. He still tried to use words like "reeks" and "ugmo."

She motioned Mary Beth to keep riding past all the glinting machinery, and they pedaled up to a big eucalyptus tree that had dropped a lot of its bark and filled the air with medicine smell. The tree was the first of a long row of eucalyptuses that spread away at an angle for maybe a half mile toward some mountains that were faintly visible in the smog. They parked their bikes behind the trees and peered around a trunk to watch the clubhouse.

"You sure that's it?" Mary Beth asked breathlessly.

"Can't you see? The Indians are home."

"You think they live there or it's just a clubhouse?"

"Don't know."

"Aren't you scared?"

After all her talk about courage, Maeve found she couldn't back down now. "We're not doing anything wrong."

But that wasn't going to last long, she thought. There was a low chain-link fence around a backyard, separating the weeds and dirt inside from the weeds and dirt outside. There weren't any more houses beyond this one, just a dry wash, a heap of trash out on the hot plain, and the faint mountains beyond.

"I bet we can go look in a back window," Maeve said.

"I dunno."

"I'll do it. You keep lookout."

"Okey-dokey."

Maeve knew if she hesitated now she'd never do it. She walked casually out along the eucalyptus treeline, which she guessed had been planted as a windbreak, though there was no evidence of any fields or groves to be protected. The house had two back windows, both curtained, but there might have been a little gap in one. She glanced back at Mary Beth, who was holding a hand hard over her mouth as if trying to keep herself from screaming, and then she stepped between two of the trees and sauntered confidently toward the fence.

"Two-four-six-eight, LAPD's never late!

"One-two-three-four, break down your wooden door!"

That seemed to be the chant anyway, as the small parade of African-American protesters with homemade signs made its way down Slauson, working themselves up into a rage. Almost all of them were men.

REVENGE AB-IB! a sign said. STOP KILLER COPS!

There were fifty or sixty of them, marching in step to the chant, and all of a sudden they did something Jack Liffey had never seen demonstrators do. At some signal they broke into a stutter-step, then a high kick with the right leg and a hard stomp downward. They did it again, then took a few normal marching steps, then in perfect unison performed another pair of the Zulu high war kicks with the left leg. They must have practiced it for quite some time to get it right. He'd seen it in an old film once, and he'd thought how heart-stopping and intimidating it was.

The parade neared the vendors of cheap carpets and sweet-potato pies at the corner of Crenshaw, and they reverted to an ordinary walking pace, chanting their two-four-six-eight again, normalizing the scene so abruptly that it was as if the war-kicks exhibition had all been a hallucination. They came abreast of a few stone-faced policemen who were stopping traffic on Crenshaw to let them pass. Onc of the cops was black, but it took a moment to work that out because of the big plastic face shield he was wearing.

Suddenly there came a cry and the demonstrators high-step-stomped through the intersection, shouting something he couldn't make out. Even here in the world of cell phones and MTV, the Zulu strut carried a kind of bizarre menace, as if thrusting onlookers into a dimension where ordinary defenses might not work.

Jack Liffey would have given a lot to have access to the thoughts of the black cop. Was there an inner blink, a wish to identify? As the marchers moved on, he thought about the inspiration for the event. He wondered what Ab-Ib was like as a person, if the knuckleballer had a social conscience or just wanted to milk the incident for publicity. That curiosity had almost been enough to make Jack Liffey pick up the sports pages that morning, but not quite.

"Maybe it's just made up."

There were a dozen chunky boys in the schoolroom when he

came in, most of them seniors and juniors. For some reason the club had had trouble this year recruiting the younger boys. They all had dog-eared Bibles open, and Gary Chapman, the Reader Trustee up front, looked relieved that the man had arrived.

"Coach K!"

Flat hands were held up near him, and Perry Krasny distributed subdued high fives along the row as he passed up front. A lot of them were his kids from the JV team. Usually he let them meet alone, but Chapman had sent for reinforcements to sort out some kind of trouble.

"We thought we'd better refer this upstairs." The crew-cut boy handed him a typewritten document, four or five sheets stapled together. "Dave got it from somebody in English."

Krasny stayed on his feet and pursed his lips as he read the paired statements.

LITERALLY TRUE?

God creates animals and then man. Genesis 1:25–26.
God creates man and then animals. Genesis 2:18–19.

Noah takes seven pairs of each type of animal onto the ark.
   Genesis 7:2–3.
Noah takes one pair of each type onto the ark. Genesis 6:19.

Jacob's offspring in Egypt totaled 70. Genesis 46:26–27.
Jacob's offspring in Egypt totaled 75. Acts 7:14.

Aaron dies on Mount Hor. Numbers 33:38.
Aaron dies at Mosera. Deuteronomy 10:6.

He flipped through the pages. Most of the Bible had been covered, right up through the New Testament. He let his mind gear up and stopped thinking about what he was reading.

"Well, gentlemen, I'm sure there's an explanation to offer you, but I'm not a biblical scholar. Instead of focusing on these supposed contradictions, however, I think we should ask ourselves where they come from. And the motives of whoever put them together."

Those fierce eyes came up, and they all saw Dave Cooper shrink a little. Krasny smiled. It might have been the smile of a very large predator that was ready to eat.

"Go get him," somebody said.

Basically, attacks on Bible literalism worried him a whole lot less than the dangerous multicultural myths that the kids were encouraged to swallow on a daily basis. He had to start where they were. Any sign of rebellion was a worry. And look who'd been the conduit for this doubt and confusion, he thought. Dave (Fast Fred) Cooper was second-string linebacker and, like a lot of defensive players, a bit of a troublemaker.

"This list comes out of the same world that gives us presidents who smoke dope and lie about it, a world that offers an epidemic of personal irresponsibility and racial quotas and cheating on welfare and fatherless children and gangbanging in the streets. And the unbearable, unendurable sadness of secular unbelief. On the other side. . ."

He rested his palm on a Bible on the desk. He didn't often go this far with them. Usually he saved the angrier stuff for one or two who were more advanced.

". . . is us. People tough enough to face the big questions in our society. Can we agree that this discussion does not leave this room?"

They all nodded, cowed.

"The big myths on one side, the courage to look straight at obvious truths on the other. Let's set these Bible questions aside for a moment and look at one of the truths that it's time to face. It's something we see every day in the lunchroom. The Latinos eat with their own kind by the notice board, the African Americans eat with the African Americans down by the busing table, and the Orientals sit at the front table there, with the whites out in the middle. There's nothing wrong with that; every species seeks its own kind. We tried to integrate as a society, but everybody saw how artificial it was and now some of us have to look at the consequences of the failure.

"It isn't going to be easy, I kid you not. To be fair, we may eventually have to divide the country up. Give some of the Southwest back to Mexico and some of the Old South to the blacks. Then we can start to get over this terrible mess that's got out of control, all the unsafe streets and stolen stereos and fatherless kids, and we can begin to build up our own Euro-nation."

He glanced around.

"*Or*. We can go on mouthing the liberal mumbo-jumbo about how wonderful secularism and integration are and how well they're working. And we can let the whole country slide down into the swamp. Which side of that big divide do we want to stand on?"

No one took it as a genuine question, though Dave Cooper felt he had to say something to explain his interest in the dangerous document. "I just wanted to know the truth."

"Of course." Perry Krasny smiled his terrible smile. "Where *did* this come from, by the way?"

"Norm Berquist gave it to me. He's a social science major. He used to be a goth."

Krasny knew Berquist from a geography class he subbed in once in a while, a real smart-ass. The boys facing him were all athletes. He was tempted to characterize Berquist as a pussy and a geek, but he thought better of it. "Perhaps we should pray for his soul, this social science major. I don't think social science will ever answer one one-hundredth of the questions that the Lord answers in this perfect Book. Pledge of Honor, gentlemen. Stay with that and you don't have to go looking for the truth, it will come to you."

Jack Liffey was disappointed when he found no one out front of the Brighton house. He'd enjoyed chatting with Ornetta, and it was really the little girl he needed to talk to. Even the Rolling 60s Gangsta Crips had given up their vigil, and the scorch on the lawn had been doctored up with a patch of sod and some fertilizer.

"Mr. Davis," he called in through the screen, after rapping ineffectually. The sound of typing toward the back of the house broke off, and presently the old man hobbled to the door on his cane.

"Ah, Mr. Liffey." He unlatched the screen door and they shook hands gravely.

"Before I talk to the Young Turks at Umoja, I wonder if you could give me some idea of who I'll be seeing?"

The old man smiled faintly as Jack Liffey came in, and they sat in the sparkling Danish-modern room, watched over by the long-nosed African god. "I'll try. Kidogo is Amilcar's age, a fine young man, even if I might disagree with some of his . . . emphasis. He and Amilcar were friends all through high school, played basketball and went hiking together. He's smart as a whip, but he decided against college. He'd got it into his head that the point of college was to try to make him white. I think you'll probably meet Mwalimu wa Weusi, too—he's the head of Umoja. His name literally means Teacher of Blackness."

The old man smiled lightly.

"We can all surmise what he meant when he made it up, but I'm told a fluent Swahili speaker would interpret it as a clumsy explanation for something like a witch. So would my wife, undoubtedly, but really he's not a bad man at all. He has genuine charisma and he helps a lot of kids stay out of gangs. He's wary of whites, but I doubt if he'll try to mau-mau you."

Jack Liffey was a little surprised to hear how positively Bancroft Davis regarded Umoja. "That'll help situate me. Would you mind if I spoke to your granddaughter for a few minutes?"

The old man looked surprised.

"Amilcar might have confided in her."

"She's out back. Don't let her talk your ear off."

"That's what ears are for."

Ornetta sat cross-legged on a small patch of grass beside the vegetable garden, staring off dreamily at a pepper tree. A number of brightly colored stones were set out into a pattern of some sort in front of her.

"Hi there," Jack Liffey said. He sat down and got as cross-legged as he could, facing her across the stones. A big 747 came over, descending toward LAX but still fairly high.

"Hi, mister. You want to hear the story about the secret language of cars?"

"I would like nothing better."

He wondered how long it took to get all the beaded rows into her hair, and if the beads had to come out from time to time for a rework.

"They was this country girl her name Piretta, live out on a farm way in the country with her mama and her daddy and all they animals in a big white house with a chimbly. One day in the barn Piretta find her a little magic bottle.

"She feel a bump inside there and a voice go, 'Rub me and let me out!' She real scared, but she rub and, *whomp*, out pop a big black man like a rassler on TV and he got a big white do-rag on top, call a turband."

"Wow!" Jack Liffey exclaimed.

Ornetta moved one of the colored stones in front of her with great concentration, as if only *that* stone unlocked the secrets of the story. Her heroine seemed to have released a very strange genie who wouldn't give her gold or jewels or anything nice that little girls wanted, but only magic powers and only the magic powers he chose. She was going to be able to hear the secret language of cars. Piretta was truly disappointed, because that was not what she had in mind at all.

Ornetta fell silent for a moment at a burst of gunfire in the distance, but there was no sequel. She moved a shiny green stone a few inches before going on shyly to tell him that Piretta's first surprise with her new powers came when she started to do her chores that afternoon and wash the old Cadillac that her father used once a week to take them all to church.

"'Bout *time*, girl.'" Ornetta mimicked a voice as deep and irascible as she could. "Piretta she jump a foot. 'I was feelin' pow'ful dirty,' Mr. Cadillac go. 'Do me some more, child, over here on this side.'

Piretta was outraged at this bossy car, who called her "child" and wouldn't even thank her, even though she did an extra-special job washing him, and after dinner she sneaked back out to the barn and overheard the shiny car lording it over the beat-up tractor that Piretta's father drove every day.

"'You a fool,' go Mr. Cadillac. 'All day I sit here in the cool shade and you work yourself near to death. Look at you. You dirty and broke down and got bumps all over you. You paint comin' off while I sit here all wash and clean and rest up.' "

A police siren wailed a block away, then another, but both sirens choked off abruptly. Ornetta moved another stone, swapping it for a different one that looked pretty much the same. Jack Liffey wondered if all this divination was her way of fending off the dangers out in the world.

As the story went on, it turned out Piretta liked the tractor, which she found kindly and shy, though a bit gullible. The Cadillac was full of mischief and convinced the tractor to play sick so it wouldn't have to work so hard. Piretta went to bed that night worried about what she'd heard. She knew her father had to use the tractor to take their pumpkins to market the next day, but she couldn't think of a way to warn him about the trick they were going to play on him.

The next day Piretta peeked in the barn door, and the tractor coughed and sneezed and refused to run. Her daddy cursed a little and then hitched the market wagon to the Cadillac, and only Piretta could hear that proud car howling in outrage.

Some boys bustled past down the alleyway, loud and bellicose, and Ornetta rotated two of the stones like TV knobs until the boys passed. Jack Liffey noticed how heartbreakingly delicate the girl's wrists were, as if you might snap them off accidentally with a touch.

The farmer drove off to market with the Cadillac towing a trailer of pumpkins and then came back for more and more, all day long.

"That night the Cadillac dirty and bumpy and so tired it can't keep it headlights on. And Piretta waiting for it in the barn, and she go, 'You sure Mr. Smarty now, ain't you, Mr. Cadillac? And you gone stay dirty, too, till you learn how to say thank you.' "

Jack Liffey laughed and clapped, genuinely delighted. "That's a wonderful story." He poked around gently, trying to figure out if she'd read it somewhere, but like any good magician she wouldn't reveal her tricks.

"Ornetta, I have to go soon, but before I do, can I ask you something about your Uncle Amilcar?"

She breathed deeply and her grin faded away. Then she nodded solemnly.

"Do you remember the last time he came home from college?"

She nodded again, looking down at the stone pattern, as if whatever he needed to know might be found there.

"Did he tell you anything? Was there some trouble about Umoja?"

She shook her head. "Uh-uh."

"How about with his friends? Did they have a fight?"

Again she shook her head.

"Do you know any reason somebody would be mad at him? It might help me find him."

She moved several stones around, and finally she was satisfied with the arrangement. "Everybody always ax about Ami," she said. "Nobody ax about Sherry and she people."

seven

Unacceptable Offerings

"So you wait there, look at the pictures, you hear wh'm sayin'?"

The Umoja headquarters was several old storefronts on Manchester, tied together above the windows by a black-green-red tricolor stripe of fresh paint. To one side, like a bookend, there was an appliance repair shop, and at the other a derelict eatery with a fading YOU-BUY-WE-FRY sign.

Just inside the hot entry room, a young man in a colorful pillbox cap frowned at him from a little desk, like a dedicated postal clerk stuck with a troublesome patron. What the young man had waved Jack Liffey over to look at while he waited was a gallery of old photos, so he looked at the old photos.

There was Marcus Garvey, waving to a crowd from an open car. Then a number of other black men in similar crowds, mostly prewar, judging from the cars and clothing. He read the captions.

Marcus Garvey, United Negro Improvement Association, Harlem.

Father Divine, Peace Mission, Harlem: Sitting on a big throne that jutted above the backseat of a touring car that was surrounded by a cheering throng.

Grover Cleveland Redding, Abyssinian Movement, Chicago.

Noble Drew Ali, Moorish American Science Temple, Chicago.
This one bearded and in a fez, among many other blacks in fezzes.
W. D. Fard, Muslim Temple Number One, Detroit.
Elijah Muhammad, Muslim Temple Number Two, Chicago.
Malcolm X, Organization of African American Unity, Harlem.
Mwalimu wa Weusi, Umoja, Los Angeles.

There really were separate cultures, Jack Liffey thought. He hadn't even heard of some of these leaders. One black nationalist was conspicuously missing. Jack Liffey turned back to the receptionist. "Where's Ron Karenga and US?"

The young man furrowed up his eyebrows even more, "Check it out. You go to a Ford dealer, you expect a lot of pictures of Chevys?"

"Point taken."

There was a framed multicolor motto beside the gallery: GANGSTA RAP NOT WELCOME HERE. THESE ARE THE REAL HEROES.

He took to peering closely at the shot of Malcolm, probably taken toward the end of his life. The man had been caught looking exhausted to the core, as he leaned out over a lectern. A Young Turk stood beside him, his eyes wide as if spotting the assassin in the crowd.

Jack Liffey heard voices, and a young man in sweats hurried out of a side room, leaving the door open to what looked like a classroom. A blackboard was covered with what was probably Swahili, and three young men pored over an ancient computer on a scarred desk. One of them wore the same tricolor cap as the receptionist.

"*Numba yanga haina malango,*" one read off the screen.

"Something about a house."

"My house has no door. It a Swahili riddle, fool."

"Huh?"

"It mean an egg."

Outside, a whole parade of fire trucks went wailing down the boulevard, one after another, not just the two you usually heard. Something pretty big was burning.

Maeve Liffey hefted a big plastic trash can that was nearly empty and set it under the high window where she could see the curtain was parted. Her heart thundered away so loud she was afraid they could hear it from inside the house. She knew Mary Beth was watching from the trees, so she stifled an almost irresistible urge to flee as fast as possible.

The plastic can had a lot of disconcerting flex under her feet as she climbed onto it. She pressed her palms against the rough sun-warmed stucco to stabilize herself and inched upward until her head just cleared the sill.

A TV was glowing blue across the room. It took her eyes a moment to adjust to the interior murk, and then she found she was looking across a dining table piled with dishes and cooking pots and ravaged pizza boxes that had probably been there for weeks. Beyond was a front room where half a dozen big men lounged on a sofa and pillows on the floor to watch the TV. One seemed passed out flat on his back on a reed mat, his mouth wide open to collect flies. There were more tattoos per square foot than anywhere she'd ever seen. Most of the guys wore armless T-shirts and jeans that didn't look any too clean, but one of the bikers was bare-chested, and the man passed out was only wearing jockey shorts and had the hairiest shoulders and chest she'd ever seen, like somebody had glued toupees all over him. The bikers all had beer cans, and they were watching one of those talk shows where people sit side by side to humiliate one another. She could hear the TV voices buzzing lightly against the glass.

A car passed on the street, and one guy on the sofa looked over at the front window and said something. He held up a hand and the man beside him high-fived him, so Maeve guessed whatever he'd said had been judged witty.

She was just wondering what *exactly* this was going to tell her about the disappearance of Amilcar Davis, beyond the fact that he was not chained up in the corner of their living room, when the trash can started to bend in on one side. It was like a slow-motion nightmare. She willed the plastic to stop its inexorable sag and clawed at the stucco to take her weight off that side, but she went right on sinking slowly at an angle until all at once the can sproinged and she fell straight down onto it. She cried out in alarm, unable to stop herself,

and found herself on her stomach, draped over the side of the toppled trash can, catching her weight on a smarting knee on the dirt.

Oh, please, *please*, she thought.

She heard the back door open and then there was this inconceiv-
able person looming over her, with a grin and a pointy beard and
arms like trees that were covered with blue eagles and daggers and
other things. A gigantic hand closed on her thin upper arm.

"Little girl, if you're so all-fired het up about what's inside here,
maybe you best come on in."

"Mary Beth, run!" Maeve shouted.

The Mwalimu himself came out to usher him into the inner sanctum.
He was tall and imposing, maybe sixty, bearded and dressed in full
African regalia. He didn't offer to shake hands, either in standard
fashion or Movement style.

"Welcome to Unity House, Mr. Liffey. We're not as hostile to
your people as you may have been led to expect."

"I'm never sure who my people are," Jack Liffey said, as he followed along a shabby corridor, with the Mwalimu's gold-red-green
robe billowing ahead like some huge flightless bird. He wondered if
it was cooler under there. The place had no air-conditioning, and the
deeper he went into the complex the stuffier it got.

"You have that luxury. The oppressed do not."

"Yes, okay."

The office was fairly shabby too, except for an imposing African
mask of a woman's head, with what looked like long seed pods bal-
anced on top, and a large cloth covered with repetitious black-and-
white designs that hung flat against the wall. There was a small
desk, but the man chose to sit in an old easy chair and motioned Jack
Liffey to a threadbare sofa opposite.

A cheap old transistor radio was fizzing softly on a side table, and
the man bowed for a moment to put his ear near it and then came
upright.

"Kidogo is out right now, but he'll be back shortly. I assume it is
he you wish to meet."

"It is *he*," Jack Liffey repeated.

The man smiled. "I have a doctorate—in what we used to call Black Studies, from the University of Michigan," Mwalimu wa Weusi said.

"Then you probably knew Amilcar's mother in Ann Arbor."

"Oh, yes. Even though we were on opposing sides of a very old dispute. We had one common point, in that we both claim W. E. B. Du Bois. Beyond that, Ms. Thigpen always put the working class and the writings of a dead German Jew ahead of her own people."

"I'm not sure you can call Karl Marx Jewish."

He shrugged. "Race is always a bit of an artificial construct, isn't it? Obviously I have some European blood, but this country sees me as African American completely and forever. As long as they do, I haven't much choice."

Which deftly avoided the issue of anti-Semitism, Jack Liffey thought.

"You will admit it's curious that Amilcar's family chose to send a white man to investigate his son's disappearance," Mwalimu wa Weusi added.

"I caught the case from an African-American detective. He punted when it looked like he might have to interview some neo-Nazis out in the Inland Empire."

"Did you get along well with them?"

Jack Liffey smiled. "I don't think I'd like them any more than you would, but the trail seemed to lead more in this direction. Reports suggest that Amilcar and his girlfriend had a bad experience right here in LA the weekend before they disappeared."

"I don't know anything about that. Perhaps Kidogo can help you."

He raised a finger for silence and then dipped his head again to the radio.

"Not yet," he said, after a moment, sitting back up with a grave look. "Abdullah Ibrahim is about to hold a press conference," he explained.

"Is he one of yours?"

"He's NOI, but we honor him. He made his fortune, but he didn't move out to Malibu to swim with the movie stars."

"NOI?"

"Nation of Islam."

"Ah, of course. Did they ever adopt orthodox Islam? I can't remember."

"After Elijah Muhammad died, his son Walid moved them in that direction, but Farrakhan won the internal struggle and took them back to that inventive tale of the evil scientist Yakub who conjured up the white race by accident. I believe Farrakhan reports that this all took place after he visited Elijah on a flying saucer."

He didn't crack a smile and Jack Liffey couldn't work out his attitude. They sat in silence for a moment. Generally, silence did not make Jack Liffey uncomfortable—it provided a nice edge when he was questioning people—but this time it did. "Tell me about gangsta rap," he inquired. "I saw your sign out front."

"Whatever the sign says, I would defend it in the white media. But just between us I think it's obscene nihilism. Glorifying a thug life. There's something abhorrent about watching a people dance to their own degradation, all for the profit of white music executives."

"A lot of young people seem to respond to it."

"Yes, the white press always argues that the gangsta images are simply holding up a mirror to reality. But a drowning man doesn't need a mirror. He needs a hand, a way out, a swimming lesson."

The answer was so studied that Jack Liffey guessed it was part of a canned response he had given often.

"We have to get our own community together before we can meet the world on its own terms. Once we do, we can define our own interests for ourselves and offer our own cultural truths to the world. African Americans have been at the root of just about every great form of art this country has produced—jazz, blues, rock."

"Not cinema," Jack Liffey offered. "The Jews did that."

Their eyes met, and he thought he sensed a spark of amusement. "Yes, they did," the Mwalimu conceded. "And as a people, the Jews have suffered greatly. Pogroms, the Holocaust—we appreciate all that, but we are no longer in a period when alliances are of much value to us. We are about self-reliance now."

"More power to you," Jack Liffey said. "But I'd like to share jazz, if you don't mind, even if the Irish seem stuck with Riverdance."

* * *

Maeve Liffey sat on a folding Samsonite chair in the middle of the living room with a big fat rope tied around her waist. It looked like the kind of rope they used to moor ocean liners, and it had about thirty feet of slack wending across the floor to where the other end was tied around the toilet in the bathroom. It had taken two of the overmuscled bikers to cinch up the knot against her belly so she had no illusions about working it free in some moment of opportunity.

"So you looked in the window and you liked what you saw?"

It was the huge one who'd hauled her inside, whose name she'd heard as Lunchmeat. A skinnier and fiercer one nicknamed Greek sat in a beanbag facing her. He had the word UNEMPLOYABLE tattooed across his forehead, with a swastika under it.

The initial panic had almost made her faint as she'd tried to dig in her heels outside, but Lunchmeat had lifted her off the ground with one hand and carried her inside like a tote bag. Her panic had now given way to a kind of frantic calculation of possibilities. It was hard to discern what went on in their heads. She felt like a dog in a room full of humans, trying desperately to read their unspoken intentions.

"No, I don't," she said.

"You don't like us?" big Lunchmeat said, with mock wounded vanity.

The TV was blaring away in the background, identical twin women bragging about how they had fooled their husbands and swapped beds at will. The husbands were much less cheerful about it, and the big security guards restraining the husbands looked a lot like the bikers.

"What's your name?" Lunchmeat asked.

"Nancy."

"Nancy what?"

"Drew."

Lunchmeat bulked over her and bent way forward, sniffing at her hair. He had the reek of an old ashtray.

"Don't little girls smell *nice*. Ain't even no perfume to it. Greek, come smell her."

The thinner one launched himself toward her and buried his face in her lap. She went rigid as he nuzzled where he shouldn't, and a chill overtook her whole body.

He pushed back up off her knees. "Ain't like no woman yet, not even a little bitty can of tuna fish. You peek in our window to work out what fucking a bunch of us is gonna feel like?"

"*No!*" She realized she'd better come up with something plausible fast.

Lunchmeat took a fistful of her hair and sniffed it some more. "Nice. Umm."

"You know," Greek said, "you come into our place, we can do what we want with you. It's the law."

"It is *not*."

" 'Course it is. We talked about it back in social studies in high school. Guy breaks into your place, you can shoot him. I remember one ignoramus asks, 'What if the guy's only half in the window?' and the teacher goes, 'Just shoot the *inside* half.' " He guffawed.

"That's not true."

"So we get to do what we want with you and *then* shoot you. No point wasting it, huh, girl?" When she let herself look at him she could see he was eyeing her breasts. She was mortified that she had on the sexy lacy bra she'd sneaked out to buy one day when her mom was busy.

"I didn't break in," she insisted.

"You're in now."

"What you after if it ain't a good time?" Lunchmeat asked.

There was nothing to lose now, she thought. "I thought you might be holding Amilcar Davis for ransom."

"Milk-car?" Lunchmeat said quizzically.

There was some sort of outburst on TV and a guy across the room hollered, "Look at that! Mother*fuck*!" but no one was paying attention.

She could see understanding dawning on Greek.

"She's talking about that nigger who was double-dating with the queers."

"Man, one of those guys must have been personally related to the president," Lunchmeat said.

"He means the cops been here three fuckin' times already, pussy, even the Feds."

"There's a big reward," she improvised. She almost went for a million but thought it was probably over the top. "A hundred thousand dollars."

"Fuckin'-A," Lunchmeat said. "For that, I'd turn my own ass in."

"Too bad we ain't got him."

"If you aren't holding him, I was mistaken," she said, in a brave stab at normality. "I'm really sorry. You can just let me go and I'll forget it and look somewhere else."

"What're *you* worth?"

"My dad's poor," she said quickly. "He's laid off."

Lunchmeat had moved around in front of her but she saw his keen interest collapse, as if he'd just pawed through the stolen wallet and found only a few singles. Wouldn't a rich girl say the same thing? Maeve thought. This guy was *really* not very bright.

"Then we got to have some fun with you," Greek said. "Cash or gash, that's the rule."

He'd imagined Kidogo showing up in his own sct of multicolored robes, but in fact he dribbled his way into the office nonchalantly in a purple Laker jersey that was soaked through as if he'd been playing all afternoon. He fit the costume. He was thin and at least six-nine, and the ball kept rapping down on the floor like a finger hammering on the same bruise.

"*Habari gani*?" the Mwalimu greeted him.

"*Mzuri sana*. 'Sup? I heard you wanted to see me."

"Amilcar's father asked us to talk to this man. His name is Jack Liffey and he's searching for Amilcar."

The young man's eyes didn't come around, but he nodded. "Anything for the man Ban. Let's go out in the court, white person. 'Stoo hot here."

Jack Liffey followed him along the hallway, Kidogo dribbling slowly all the way, then out into a small asphalt yard, just big enough for a half court, with a hoop set above a blank wall. At least it was marginally cooler here. The young man kept his eyes averted, and

Jack Liffey reflected that diffidence and homicidal hatred could look a lot alike.

"How's your basketball skills?" the young man asked.

"Just south of nonexistent."

The young man sent him a no-look pass, a little harder than necessary. "If you can put it through, I'll answer a question."

"Hell, with my height I ought to get a stepladder." He took a shot, an air ball that arched embarrassingly short. He hadn't touched a basketball in probably twenty years and realized that he'd seen so much expert play, at least as often as he'd stumbled across it on TV, that his subconscious had forgotten that the ball had any weight to it.

Kidogo took a step to reclaim the ball.

"So don't answer the *first* question," Jack Liffey said. "It was, What's the square root of thirty-four?"

Kidogo smiled, despite himself, went up on a jump and put the ball through without touching net. Then he retrieved the ball and bounced it to Jack Liffey again. It took him two more tries to get it through the hoop, inelegantly, with a high bounce off the rim.

"The last weekend Amilcar was home, there was some sort of problem here in LA. Maybe a run-in. People on campus said he was pretty upset about it."

Kidogo took two steps and leaped, swung around in midair, and did a reverse slam dunk.

"Nice," Jack Liffey offered.

The young man still hadn't made eye contact. "The trouble wasn't here. I saw Ami that morning at the bookstore, Eso Won, and everything was fine. Him and Sherry were gonna have dinner with me and my woman at Elephant Walk in Leimert Park, but he called about five. It was from a pay phone, I think. I could hear traffic. He was angry and said he couldn't make it. They were going home to Claremont."

"Do you know where he'd gone after you saw him in the morning?"

"Nope."

"Did you tell the police this?"

"They never asked."

"Is there anything else you know that could help?"

He seemed to think about it for a moment. "You must think you one tough motherfucker."

"Why do you say that?"

"Pushin' in here, askin' questions where you ain't—say—*real* welcome."

"You know, up to now I've found African Americans almost faultlessly polite to me all my life. It's usually white racists who can't manage civility."

"Must be they little bitty dicks," Kidogo said, but there wasn't any real menace at work. The chip on his shoulder was just something he had to wave around a bit to prove something to himself. Jack Liffey felt sorry for all the pain his attitude was going to cause him for the rest of his life.

"I'll tell them that, if I see any." He could see he'd got all the information he was going to get.

"I don't hate whiteys," Kidogo said, all of a sudden. He lofted another swish through the net and met Jack Liffey's eyes for the first time, a neutral expression that suggested he had expended all the patience he had available. "I just want a situation where we can be with ourselfs and make our own decisions for ourselfs without some white muckty-muck coming and telling us what's good for us to be down for."

"I hope you find the world where that's possible, I really do," Jack Liffey said.

It was late but still a bright dusk as he got home, one of those hot California summer evenings that swore to you they'd never pass away until all your dreams were fulfilled. If only his dreams were still simmering away on the back burner.

Water was running, and a steady discharge of steam seeped out under the bathroom door. She usually bathed first thing in the morning. He turned the knob softly and saw Marlena's strong brown shoulder in a fog of bubbles rising off the tub. She appeared to be scrubbing hard at her privates.

"Eeep." It was a tiny squeal of surprise, and two fingers went to her lips as she sat back.

"You forget. I've seen that lovely body," he said.

A froth climbed her breasts like frosting on a cake, and she tried to smile at him, but something was wrong.

"You okay?" he asked.

Just then the phone rang, and she said, "Please get it," with such urgency that he thought she might be expecting word of a death.

"Is this Jack Liffey?" a man asked.

"Speaking."

"Jack, this is Tom Leary."

It took Jack Liffey a moment to focus and make the connection—his cousin out in Claremont—and then sense the note of tragedy in the man's flat suburban voice.

He nearly shouted into the phone. "Is Maeve all right?"

"I don't know. It took a long time for Mary Beth to tell us what happened." He hesitated.

"*Please.*"

"Yeah, sorry. Maeve got caught up with some motorcycle types out in Fontana, and she hasn't come home yet."

Something heavy and cold sank to the pit of Jack Liffey's stomach and kept right on going down.

"Did you call the police?"

"Right away. They just called me to say they checked and nobody was at the clubhouse Mary Beth described. She's a little hysterical right now, but she swears that's where Maeve was. The girls were playing some kind of detective game, and Maeve was peeking in a window when a big guy with a beard caught her and took her inside. I'm sorry. It took awhile for Mary Beth to bicycle back here and tell us."

"Was this the Bone Losers?" Jack Liffey asked.

"Yeah, that's the name she used."

How on *earth*? he wondered. She must have seen his paperwork, but what was she up to?

"I'm on my way."

He swung open the bathroom door. "Maeve's in trouble. I've gotta go, and I'm taking the Franchi." The Franchi was a big black twelve-gauge shotgun she kept under the bed. It had a pistol grip, operated either as a pump or a semiautomatic, and was a lot more intimidating than his pistol. He noticed she was crying as she sat helplessly in the bath, but he didn't have time for that.

Jack Liffey drove east on the 10 as fast as he and the Concord could bear, panic and dread gnawing at his stomach. This had always been the nightmare: something gruesome swooping down out of nowhere to gobble up his vulnerable daughter. But what had she been up to, playing detective? Kathy would certainly blame him for that. Far off to his right, he noticed dark columns of smoke rising up and then shearing off westward at several points in South Central, offerings unacceptable to the gods.

eight

A Failure to Communicate

She had no idea where she was. With the scratchy fat rope still tied around her waist, she had been carried into a beat-up van and driven miles to a piney little house up a canyon where a lot more of the weird motorcycles were parked.

They were effectively lashed together, she and the beer-smelling gorilla named Lunchmeat, standing outside among the bikes. He had the end of her rope wrapped once around his tattooed forearm. She tried to imagine him as a child, smaller but still chunky, holding back his tears as he was beaten and thrust away by a boozy father as big as he was now. She couldn't really do it, and she couldn't picture where he lived, either, though she tried to imagine him in a cheap apartment with his possessions stashed around in old fruit crates, his shirts hung on nails hammered into the walls. He was too far out-side her experience, but she needed to imagine who he was. She knew her safety might depend on figuring him out.

The nearest lights she could see from the yard were far out in the valley, obscured by haze. A big road was out there, too, probably the 10, with pinpricks of light crawling along it.

" 'The darkness drops again! But now I know that twenty centuries of stony sleep were vexed to nightmare by a rocking cradle!' "

The skinny one named Greek had his head thrown back, his arms flung outward, and was bellowing some poem into the night, lit up where he stood by the yellow light spilling from a window. Sweat dripped down his stringy hair and flew off as he tossed his head. On the way up the canyon, Greek had sat beside her on the floor of the van, and she had tried not to watch him rip a small piece off a Chore Boy copper pan scraper, stick it into a weird glass pipe with a little yellowish rock, and smoke it hard and fast.

Maeve tried to act nonchalant as she stood among the monstrous motorcycles, but she was really nearly catatonic with fright, and her legs were too rubbery to trust. Bats darted around silently overhead, zigging as if they were bounding off invisible walls. She took a deep breath and forced her thoughts and imaginings to stop flitting around like the bats. What to *do*? Calling out for help seemed pointless, though she certainly hoped Mary Beth had the police heading after them by now.

"Pay attention, little one," Lunchmeat said. He squatted to get up close and personal with the engine of a motorcycle, supporting his immense leaning bulk on one hand. "This here is a 'sixty-eight shovelhead. You can tell by these two bolts in the cylinder head."

He might as well have been talking Sanskrit, but she did her best to absorb the information.

"In 'sixty-eight, the Japs brung in their big Honda, and the shovelhead was Harley's answer to the big rice-burners. And see this one here, it's got electric start. The wussies got to have it these days. Won't do no jump starts no more."

"Will there be a quiz?" Maeve heard herself say.

He chuckled. "You got a good spirit on you, Nancy Drew."

" 'The blood-dimmed tide is loosed!' Owww! *Goddamn*!" In midverse, Greek seemed to have lost his balance and fallen against a motorcycle. He was hopping around on one foot, rubbing his knee like crazy.

"Look here, Nancy. This is the blockhead engine that the company calls the Evolution. It's all smooth on the heads. This is my own baby; I call her Big Potatoes."

"Why's that?"

"That's the Harley sound, *potato potato*. When that big V-twin mothah's started up and idling away between your knees, it's rough as a rasp, going pa-*too*-toh, pa-*too*-toh, and you know for sure you're on a real man's machine."

She'd never felt so lost and helpless in her life.

"We make a pretty unlikely pair of vigilantes," the young man said. He rode nervously beside Jack Liffey, cradling an aluminum baseball bat. The nose ring was gone, and he was dressed in ordinary jeans and a sweatshirt that said only COLLEGE.

"Who would be a *likely* pair of vigilantes?" Jack Liffey asked. He was pretty distracted himself, his muscles so tensed he knew he would be wrung out like a rag before very long.

"True, true."

He had grabbed up Marlena's cell phone and called David Phelps on the way, and Phelps had gone through a friend-of-a-friend-of-a-friend to get an address for the Bone Losers, somewhere out into the foothills of the San Bernardino range not far from a place improbably called Muscoy.

Phelps eyed the big, ugly shotgun that rode between the seats. "Is that legal?"

"If it's unloaded, it's legal to carry it."

"Is it unloaded?"

"No."

"I see."

"It's only legal in the trunk anyway," Jack Liffey added, as if he didn't want the young man to get in trouble by quoting him wrong one day.

"I'm kind of opposed to violence," David Phelps demurred, though still anxious to be agreeable.

"So am I."

Phelps studied him carefully. "You look 'Nam age. Were you over there?"

"Uh-huh, but I was just a technician in an electronics trailer out in the jungle."

"So you've never shot anyone."

Jack Liffey didn't answer and time stretched out a bit.

"Uh-oh. This isn't a death mission here, is it?"

"We're going to get my daughter. As Malcolm X said, by any means necessary."

"Uh-huh, okay. But did you actually shoot somebody before?"

"Yes." It was a long story and he didn't have time for it, and he wasn't very happy about it. "Sometimes, say when you're falling out of an airplane, it doesn't do much good to insist you're opposed to gravity."

"Got you. Yes, sir." He could see the young man's sense of calculation was working overtime, and it was running hard up against his agreeable nature. "Let's hope we can negotiate this. That's what I'm here for."

"Let's hope."

Then they rode in silence down the darkness, threading fast from lane to lane through what was still a fair amount of traffic on the 10. The old Concord wasn't worth much money anymore but it still had a V-8 and it could crank. The inland valley was so smoggy, taillights materialized slowly a mile or two ahead in the murk, starting out orange and growing redder as he swooped down on them.

David Phelps rotated the aluminum bat, as if giving its presence there a second thought. "Whatever happened to ash bats? Aluminum makes a stupid tinny sound when you hit a ball."

"Uh-huh."

"It's like they have to inject their damn technology into every corner of every sport to make you buy new stuff. Fiberglass pole vault poles, high-tech basketball shoes, carbon tennis rackets. Why not just shoot balls out of guns at each other?"

"Do you really care about the purity of the baseball bat?" Jack Liffey asked.

There was a long silence as the young man stared down at the bat in his lap. "Did you know it was a gay football player who invented the high five?"

"And Michelangelo was gay, and Einstein, Marconi, and Lindbergh, too."

"Just Michelangelo. But a helluva painter."

* * *

"Kid, what's up?"

A tug on the big rope yanked her a foot out of the corner of the rustic pine room where she'd retreated. The air was full of cigarette smoke and the smell of stale spilled beer. Greek snored on his back on the floor and Lunchmeat was sitting on a worn leather ottoman, absently flipping the other end of the rope as if he was about to start a skip-rope contest.

She would need all her wits about her now, she thought. She had already wound two turns of the rope around her waist without his noticing. She had a plan, actually a very simple plan. She would get him back outside and ask him a barrage of questions about motorcycles until she found some way to entice him into occupying both his hands with one of the bikes so he'd drop his end of the rope. That would give her a chance to pirouette slowly, wrap the rest of the rope around herself, and bolt out into the darkness, where she thought there was a ravine with a small stream and a lot of plants that might give her shelter until morning. *Unless*—she thought with a shudder— he had his way with her first.

She thought of Brad again. He had slapped her in a moment of anger and deeply disturbed her childhood faith in human goodness, yet even now she couldn't believe that anyone would be so depraved as to take sexual advantage of a girl like herself. There was even an undertow of guilt whenever her thoughts lit on the subject because of various idle sexual fantasies she had had over the years. But the reality turned out to be pure abhorrence, nothing at all like the fantasy.

"I want to go home," she blurted out, her voice a lot smaller and shakier than she'd ever heard it. She had a feeling that it might be good not to let on how frightened she was, but the words just spilled out of her.

He flipped the slack rope absently, and a traveling wave crossed the room and buffeted her as it arrived. "I didn't mean none of this to happen like this, but, sheesh, I just don't know what to do now. You look like a good kid, Nancy."

The name threw her for a moment. "You've never heard of Nancy Drew, have you?"

"Huh? You somebody important?"

"No, no." She figured being somebody important would only make things worse. "My dad is poor but he's a detective, you know. He doesn't ever give up when he's after something so you don't want to do anything to hurt me."

"Don't be kickin' at me, kid," he said dully. She could see that appreciating the consequences of his actions was probably not Lunchmeat's strong point.

"Back home in Fon, we was just gonna have us some fun scarin' you. Girls like you is always tryin'a pump our gas and shit. But this pal of ours in the police called up and said the black-and-whites was coming and we had to book out, and then Greek gone and got himself so fucked up on dust I don't know what to do."

"Just let me go. I'll say I was lost all night in the hills. Honest."

He made a face. "I wish I could, Nancy. I really do. But it's all turned into a big fuckin' deal somehow. Maybe I best just throw you off Icehouse Canyon."

A chill went all the way up her spine and clasped the back of her neck. If he meant what he seemed to mean, it stunned her that he would suggest it so casually. Neither of them seemed to want to talk for a while. Greek snored away with a steady ripping sound, and another biker lay face down on a sofa, as still as death. The dark hot world outside the unscreened window was absolutely silent.

"How come you're not married?" Maeve asked. It had taken a big act of will to gather herself together bit by bit.

"I was once, but my old lady went and found somebody else. I would of jumped him and beat his brains out but they took off and only left me a note. I'm not a bad guy. I just never had no chances."

"Did you love her?"

His face screwed up and he chewed and worked his cheeks, as if, in order to consider a question like that, he had to fire up an engine that didn't get a lot of use. "Yeah, I guess so," he essayed finally.

"I'm sorry."

"She was pretty as a picture till she let herself go and got fat."

"What's your real name?" Maeve asked.

"Ratke," he said. "Phil Ratke, recording treasurer of the Bone Losers."

"What do you do, Phil? I mean, your job."

He gave another absentminded toss of the rope, and she felt the wave reach her like the swell off a powerboat. "My dad was a puddler at Kaiser. He was in the steel all his life. I had me two years there, too, before they closed down and sent us all home. I sold paint for a while, but a big Home Depot come in and killed the paint store."

"Couldn't you move to the big store?"

"Nancy, do I look like the kind of guy they want at the desk, selling lawn chairs to Joe Suburb?"

"Sure." The Nancy business was beginning to embarrass her, but she didn't see how she could fix it.

He frowned. "Naw, you know I ain't. After that I drove a bus till I busted one up and they found out I'd had—ah, about two sniffs of beer in the twenty-four hours before. I ain't worked steady in a year now."

"What did you study in school?"

The question occasioned another long hitch in the machinery.

"I mean, when you were in school, what did you want to be?"

"I wanteda be me. I dunno. I guess I wanted to be a rich retired golfer."

Maeve chuckled softly. "Do you play golf?"

"Fuck, no. I just don't wanna do nothing but ride my bike."

"What about motorcyle repair?"

He shrugged. "Them Japs—it's all electronic ignition and shit. Takes a computer to change the fuckin' oil. Pardon my French."

"Could you show me some more about those great American motorcycles?" she asked, as if casually.

"You want to look at the bikes?"

"Sure. I may as well learn something."

He looked at her anew, as if changing his mind about something. "You're one tough kiddo, Nance." He took another turn of rope around his forearm and nodded toward the door. "Why not? I never showed you the real jewel out there, the finest riding bike they ever built."

"Is it yours?"

"Naw. It's Jake-o's. He's the Supreme President of the Bones, but he's gone off on a little vacation to Quentin."

They went out into the spooky dark of the yard, and then he reached back in the door to open the blinds and let light spill over the bikes. Far away she heard an owl and then a train whistle down in the valley, like an eerie reply to the bird. The air was still hot and dry with a gusty wind full of grit that she recognized as a Santa Ana blowing west off the desert.

"Living out here is bad for your skin," she said.

"So's dyin' out here," he said, and guffawed a little. She felt a chill but decided she preferred not to explore that subject.

"Which one's the super bike?"

"Over here."

It was sitting by itself under a canvas tarp. He threw the tarp off and she saw an older-looking motorcyle with a windshield and a huge molded seat. Big metal containers hung on both sides of the rear wheel like saddlebags.

"That's a 1963 Electra-glide."

"It's a panhead engine, isn't it?"

"Wow, girl. You pay attention."

Then the night was torn open by an explosion. It was very close, and her head snapped around to see the 1963 Electra-glide recoil from the blast and lean away from them. The seat was torn up and the motorcycle seemed to consider toppling, but thought better of it and righted itself.

"On your face, asshole!"

She knew that voice. "Daddy, no!"

She heard a *ka-chunk* that she recognized from a hundred cop movies as the sound of a shotgun being pumped. The explosion came again, and the middle of the motorcycle disintegrated. She expected to see it explode in fire, but it didn't. What was left of the frame just fell over with a crash of metal. She couldn't see her dad, but it was definitely his voice.

"On your face *now*!"

* * *

He saw a biker the size of a middle linebacker standing there with a tarp dangling from one hand. He saw a big rope around his daughter's waist and a droop of the rope going back to the biker. He had fired away from the biker, but it was a near thing in his head. David Phelps stood nearby with the aluminum bat at parade rest. The motorcycle had offered itself as a convenient target for his wrath. It was an emblem that some deep reserve of self-mastery told him he could ventilate a bit just then, take the edge off his fury and feel some satisfaction without spending the rest of his life in prison. Those two shots had shaken up his psyche, though in a new way. They had blasted away the initial rage at seeing his daughter tied up, but they'd also initiated something that he had not anticipated, a swelling bloodlust that picked him right up off the surface of the earth and seemed to want a whole lot more out of him.

The biker went face down slowly, and the barrel of the shotgun dug into the back of his neck. Jack Liffey found that his own scratchy throat was bugling some terrifying cry that he did not even recognize as human speech. There was a bleat in his left ear, perhaps his daughter's voice, and a further human noise on the right, but he was up on a knife edge now, far above them all. He hung there in a fiery place where he had never been.

He liked it a lot. The shotgun in his hands begged to be fired, rumbled and trembled and squirmed and pleaded with him. *I've got all this pent-up force*, it swore to him. *Release me, let me show you. You'll love what I do.* The hillock of flesh was face down in the dirt as if just finishing off a push-up. Jack Liffey wasn't given to extravagant acts but there was a dark urge propelling him toward this one, toward that wretched being at his feet. He felt the trigger flex. He teetered. Go, go! Suddenly a sharp blow knocked the shotgun sideways and the instrument fired deafeningly out over the canyon. Jack Liffey found himself trembling, his head woozy, and gradually he became conscious of David Phelps clinging to him on one side and Maeve on the other.

"He didn't hurt me! I'm okay, Daddy!"

"Oh, man, *please* don't kill me."

As his vision started back from pink, Jack Liffey began to laugh. The earth firmed up. It was all clear as a snapshot and it was absurd.

His daughter, a fat rope around her waist, clung to one of his arms, and a flamboyantly gay young man with a baseball bat clung to the other, while a tattooed mound of Jell-O lay at his feet, groveling shamelessly.

"'What we have here,'" Jack Liffey said, as he squeezed himself back into a more normal frame, "'is a failure to communicate.'" The prissy words of the weaselly little guard in *Cool Hand Luke* were all that came to him just then.

"Uh, anything you say, man."

Maeve started pleading rapidly, trying to take all the blame. She had been totally dumb, she insisted, she'd set out to play at Nancy Drew and intruded on the privacy of the bikers; it was her own butting in that had created such a terrible misunderstanding. Jack Liffey hushed her with a finger to his lips.

"You're not Nancy Drew?" The biker seemed confused, but the shotgun came back on him and his mind only had time for the weapon.

"Let him be, man," David Phelps said. "Ease off."

"Sit up, but don't get up," Jack Liffey said. "This isn't over."

"Anything, ah, sir, *really*. I didn't do nothing to the kid."

"He didn't, Daddy. They just scared me, honest."

Jack Liffey took the heavy mooring line in his free hand and looked dubiously at it.

The biker rolled his eyes. "Just a game, sir."

"*Please*, Daddy. Don't hurt him."

"We've got a couple things in the balance here." Jack Liffey's voice had become lethargic. "We've got felony kidnapping of a girl. Do they give the death penalty for that anymore? I can't remember." He glanced at the motorcycle. "And we've got a wounded piece of metal, result of the discharge of a shotgun—maybe more to come. I don't know what sort of jail I get for that, not very much if I reckon the sensibilities of most juries. Maybe a medal. But I'm feeling magnanimous here all of a sudden. That's 'forgiving' in little bitty words. We might just call all this even. What do you say?"

The biker glanced briefly at the mangled toppled bike, and there was an instant when he seemed to be considering the grievous loss.

"Felony. Kidnap," Jack Liffey reminded him.

"I guess it's even, man. And—uh—we didn't touch the missing nigger and his girl neither."

"I never thought you did."

"What are we going to tell your mother?" Jack Liffey said, when they were all back in the car and safely heading west on the 10.

"I don't know," Maeve said glumly. She turned to David Phelps, in back. "Who are you?"

"I'm the Lone Ranger," he offered.

She glanced briefly at her dad. "In this movie, I think you're more like Tonto."

"Sure, Kemo Sabe. Just take me home, please."

nine

Señor Coyote's Swing Rope

It was very late, he knew that much. His Timex had staggered to a halt about ten, as it did every once in a while, particularly when it might have been nice to know the time. He had to live with his intuition that it was about 3 A.M., at least until he caught sight of a roadside clock. Strangely, a cortege of big American cars roared past on the 10, honking and bedecked with black pom-poms and streamers of black crepe. On the rear window of the last car, a low-riding Oldsmobile, someone had scrawled *Just divorced* in poster paint; blink and it's gone. He had to smile. Celebrating social breakdown had reached the point where it was probably time to invest in bitter herbs and small arms.

"So what are we going to tell your mom?" he asked, coming round to it again. Maeve was still so wired she looked wide awake. They'd dropped off David Phelps and then roused the Learys, where they fetched Maeve's tiny suitcase, mollifying the cousins as best they could. Poor Mary Beth had found herself grounded for a month.

Maeve gave an exaggerated wince. "Do we have to tell her anything?"

"Yes, we do."

"You and your rigid ethics," she complained.

"They've become somewhat more flexible over the years." He tapped thoughtfully on the steering wheel. "Perhaps we can wait a little before giving her *all* the details. How do you feel about staying away from Bradley for a while longer?"

She lit up. "I feel really great about it. You know I love being with my daddy."

Her affection eased his edgy mood. She could always do this to him, and she knew it.

"Give some thought to how we're going to present this day of infamy in the long run," he suggested. "I think I've got a bit of leverage now to see you more often—I mean, after the run-in with Bradley—so I don't want to squander it."

"*That's* the kind of ethics I like."

"Not necessarily flexible," he suggested. "Just kind of portable."

She smiled, and rested her head against his shoulder, and then went out like a light.

By the time they pulled into the driveway in Mar Vista around 4 A.M., Maeve was snoring away. He was surprised to see no lights in the bungalow. He knew Rogelio was away, but Marlena usually left a few lamps on for the bogeyman. Her Toyota wasn't in the driveway either.

He woke Maeve with difficulty. She was drooping so badly that he had to bear most of her weight up the steps. Intentionally, he made a bit of noise as they came in so Marlena wouldn't be frightened if she happened to be there.

"I'll let you handle the mother issue," Maeve said groggily.

"Sounds good."

She went straight to her room. Jack Liffey peeked into the master bedroom and found it empty. He drifted toward the fridge where they kept a note pad, all of a sudden repicturing the tears he had seen running down her cheeks in the bathtub before he'd rushed off to save Maeve. The last few hours had blown the image of a distressed Marlena right out of his mind. There was a folded note under the magnetic carrot.

Jackie: I won't be back for a couple of days. Then we got to talk. Sorry.

A chill blew through him, while guilt padded around him like a wolf, nipping at his ankles. It could only be another man, he thought. He hadn't been attentive enough. He hadn't been loving enough. He hadn't been asking what she'd been doing the last few weeks. In the big picture, he hadn't made enough of an effort to overcome their contrarieties, to listen to her reports on the soaps and the doings at the hidden flying saucer hanger at Area 51 and who really killed Jon-Benet Ramsey.

He closed his eyes for a moment.

"Daddy, where's Mar?"

Maeve stood behind him, woozy and innocent in her cottony pink nightdress.

"I forgot," he said evenly, as he pocketed the note. "She was going to visit some relatives."

"Who?"

"You know what? I think she told me this morning, but your adventure has just burned my brain completely blank."

"You shoulda been a lawyer," she said. "You always turn it around to me."

"I shoulda been a merchant prince. Then I could *buy* lawyers. Full board in the morning, pancakes and sausages."

She tiptoed up to kiss his cheek. "Goody. Good night, Daddy."

The man with the salt-and-pepper beard slid into the booth at Sally's, eclipsing a few of the bright lozenges that the morning sunlight was burning onto the red and white oilcloth. He laid a folded-open *Simi Record* on the table, as if casually. "Yo, coach."

The place was busy as usual and Perry Krasny just glanced at the paper, a glance that told him all he needed.

S.V.H.S. STUDENT

BADLY HURT IN

SOLO CYCLE CRASH

Norman Berquist, 17, a senior at S.V. High School, was badly injured in a solo motorcycle crash late last night. . . .

Maybe the little shit would think twice now before passing out his malicious atheist literature.

"How's the wife, Bri?"

"Just fine there, K."

"Have a cup of coffee."

"Sure."

Krasny waved for the waitress.

"I'll bet you still tell the kids you got that scar jumping on a grenade to save your platoon," the bearded man teased.

Something hard entered Krasny's eyes. "What would you know about things like that?"

"I know I'm getting worried about our affairs starting to snowball out of control."

The waitress ignored them and went on talking to a handsome man in a business suit. He looked like someone who hung out a lot at a gym. Krasny picked up his coffee cup to wave it, but the napkin stuck to the bottom and that seemed to infuriate him. He ripped the napkin free with his left hand and crushed it into a ball.

"What have you done about the detective?" Krasny asked.

"Well," the bearded man drawled, "we *could* take care of him the old-fashioned way—" he glanced at the bud vase that held a single dusty silk chrysanthemum, picked it up, and spoke into the flower as if it contained a microphone—"but that would be wrong."

"I'm completely stuffed." She pushed back from the table and gave a little involuntary belch. "Oops! That was a doozy."

"*Excuse me* is sufficient," Jack Liffey suggested.

"It's funny. If you burp, you can say *excuse me*, and if you sneeze or yawn or hiccup. But if you fart, you're just supposed to pretend it didn't happen."

He gave it some thought. "I think Emily Post regards *excuse me* as inappropriate in a number of situations, such as keeling forward and ending up nose down in the soup."

"Changing the subject again. Did you know Mark Twain wrote a whole book about farting? Did you light farts when you were in college? The bad girls do it at school, sitting up on the counter in the bathroom, right through their panties."

"I thought, with all your adventures yesterday, you'd be a bit chastened this morning. How do you know what the bad girls do?"

"What's chastened?"

"Subdued."

"No, I'm irrepressible."

He smiled. "I've noticed. And you change the subject pretty handily yourself. We need a long hike to walk off all these carbs. There's a canyon up toward Point Mugu that has a real waterfall."

"You've told me about it, but you've never taken me there."

"I save it for my best girlfriends."

"Then we're there, Dad."

He was clearing the plates when he heard a clatter and rattle on the sidewalk in front. He wondered if Marlena had come back, and how he would handle it in front of Maeve if it plunged into an emotional crisis. But he quickly decided that if that sound came from Marlena, she was dragging something pretty strange along with her.

He peeked out the front and saw Genesee Thigpen pushing an aluminum walker, with Ornetta skipping around her. There was an old black Mercury parked in front. He noticed someone had stuck split tennis balls on the rear legs of the walker to help it slide and cut down the noise somewhat.

He hurried outside and greeted them, offering the old woman his arm. She clamped him in a startlingly strong grip.

"What a wonderful surprise," he said.

"Gramma come early," Ornetta explained, "so you won't be got yo' hat yet."

"We weren't gonna leave for a while," he answered. "My car's still busy having its secret talk with the lawn mower."

Ornetta grinned and pranced toward the steps. Maeve came out and Jack Liffey introduced them.

"Daddy told me about you. You're the storyteller!"

The girls smiled at each other, like lost Martians meeting on a far world.

"Maevie, hi you!"

They held hands. Jack Liffey was astonished how easy it could all be. Why did men have to circle around, sniffing butts and growling?

The old woman let go of his arm when it turned out to be impossible to hold on and push the walker at the same time. She made her own way up the walk, step-step-slide.

"Ornetta's got something to tell you," Genesee Thigpen pronounced between footfalls.

"She's already hinted to me I should check out the Sherry Webber end of things. I just haven't had time to act on it." He didn't want to talk about the adventures in Claremont. "Can I get you some coffee? Some food?"

"Coffee would be most kind."

"Where's your husband?"

"He's at home. He wants Ornetta and me to stay with my sister Taffeta in Oakwood for a while."

Oakwood was a tiny African-American enclave not far away in Venice, which, along with a section of downtown San Pedro near the shipyards, was as close as the realtors ever got to letting blacks belly up to the ocean. Everywhere else they were dammed back into the interior by elbow-to-elbow white engineers and dentists guarding the beach towns.

"The cross burning?"

"Uh-huh, and other things. He wants us safe away from the house."

"What other things?"

She abandoned the walker and took his arm to hobble up the steps onto the small veranda, where she chose to take a breather on the oak glide. He sat on a beach chair while she huffed a little, the glide swaying gently.

"Threats. But we're experts on that."

"I'll bet. Let me get you some coffee. I warn you, it's strong. Sugar or milk?"

"Milk, please."

"Coming up."

Inside, Ornetta and Maeve had disappeared into Maeve's room and he could hear their voices overlapping eagerly behind the door. He was immensely pleased they got along so well and so quickly. But he knew the younger girl was sharp as a tack, maybe even sharper than Maeve, though the notion that anyone could be smarter than his daughter was hard for him to entertain.

He carried out two mugs of French roast and sat gently in the folding chair as the old woman waited with her eyes closed.

"Coffee is served, ma'am."

"It's so good for Ornetta to be with someone near her own age."

Ornetta giggled and leaned closer. "Señor Man think to hisself, I'ma set this box trap in the garden and cotch up Señor Coyote, keep him from stealing my tomatoes the way he do."

Ornetta's glee was breathtaking to Maeve. She rocked back on her haunches on the hooked rug, wiggling back and forth with an excess of pure energy, and Maeve recalled what her father had reported to her about the revolt of the rhinestone animals and the secret language of cars. She wondered where these fables boiled up from.

The girl giggled again and moved her shoulders around until, in some way that was hard to identify, her body language suggested a cocky coyote stalking up on a box-and-bait trap. Señor Coyote went for the bait and, of course, got himself caught when the box fell.

"So Señor Man, he step right back from where he hid and he go, 'Yo, Señor Coyote, how you do in there? I'ma just take and hang you up on this here rope by yo' hind foot, and when I get back from the market, I believe I'll have myself a bowl of coyote stew.' And he go off to sell he tomatoes and buy hisself some stewin' okra."

Half of Maeve's mind was so enthralled that she kept giggling out loud, and the other half retreated to mull things over, the way her mind always did. She wanted to understand why she was so attracted to this girl she'd just met, as if a giant magnet tugged at her from across the rug in some *Looney Tunes* cartoon. Some people had that appeal, just laid it on you without even knowing their power, and most others didn't, no matter how hard they tried. She had done her best to like Mary Beth, for instance, but it hadn't really taken root. Something about the girl had been too lost and helpless and *unserious*.

Maeve wondered if the attraction came from energy, which Ornetta had in surplus, but she didn't think that was sufficient. She'd known other high-spirited girls who made her want to shrink right out of their presence, cheerleaders who were all bubble and enthusiasm but only about an inch deep. She didn't think it was just self-confidence either. Her seatmate in homeroom, Nora Blackstone, was as confident as they come, and Maeve couldn't stand her. But she knew she wouldn't be able to get enough of Ornetta—she felt somehow that no matter how long she knew Ornetta, the younger girl would always have something delightful to tell her or show her or teach her.

Ornetta swept her slight olive arm back and forth in the air.

"And Señor Coyote, he be swingin' on that rope way up in the air and laughin' up a storm when he see Señor Squirrel come hurry up the path.

"'What you laughin at?' go Señor Squirrel up to Señor Coyote.

"'Señor Squirrel, I ain't laughin' at you, no way. I just havin' so much fun swinging back and forth up here on my fine swing rope. This the best swing rope I ever seen.'"

"'Ooooh,' go Señor Squirrel. 'Can I swing too?'"

"I gather Ornetta told you there was some trouble with Sherry's family in Simi."

"She hinted. But she seemed conflicted. I have a hunch Amilcar asked her not to tell."

"What Ornetta knows is a bit stronger than a hint."

"Okay." He sat facing the old woman and gave her the time to gather whatever it was.

"This is what I heard. Sherry has two brothers, one older and one younger." She sighed. "They told Sherry she was no longer their sister if she kept going out with a black man. They said something that day to threaten *him* too, or maybe all this came from some of their friends; I don't think Ami told Ornetta exactly what happened. But it really made him take stock. Ornetta just admitted this to me recently. Hold on."

"I'm holding."

She frowned and took a sip of the coffee, cradling it gently. "I've heard they've got some . . . organization up there in that town. Maybe it's serious, maybe not."

"Is there reason to think they might be behind the cross burning on your lawn?"

"In America there's always reason to *think*, Mr. Liffey," she said sadly.

He saw that he was going to stay stuck at *mister*.

"I grew up in the Communist Party, believing all my life in the solidarity of the working class," she said, with a fierce kind of determination. "And I saw it. I saw white workers come out in the streets for the Scottsboro boys and Emmett Till and a lot of other black folk. This was Detroit, you know. In the thirties those white workers were only a few years out of Tennessee and Arkansas." She stopped and sighed again. "They did good, but I can see now that a lot of what we told ourselves in the Party was just self-hypnosis. Those working men needed a whole generous helping of nudge to get on the right track, and now that the Party's gone nobody's doing any nudging."

She thought about things for a moment while a flight of seagulls wheeled over the house, complained idly about the heat, and then took off inland. "I went to Mississippi with Bancroft for one entire year, Mr. Liffey. That was 1965. I went down there as an activist from Detroit who just happened to be a Negro, and when I came back north I was a plain ol' nigger. That mean, mean year did something to me inside. I hope I never again get that close to the face of a woman spitting hatred into my eyes."

He puffed his cheeks a bit. There was nothing you could say to that.

"Have you ever been to Mississippi?" she asked.

He shook his head. "When I was a freshman in college, a SNCC worker came and talked to us in the student union and invited us to join him down there in the voting rights program. You know, I was the first person in my family to go to college. I'm from a working-class town too, and I had enough on my plate right then getting used to a strange new world that was full of kids who'd read all these books I'd never even heard of. But I always regret I didn't go south."

"Oh, no, sir, don't you do that. You might have got yourself a headstone on some levee right now, marking where the good ol' boys dumped your remains. Sometimes they picked on the white boys worst, to send a message."

"How will I ever know now if I'd have had the courage?"

"Some things just plain aren't worth knowing, not if you've got a choice."

They heard a burst of giggling from the side room. The old woman sipped tentatively at the coffee and, seeming to approve of it, took a long drink.

"As long as they appear to be happy in there together, could you do me a favor?" Jack Liffey asked. "Tell me about Mississippi."

"Señor Man he come back from the market on he mule, and he eyes bug out real big and he be, like, 'Oh, I *so* sorry, Señor Coyote, I lef' you hangin' up there in the hot sun all day long, and you gone and shrunk down to a bitty morsel of yo'self.'

"But Señor Man had him a bitty bowl of stew that night anyway, even if it tasted kind of funny for coyote."

Maeve giggled and nodded. "Let me try to tell you one now."

ten

Four Muscles

He headed west out the Reagan Freeway, which most folks still called the Simi Valley Freeway. There had been a Nixon Freeway, too, until the days after Watergate, when it had quietly reverted to being the Marina Freeway. In general, LA didn't seem to like naming things after people, the way eastern cities named so many of their bridges and buildings and roads, perhaps because a lot of folks here were sensitive about the big ego bruise of Hollywood.

The Reagan ran up the center of a valley that was wall-to-wall white flight. Art Castro, who'd once lived out here for a year—until the lights came on and he realized he was miles from anyone else who spoke Spanish—called it the land of earth tones and left-turn arrows. Now Jack Liffey saw what he meant. Those sandy, lizardy colors were everywhere, on minimalls, freeway sound barriers, and endless reaches of two-story homes. He bet the glut of left-turn arrows was out there too, making even tiny alley intersections into eight-ways and slowing traffic to a crawl—something else urban folks didn't like very much about the suburbs.

He merged right as he saw his exit approach, thinking it might have been simpler just to move out here and go with it all—lawn sprinklers and chain restaurants and band saws in the three-car garages. It probably brought you face to face with something elemental in yourself when you knew there was no place farther to run. Marlena, he thought all of a sudden. He saw her naked beside a strange man, and all the hair on his shoulders and neck stood on end. Is that what her note signified?

Then he was distracted by the abrupt approach from behind of a station wagon recklessly slewing across the freeway. When the vehicle blew by him he saw three pairs of bare buttocks flattened against the window glass. It was the next stage up from mooning. Pressed ham, the frat boys had called it when he was in college. He gave them Nixon's stiff V-sign out the window, but he doubted anyone was looking.

As he pulled off at the bottom of the ramp, he saw a pair of really big vultures circling over the housing tract where he was headed, presumably awaiting the final death of the human spirit out here. The house was two stories of earth tone—thank you, Art Castro—one of those unnamable colors caught between peach and beige. There was the obligatory Sam Spade fanlight over the upper window and the usual postmodern refusal to lay anything out in graceful proportions.

In the driveway, though, there was a window into a different reality: a 1950 Mercury coupe in deep candy maroon, lower and squatter than he remembered, with a Dartmouth decal in the rear window. He hadn't seen a car like that since high school in San Pedro, where the Yugoslavs and the surfers had scorned them as taco wagons or bean bandits, but he had always responded to them with a little catch in his heart. He loved the very idea of a customized lowrider; it was so nutty and unfunctional. None of his friends had ever had one. Did anybody still do this to cars? He supposed all the handiwork of the fifties and sixties had to come to rest somewhere.

As he walked up the drive, Jack Liffey heard a repeated metallic *ka-ching* from the backyard, which sounded familiar but which he couldn't quite place. There was no fence, so he walked around the side of the house to see a blond teenager in a strap undershirt speed-pressing a fairly light barbell. He was surrounded by workout equipment under a patio awning, but he wasn't particularly bulked up.

"Hello. Are you Burkard Webber?"

The boy was a little startled and let the weights dangle. "Yes, sir, I am. Can I help you?"

That decorous politeness alone was a pleasant surprise. He had a big square jaw and a handsome curl of blond hair that swept back off his forehead like some lost Kennedy. The girls would be after this one, Jack Liffey thought. There was a squeal out in the backyard, and he noticed a little boy and girl sitting at a tiny tea table, arguing over a stuffed purple lizard.

"My name is Jack Liffey. I'm a detective looking for your sister." He left what sort of detective ambiguous.

The boy went very grave and set the barbell down on a mat. "I'm glad you're still looking. You're always afraid these things get forgotten."

"Can you tell me about the last time you saw her?"

"I only saw her for a minute. She came by with her boyfriend to talk to my parents about their plans for the summer."

The boy used a grease pencil to mark off his exercise on a big white sheet of foam core leaning against the house. Handsome, polite, and systematic. Blend in the Mercury out front, and Jack Liffey felt he could have dropped through a crust of time into an *Ozzie and Harriet* episode. He chose his next words carefully, a bit off base for the times, not politically sensitive but not quite openly bigoted, either.

"That would be the colored boy from Pomona College?"

The boy didn't react. "Ami Davis. We talked for a few seconds about what the Lakers were going to do without a shooting guard."

"Did your parents get along with Davis?"

"Sure. You mean because he was black? This isn't Alabama, Mr. Liffey."

"And did you and Rolf get along with him?"

"He was a nice guy."

It wasn't quite an answer. "*Was?*"

The boy shrugged apologetically. "They've both been gone a long time now. I've adjusted to thinking Sherry may be dead. We may never know."

There was a wail from the tea party, and Jack Liffey watched the two little kids toss the dinosaur up in the air and try to grab for it. "Your sister and brother?"

"No. I'm watching them for Mrs. Holtz across the street."

"What does baby-sitting go for these days? I remember charging fifty cents an hour."

The boy smiled in a bland sort of way. "Oh, I don't charge. It's a favor."

"That's good of you." It *was Ozzie and Harriet.* "Are there a lot of coloreds in your high school?"

"There's maybe six. One girl's in AP English with me."

Jack Liffey sat on the weight bench, where a much heavier bar rested crosswise on the bench-press rack. A medallion on a chain dangled from the end of the bar, and he picked it up to inspect it: a circle enclosing the petals of a rose enclosing a heart that had a cross inscribed in it. On the back, raised lettering had eroded from long friction against his chest.

"Ah," Jack Liffey said. "You're a Luth-e-pan."

The boy smiled again. "They all wear off that way. My family's Lutheran, and I guess I used to be. I'm in a Bible-reading club at school where we take the Gospels a little more to heart than the Lutheran pastor does."

Jack Liffey wondered if that meant they always kept three long nails at the ready. "A Bible club's a real change from when I went to high school. Are most of your classmates religious?"

"Only a small minority care enough to do anything. Have you read the Bible, sir?"

The little kids had gone into a tug-of-war over the toy and were leaning back and really getting into it. The screams became unbearable, so Burkard Webber hurried down the grass and squatted to separate the two. He seemed to have a genuine rapport with the children, and he rested a hand on each of them as he talked. When they were calmed down, he came slowly back across the grass.

"I've read a fair amount of the Bible," Jack Liffey offered. "Once somebody gave me the revised translation, and I realized how much easier it was to follow the stories when they're not in King James English."

The boy looked pained.

"You don't really think God spoke seventeenth-century English?" Jack Liffey asked.

"Not exactly."

"Don't most scholars think the King James panel made a fair number of mistakes in translating all that Aramaic and Hebrew?"

He was probing just enough to see where the boy lived, but he didn't really want to start a holy war with a seventeen-year-old.

"We believe God can inspire a translator every bit as much as a writer. 'He is the Rock, his word is perfect; for all his ways are judgment: a God of truth.' Deuteronomy 32:4."

No wonder the Lutherans weren't strict enough for him, Jack Liffey thought. But he could see he'd gone far enough. "Sure. Your parents still go to the Lutheran church?"

"Oh, yes. They're German Lutherans through and through. Our name was actually Weber"—he pronounced it *vayber*—"until Grandpa decided to Americanize it during World War One. He called it the Great War."

"Where was that?"

"Wisconsin."

"Did you grow up there?"

"No. I was six when my folks left Racine to come out west. Rolf remembers it better. He was ten."

As if on cue, an older boy trundled open the sliding glass door and looked out. He was just as blond and just as clean-cut, wearing crisp chinos and a blue button-down shirt.

"Rolf, this is a detective looking for Sherry."

"Jack Liffey." They shook hands solemnly. The older boy seemed even graver and more reticent than his brother. "Were you here when Sherry and Amilcar came to visit in June?"

He nodded. "I'd just got back from college. They only looked in as a courtesy. They were on their way to spend the weekend in Ojai."

That was new. "You're sure about that?"

"I think that's what they said."

"You wouldn't have any idea why Amilcar told his niece later that he'd had a hard time out here?"

"Gosh, no."

"Maybe they argued with your parents?"

He shook his head, hiked a leg of his chinos, and sat on the edge of a folded Ping-Pong table. He had so much neutral languor he seemed drugged. "It couldn't have been much of an argument in the two minutes they were in the house."

"Are your parents around?"

"They're in Europe right now. They didn't want to go, but the trip had been planned for more than a year and it didn't look like anybody was going to find Sherry right away. We know where they are every minute if we have to reach them."

"Our mom and dad have gotten pretty heavy into genealogy," Burkard added. "They're looking up the village where the family came from."

"So as far as you remember, Sherry and Amilcar drove up, parked their car, got out, said hello, and left for Ojai."

"Uh-huh."

"That's about it."

Jack Liffey tried a few other tacks but was just as becalmed whichever way he steered. The infants had started up their tug-of-war again without anyone's noticing because all of a sudden the big lizard was in two pieces and a cloud of feather stuffing filled the air.

The Webber boys both hurried down to take care of the situation and he watched their kindly interventions. They looked like Jan and Dean, tidy and sober, polite and reserved, Christian and proper. Whatever they were hiding, he couldn't quite see these two spitting rude names into Amilcar's face or lugging a big wooden cross into South Central and torching it up.

He asked to use the bathroom and got lost on the way, long enough to check out a bedroom with a Dartmouth pennant, a rack of slot cars and sports equipment, a lot of computer gear, a short surfboard, and a very big black Bible. No Nazi flags, no lightning-bolt posters, no bedsheets with eyeholes.

"I guess I'd better check Ojai. Is that your Merc out front?"

Rolf grinned a little, his first display of emotion. "Cool, huh?"

"Did you customize it?"

"Oh, no. I bought it that way. It's been around for a long time."
He walked Jack Liffey around front and plucked an errant leaf off
the hood. "Chopped and channeled. You know how they do it?"

"Uh-uh."

"The last owner told me. He was a policeman who bought it out
of impound, but he'd worked on cars when he was younger. They cut
off the roof and shorten all the roof pillars about six inches. That's
chopped. Then they channel it. That means they cut a slice all the
way around the car about here." He indicated about mid-thigh.
"They remove six inches of sheet metal and weld what's left back together. Then they sand it out so good you can't see where the weld
went. It changes the whole look of the car."

"It sure does. What's under the hood?"

He shrugged. "They weren't into engines so much. It's meant to
cruise slow. It's got the standard straight six with a three-speed.
They did change the linkage to make the three-on-the-tree into a
floor shift."

"Did you have it back east?"

He shook his head. "I let Burk drive it when I was at college."

"You're certainly a good brother."

One detail caught Jack Liffey's eye before he left, a discreet decal in
a corner of the back window that read 16/8. It reminded him of the sinister 88 skinhead kids used as a private code. The eighth letter twice,
HH, for Heil Hitler. But 16/8 worked out to—what?—PH. Acid-base?
Peter Hitler? Probably just a parking spot at the high school.

"Thanks for your time, Rolf. What have you been studying?"

"My major was history. I did history of religion, with a senior thesis on the holiness movements."

Jack Liffey pointed at his '79 AMC Concord. "You think these
customizers could have done anything with mine?"

The young man wrinkled up his nose. The car was so beat up it
was barely recognizable. In addition to the plastic windows, both
right fenders had been replaced with junkyard cousins primered orange. "I don't think they'd try."

"Maybe they could lop the roof off, channel it drastically, and
make a planter out of it."

* * *

The car radio, stuck for years on all-news KFWB-AM, informed him that an appellate judge had just thrown out Abdullah Ibrahim's lawsuit against the police, on the grounds that peace officers were now protected absolutely by some new reasonable-belief statute that had dribbled through the legislature. But Ab-Ib's lawyer was vowing to refile on new grounds. The newscast then switched over to a woman reporter whose voice went up into a hysterical register trying to shout over a lot of sirens wailing past her. Something about a massive tactical deployment by the LAPD to head off trouble. The sirens gave the broadcast an end-of-the-world feeling that made him anxious, so he switched it off.

He'd seen two massive LA uprisings in his lifetime, 1965 and 1992, and he didn't even want to think about another one. The civil unrest—yet another of the city's euphemisms—had disturbed something very deep inside him, a despairing sense that injustice went on and on without anyone's caring enough to address it.

But mostly he tried to ignore the pain, just like everybody else. He would have been perfectly happy to pay more in taxes to feed the homeless, but no one had ever asked him, and he didn't know what else to do.

Already in a funk, he found his thoughts drifting toward Marlena again. Why had his life become so strange? Where did it become so strange? Could he go back and reorder it, just a little?

As he pulled off the freeway at Washington, a car came up beside him and a blacked-out window rolled down. A young African American put his whole torso out into the afternoon, wrapped in a Hawaiian silk shirt with big pineapples, and shouted, "It's Uzi time!"

There was no cross traffic; Jack Liffey jumped the red light and got out of there. Far away, he thought he heard gunshots.

"Your daddy pretty cool."

It was only eight or nine blocks from the little house in Oakwood to the beach, and they walked there in the gathering heat, carrying towels and paperbacks and sunblock and a little plastic cooler with

Seven-Ups and apples. Maeve was happy she'd thought to bring along her swimsuit. Her dad had agreed to let her spend a day and night with Ornetta's aunt, joining Ornetta and Mrs. Thigpen in their retreat.

"He not with your momma?"

"No, they're divorced."

"Uh-huh. You think they get back?"

"He lives with another woman, and my mom's remarried. For a while I really wanted them to get together again, but I'm kind of used to having them in two places now. It means I've got two families instead of one."

"Nana and Ban my family. Nana not my momma, you know. My momma live in a big castle in New York. I only be here since March."

She said it matter-of-factly, but Maeve could feel something wrong underneath. She took the tiny dry fist, and they walked hand-in-hand. Maeve sensed that family was something to be avoided for the moment.

"Do you like LA?"

"Sure. Everybody here livin' large." She seemed to reconsider something that was warring in her. "It hard to come from outsides. Girls I know over on Sixty-two Street, you know, you can't just cool out. You got to stay on top or they rank you down. You different, I can tell."

Maeve felt a squeeze of her hand and her heart went out to the girl. "I like you too, Ornetta."

Ornetta smiled and looked up at her, a good three inches taller. "You safe, like a sister."

Brian Franchino reacted a little as Perry Krasny stepped out onto the patio high above the canyon with a big SSK assault rifle. The rifle had a silencer on the muzzle like a big soup can. There were houses on both sides of them along the high ridge road, and a faraway V in the hills revealed tracts out in the Simi Valley. Krasny stood breathing heavily for a while and then aimed the rifle outward at a high angle and began to fire methodically. "*Get* some, motherfucker, *get* some," he chanted as he fired. Only a muffled popping could be heard, on and on to a steady tempo, in between the *ka-ching* of the brass eject-ing to skitter across the redwood deck.

"Jesus, K! What are you doing?" Franchino came to his feet. He remembered that the man's wife and kids were away somewhere. Maybe he got like this whenever he was alone. The nearest houses below were several miles away, but those 7.62mm assault rounds would carry.

Krasny said nothing, simply went on firing until the rifle's bolt clicked open on an empty magazine.

"Those shells, they got to come down out there, K."

"Bullets come down, Bri, *rounds* come down. Shells stay right here." And indeed the bright brass casings made a little scatter to his left. He set the rifle down and took a pull of his beer. "Fear not, ten-derhearted friend. The odds are very slim that anyone will be hit. Just a broken window, a mysterious hole in the stucco. An angry god working his malign will from up in the clouds."

"Sometimes I wonder if you got both oars in the sea."

"Oh, I know what I'm up to. I'm practicing for the next stage of our nation's perilous journey. As far as I'm concerned, I'll do all the dirty work that's necessary, and I'll do it forever, at least until the people catch on. Think of the thousands of years the Europeans have had to work on the moral outlines of their nations, to expel the foreigners, to fight their border wars. We got started late in all.

"I'll do whatever it takes for this new white nation to be born, and if they take me to some Nuremberg afterward and try me for war crimes so they can dip the new Euro-American state in bleach and pretend none of this bad shit ever happened, then I'll still do the whole filthy job with no regret. Two hundred years from now we'll be known by some as the Washington Lincolns of Euro-America, the guys who built it and held it together."

Krasny said all this without real rancor. He spoke in an amiable tone with a palm flat on his chest as if pledging allegiance. Far away out in the canyons there was an animal whoop with a rising trill at the end: *whoo-up whoo-up.*

"Coyote," he said. "I love coyotes, but they got to go, you know. They get in the way. If these brown and black people get too uppity after we give them their own places then they got to go too. We can nuke the whole lot of them. An idea like that hasn't hurt the Israelis, has it? Let them walk tiptoe over on the other side of the border, man, that's what I say. A few more wars where we kick the shit out of our neighbors and we expel a few million blacks and browns to these states of their own, and everything calms down and we become just like any other European country, a big respectable white nation with safe streets and a little criminal past."

"And the meantime we got to pay the rent and such."

"The meantime. Remember, when you're having a bad time and it seems like all the liberals on earth got it in for you and some particular pussy wise guy calls you a name to piss you off, remember, it takes forty-two muscles to frown—like you're doing right now—and only four to pull the trigger of a decent sniper rifle."

eleven

The Look of History

"**O**oooooh!"

The 747 settled heavily toward them, drifted sideways a bit, and then corrected with the dip of a huge wing, swelling ominously like a dream, only fifty feet above them.

"All *right*! Come *on*!"

"Do it! Do it!" A woman in a gauzy white dress at the edge of the grass danced forward and punched her fists alternately up into the path of the jet. Two young men lay on their backs in the flight path and let out cries of delight.

Jack Liffey felt the rumble in his feet, and the air weight of the big jet seemed to wallop them as they craned their necks. Its turbulence buffeted the airport fence just past them, and moments later the tires touched down with a puff of gray smoke. Later came the angry howl of reverse thrust.

"Outa sight!"

"What hath man wrought?" Mike Lewis remarked mildly.

He stood on a low grassy hill that ran down the center of the little park they were gathered in. He jotted something on a clipboard.

"At the risk of seeming droll," Jack Liffey said, "what notes are you taking?"

"It's a 747-300," Mike Lewis said dryly. "Korean Air. No contrails."

A woman's voice on Mike Lewis's phone had told Jack Liffey where Mike often hung out for a while after teaching his morning class in urban studies at the little architecture college down the road from LAX.

"Some months ago, I noticed the airplane groupies that gather here, right at the end of runway Twenty-four-R. It's the age of spectacle, after all. It was toward the end of winter back then, with a damp onshore breeze huffing and puffing into the dry air off the desert, and the planes were all leaving big spiraling condensation trails from their wings. All of a sudden, that day, I heard a sizzling sound. At first I ignored it, but on the next landing I heard it again. Well behind the jet there was a track of vapor shooting back in the opposite direction with a kind of crackling noise. It was like a bottle rocket."

"So?"

"As far as I know no one has ever described the phenomenon. Even the engineers I ask are mystified. I've observed it maybe three more times, when conditions are just right."

"Are they right today?"

"Too dry."

"So why are you here?"

"Look around this grassy knoll, Jack. The human comedy is sufficient onto itself."

The woman in the filmy Isadora Duncan gown pranced along the sidewalk, giving high knee kicks, as if intoxicated by the airplanes. The two young men on their backs offered each other high fives now and then. An old man in a pilot's uniform leaned dreamy-eyed against the fence at the base of the landing light.

"Isn't calling this a 'grassy knoll' a little sacrilegious?"

"Have you ever seen the one in Dallas?"

Jack Liffey shook his head.

"I don't know who first called it that; it's no such thing. It's just a road embankment down to an underpass, not even vaguely like a knoll. But what's your question for me? You only come to see me when some aspect of LA's grand comedy has you mystified."

"Sometimes I need to borrow something from you."

"True."

A smaller jet wobbled out of the haze and thundered overhead. "That's a 737," Mike Lewis said. "With those flattened-off CFM engines. Very quiet and fuel-efficient."

"Does the number sixteen-slash-eight mean anything to you?" Jack Liffey asked. "Let's say, relating to high school kids."

Mike Lewis wrinkled up his face.

"Uh-oh," Jack Liffey said. "You've got that you-must-be-just-off-the-bus look."

Mike rolled his eyes. "You've got to keep up. The Sixteen/Eight Club is the high school wing of the Pledge of Honor movement. You know, all those earnest fathers and husbands who gather in sports stadiums to reaffirm their Protestant values. Like most neo-conservatism, it's mostly a phenomenon of the suburbs."

"Would those values include racism?"

"Not openly. They're very genteel this time around. They talk about one-to-one 'reconciliation.' Which means, of course, no affirmative action. The whole movement is really a stalking horse for the Christian Right. It's against women's rights, gays, and cultural relativism or any other sort of relativism. Part of the famous culture war. No ambivalence, no doubt. Basically, they're against anything that changed in the sixties."

"Civil rights *was* the sixties."

"It's possible one of the clubs might spiral away into some kind of weird neo-racism. If you take earnest well-off white kids who don't even know how privileged they are and add a pinch of demagoguery, who knows where it might go? Times change. If you remember, thirty years ago a lot of those kids wanted to be Red Guards and make a revolution. How much sense did that make?"

"Weren't you an SDS leader?"

Another jet came over, and they both craned their necks. "An old DC-9," Mike Lewis explained. "Wait'll you hear the engines. They're from the era before noise abatement."

The DC-9 touched down, and when it reversed thrust the small plane sounded twice the size of the 747, with a crackling howl so loud he wanted to hold his ears.

"At least we stopped a war," Mike said. "This isn't just a theoretical question, is it?"

"Simi Valley."

"Okay. I've got some kids in my Cal-Arts class tonight who hail from that neck of the woods. I'll ask them about it. Call me late."

"Thanks, Mike."

"Look!" The lady in white pointed off to the east now, into the city. A large column of black smoke rose into the air.

"I wonder what that is?" somebody said.

"That's the look of history," Mike Lewis said somberly, pocketing his pencil.

A troop of little girls in Brownie uniforms, all carrying pirate flags, marched northward along the sidewalk that ran at the top edge of the beach. The girls parted for a young man on a skateboard, who was twirling slowly and playing "Guantanamera" on an electric guitar, the speaker strapped to his back. On another skateboard a goateed man without legs propelled himself along with little leather paddles. A male couple stood in the sand in skimpy bathing costumes and held elastic clown noses out of the way as they kissed. It was Venice Beach, being itself.

"Let's go over there." Ornetta pointed to a bare spot on the busy sand.

They strolled past a Latino family who had set up a temporary altar on a group of ice chests, bedecked with gaudy figurines and photographs and candles in cups, and were busy lighting the candles as fast as the wind blew them out.

"Mescans be somethin' else," Ornetta said softly.

"They might be Mexican *Americans*," Maeve corrected primly.

"I don' mean no dis. I ain' no African. I jus' mean they sure like they Catholic shit."

The two girls laid out their towels side by side and Maeve stripped down to the tiny black bikini that had made her mother scowl heavily at her. Her father hadn't seen it yet.

"I wanna get one of them," Ornetta said, "but I gotta get me some bosoms first."

Ornetta's shift came off to reveal a skirted green-and-yellow one-piece that made her look even younger than she was. Maeve noticed she wore some sort of charm on a string tucked down in the suit.

"Your breasts will come pretty quick. But it's not much fun when boys stare at you all the time."

"Boys is a bunch of dogs."

Maeve thought of her two days with Mary Beth. "Have you ever read Nancy Drew?"

"Who that?"

"She's a girl detective. The books have been around for a long time."

Maeve suddenly noticed four young black boys in baggy gang-banger shorts below the knee trending toward them across the sand. They were probably fifteen and had identical zigzags cut into the sides of their fades. Maeve could feel herself going tense as they got close.

"Uh-oh," she warned Ornetta softly.

"Sweet thang, come to daddy!" a boy proposed, slowing down to a hover near Maeve. The boys formed a circle around the girls, making faces, leering a little, and shifting their weight constantly as if they were too restless to settle.

"Go away," Maeve said brusquely. "Leave us alone." She crossed her arms over her breasts and wished she had bought a more modest suit.

"Whoa, what's your trip? Peace out, *ho,* we just tryin'a be friendly."

"I'm not a *ho.*"

"Uh-huh, you go and buy that li'l fuck-me thing just to cover your booty, huh?"

Ornetta touched her charm and made a derisive sound.

"Who you making noise at, little girl? I'ma tryin'a get over with the bitch that's showin out."

"You talk like a low-down dog. Why don' you go hang with the other dogs."

"Whoa, you a trip. Look at you, girl." He put his arms on his hips and turned to face Ornetta, which was a great relief to Maeve. "I bet your momma so black she got to wear headlights all night long."

"Well, your momma so black they gotta paint a white line down her so all the mens in your 'hood know where to drive."

Despite themselves, the other boys grinned and stifled laughs as they bobbed and rocked.

"Well, your momma so ugly they keep her at the zoo," the boy insisted.

"Your momma, the gorilla threw her outa the zoo, make room for a warthog."

"You keep raggin', little girl, it's gonna be me and you."

Ornetta seemed to have held her own about as long as she could, and Maeve could see her starting to wilt as she clutched at whatever necklace she wore. Maeve put her arms around her.

"Shame on you, you boys. Scaring little girls."

"You ain't even worth beatin' on, you skinny-ass bitches."

As the boys pranced away, Maeve had the feeling that probably none of the ragging had been all that serious. It was just so ugly and so different from her experience that it left her feeling helpless and deeply disturbed.

"I shoulda called me a big magic rassler, beat they ass," Ornetta said defiantly.

Maeve was about to ask about this strange statement when somebody shouted nearby and they both looked up at a large group of people pressing close into a tight group. Then she noticed groups just like it in the distance—everybody on the beach seemed to be clumping up—and through the forest of legs of the nearest group she made out the focal point, a big portable radio on the sand.

"Ornetta, look."

National Guard armored personnel carriers rumbled up what the announcer said was Alondra Boulevard in Compton. Young soldiers sat on the APCs, out in the open, looking grim in their flak jackets. The picture went out of focus for a moment and the announcer yammered away without saying anything new, so Jack Liffey muted the sound.

The frightening note he'd found tacked to the front door—this one definitely *not* from Marlena—lay on the coffee table in front of him, but he had stopped looking at it long ago. He had been watching television with only one short break for almost two hours, since a minute or two after getting home. The one break had been to take a phone call from Maeve that she was back at the house in Oakwood after a day at the beach and perfectly safe, nothing for him to worry about, and an outgoing call to Redondo reassuring Maeve's mother. The rest of the time had been an uneasy channel-surf through the local stations, which had all abandoned their regular programming to show film of a supermarket fully engulfed in flames. It was probably the worst trouble spot, because you saw it over and over from different angles; accompanying the footage were calming statements from the mayor and the police chief, troop deployments, aerial views of crowds running through the streets, and endless repeats of Abdullah Ibrahim, in his Dodgers jersey and white Muslim cap, pleading for peace. The clip came on yet again, and Jack Liffey dialed up the sound because he liked the baritone voice.

". . . *Salaam,* which means *peace,* and I ask all my brothers and sisters to increase the peace today, whatever their religion or race, whatever their outrage, whatever their demand, whatever their past of oppression or sorrow. Please stay at home today, brothers and sisters; please treat all people with the same respect you would show your own mother, your own sister, your own little brother."

His hand shook a little with emotion, rattling the paper he was reading from, and he looked up.

"I love this town. I love all its people, may Allah be praised. Do not harm even a fly in my name, I *beg* of you. *Salaam aleikum.*"

It was hard not to like the man. Jack Liffey tried another station. Fox had a helicopter hovering over looting at a strip mall. A few foreshortened figures darted out into the afternoon with lumpy shopping bags. When the camera zoomed in, the looters were revealed to be, as they had been in 1992, brown, black, and white. There did not in fact seem to be all that much looting or burning, but there were two or three hot spots, and after two major LA uprisings in living memory, the newspeople and the authorities were understandably excitable.

His eye was now caught by the note resting beside the Seven-Up can and it brought him back, a chill running up his spine anew. HELTER-SKELTER. The stubby felt-pen letters were not so much drawn as slashed across the face of a dollar bill. It was the expression Charlie Manson had thought signaled the coming race war. Scrawled after the words was a crude drawing of a cross in flames.

He sensed an earthquake-feeling kind of alarm gathering in himself. The sight of looting left him skittish and deeply disconsolate, as he had been for weeks in '92. And now there'd been this damn note on the door, as if all the urban chaos radiated from some evil locus very near him, maybe even *because* of him. He wondered if the note had come from the same people who had burned the cross on Bancroft Davis's lawn. Something terrible was slouched out there, that was for sure, stamping and wheezing in the darkness.

A car came up the driveway and he snapped alert, tingling. By the time he got to the front window, it was out of sight and he hurried to look out the side room, nearly tripping over Maeve's little suitcase. It was Marlena's Nissan. She got out, looking like she'd seen a ghost, and his heart thundered. He could tell she sensed him in the window, but she wouldn't look up to meet his eyes. She didn't carry any luggage as she walked toward the back of the house.

He decided it was best to wait for her, for whatever it was. She came heavily into the utility room at the rear and then in through the kitchen, and he was back by the TV when she found him.

"Hi, Jackie." Her voice was curiously dull, almost without affect.

"Hi, Mar."

There was a long silence as they watched each other, then she sighed. "We got to talk."

He killed the sound just as the TV helicopter spied another source of fire and scudded away after it.

"Sure." He had thought his foreboding couldn't get any worse.

She sat primly at the far end of the old sofa and stared out at the room. She sighed again. "I better just get it out. I found somebody else that makes me happy, Jackie. You know we wasn't working."

There it was. He was so stunned he couldn't quite take it in. "We were okay," he said lamely.

"No, we wasn't. You didn't want me to talk about the Church and Revelations and what my personal savior means to me."

No, I didn't, he thought. "But I accepted that you believed in it. I never attacked you."

"You didn't want me to talk about Sally Jessy neither."

That too, he thought. "I listened to you. You listened to me."

The helicopter on TV seemed to be taking evasive maneuvers, perhaps drawing ground fire, and the image switched to a talking head in the studio, a handsome middle-aged man in a polo shirt.

"We didn't talk about nothing that mattered." There was a plaintive note in her voice now. "And we didn't vibrate together, you know it."

Resonate, he thought.

"All we had was we liked to please each other in bed, that's all, but I found a man who shares the whole earth with me and makes me happy."

"I see in you a woman with a huge warm heart, Marlena, and I love her . . . you," he said.

She swallowed hard and a tear dribbled down her cheek. "I can't talk about it no more. It's gone and happened. I got to go try it with this man. I'll go stay at his place for a few weeks, give you time. Please don't be mad at me."

"Tell me one thing, Mar. Did this guy give you the black eye?"

She shook her head hard. She wasn't a good liar, but for the first time he couldn't tell. The realization that she had a lover had shifted his footing so much he was lost in his own hurt.

She put a slip of paper down. "You can call here and leave a message, but please don't come look for me. I'll call you soon."

"Mar!"

She was up and walking out, but she stopped at the urgency in his voice.

"Marlena Helena Cruz Granados, I love you more than I can say."

She sobbed and ran. He stood up, then froze and sat back down, as if a horse had kicked him in the chest. He sat that way for a long time, overwhelmed with grief and hurt and something like shame, and then on the TV a new shot of a burning post office caught his eye and he turned the sound back up to hear the crackling of fire.

"Go on, fuck it, burn!" he said out loud. All that disorder seemed to validate something in him.

twelve

Gideon's 300

"The fence pull open." Ornetta tugged out two loose palings at the bottom of the back fence so they could slip through and out into the alley. It was late afternoon. Genesee Thigpen and Aunt Taffeta had been watching the big events on TV so intently all day that they'd never got their naps, and both of them were conked out now on the old sofa, heads together against the big lace antimacassar. The girls had thrown an afghan over them.

It was with a sense of high adventure that they now turned west up the alley toward the plume of smoke in the distance. Oakwood had a different sound to it, less car traffic and more of a human susurrus, as if people were there somewhere, just out of sight, rushing around in groups and grumbling about life. The girls heard gunshots and, far away, a siren.

The half-paved alley was an obstacle course of weeds and old newspaper, a rotted mattress, a litter of food wrappers, an engine block, and a beat-up hubcap sticking up like a crashed flying saucer. The whole thoroughfare stank of pee.

Graffiti on an old garage said VENICE SHORELINE CRIPS and some other words that neither of them could make out. Ahead, just before the alley met the street, there was a social circle of older black men sitting and standing around a big orange cable reel that lay on its side as a table.

"They okay," Ornetta reassured, but Maeve saw how cautious she was as they approached.

"Cool the fever and ease the pain," an old man said to the air, as he handed a big bottle to another man.

"You know what Night Train say to me? She say, 'You never be alone as long as I'm alive.'"

The men laughed softly.

"Hey, girls, your momma know you outa your crib?"

"I'ma just buy some bread for Gramma," Ornetta said.

"I think they be shuttin the stores up, hon. You take care now."

The street was empty, and all the shops they could see had been gridded over. Plywood BLACK OWNED signs were out in force, one dry cleaner taking a big risk with MINORITY OWNED. Maeve wondered if that one was a Korean trying to fudge. She noticed a lot of fresh graffiti saying AB-IB RULES! A big billboard on the roof had been whited out hastily and DON'T DIS DR. KNUCKLES was hand-lettered across the fresh white.

They heard a rattle, and an old woman with a shopping cart full of video cassettes wheeled fast along the cross street. "They be startin' takin' the stuff," Ornetta observed.

A lowered car went by in fits and rumbles, with hands coming out all the cracked-open windows making cramped gang signs.

"That's they brains showin'," Ornetta said softly, and Maeve giggled.

Ornetta tapped the charm she seemed to wear under her shirt. "Magic powers, you keep us safe here. Keep off them bangers and fools."

"What have you got there?" Maeve asked.

"I can't show. It secret."

A deep explosion went off on the next street, making them both flinch. "M-80," Ornetta said matter-of-factly. "Some fool trippin' on the noise."

She alternated between reality and fantasy in a light-footed way that left Maeve dazed. Someone in a house nearby began to play B. B. King very loud out the window, "The Thrill is Gone."

There didn't really seem to be any danger. What Maeve sensed was an exuberance on the afternoon air, as if everything was merely going to be more animated than usual. Two young men in long dreadlocks tap-danced side by side on pallets laid down on the loading dock of some business, their shoes hammering in unison. People peered out bungalow windows, gently parting curtains and house plants. The two girls made their way west, keeping close to the locked and barred doors of the shops.

"This is exciting," Maeve said, recovering some of her Nancy Drew courage. "I bet we're going to remember this day all our life."

"Stick together, we be safe." They held hands, hiding in a doorway.

Overhead two police helicopters circled low, sweeping anemic searchlights left and right. It was still bright day and there didn't seem much point to the lights, except maybe to point a finger. Higher up were many other helicopters from news agencies and TV stations. Then all of a sudden there was a different helicopter very low at the end of the block, a big ugly black thing with no markings at all. Pods of weapons hung off little wings in front. Its sound was hushed, a *thump-thump-thump* you could feel in your chest, like something out of another world, and it hovered in one place, bobbing its tail a little like a stick insect.

"That the big boss copter, like a dragon," Ornetta observed.

"My dad used to work where they made helicopters," Maeve said, as if this gave her some claim of power over the evil specter.

A gang of black boys, younger than Ornetta, burst noisily from between two houses, running hard and waving their arms with abandon. They turned along the shops and passed only a foot from the girls. One stopped to posture in Maeve's face. "Do me, baby, the whole nine," he said, waggling his tongue and leering, as if quoting somebody older.

"Get a life, boy," Ornetta said.

"*O-bop-she-bam.*"

He hooted and ran on. Another boy sprinted past carrying a bright red one-seat kayak.

A voice spoke out of the sky, louder than any voice had a right to be. "*Get indoors, now! All of you boys! This area is under curfew!*"

There was an insistent dull *pop-pop-pop* from overhead, and Maeve thought she saw something gray streak down out of the sky at the running boys. A scream, and one was knocked off his feet. The kayak was discarded and they all scattered. Two of them circled back to help the one who had been knocked down. The big insect helicopter came even lower and trailed after the largest band of kids, popping again and again from one of its outrigger pods.

"Woo," Ornetta said in awe.

And then the hubbub was gone as quickly as it had come. The boys had vanished and the big black helicopter had gone on. The higher helicopters moved off to circle somewhere else, and the street whispered with aftertalk. An old woman came out on her porch and called, "You girls get on home now. This ain't no time to be out eye-ballin'."

"Yes'm."

Maeve dallied long enough to pick up one of the gray blobs that littered the street. It was a very heavy beanbag in some kind of slick synthetic cloth, about the size of a coin purse.

"Must have been a dragon beanbag," Maeve suggested.

Ornetta smiled. She led them down a cross street, and as soon as they turned another corner they saw police cars parked diagonally to block the whole roadway.

They crossed and hurried into a quiet residential street of apartments and tiny court homes. A large crowd, mostly young Latinos, ran past on the other side of the street, hooting and roaring. Maeve wondered how well Ornetta knew her Aunt Taffeta's neighborhood. They cut down a walking court between little Spanish bungalows surrounded by geraniums and out onto another business street.

A sedan came on fast and then screeched unexpectedly sideways to ram straight into the grillwork of a closed minimart, touching off a shrill alarm. It shocked Maeve deeply to see the crash. The car had wedged into the grille and all its doors flew open. Four young men in ski masks hurled out and attacked the remains of the security grille with crowbars. In a few seconds, glass smashed and the accordion grate came away from the wall. They piled inside the store.

From what she could tell through the masks, Maeve thought the slight-looking looters looked Vietnamese.

"Oh, yeah, I know the Sixteen/Eight Club," the young man said, with a rueful toss of his head. "I was *in* it." Kirk Grosvenor had a big handsome square jaw, much like the Webber boys. He'd have looked like a first-round pick for pro running back—even with the gold ring in his ear—except for the little lower-lip triangle of beard that musicians call a jazz dab and painters an imperial.

"Back in high school I wouldn't have been caught dead hanging with assholes like this."

He meant the other two bearded boys in the cluttered living room. Caught up in watching television, they gave only perfunctory eye rolls.

"Ooh."

Somebody had torched a gas station on Slauson, and it was hard not to pay attention as a glorious mushroom cloud billowed up over the Baldwin Hills, chasing even the news copters back. Until that burst of fire, the announcer had been repeating the official mantra that the rioting seemed to be easing up. On the way out to Simi, following the news on his car radio, Jack Liffey had heard that Abdullah Ibrahim had taken to the streets, hurrying from hot spot to hot spot to urge people to go home.

Secretly, Jack Liffey was pleased to have so much commotion going on. When he had nothing to distract him, he pictured Marlena lying with another man, talking to another man, holding hands. Not too vividly—he didn't really picture a face or specific build—but vividly enough to do unpleasant things to his stomach.

A laugh suddenly dragged his mind back to the cluttered artists' pad in the Simi Hills where he now sat.

"I was football, Presbyterian Youth League, prelaw, Bible club, the whole nine yards. But I'd always been interested in painting, and over my dad's objection I went to Cal-Arts instead of Pepperdine, and the rest is just pure unadulterated depravity."

His companions looked even more like young artists than Kirk Grosvenor, though some of that was undoubtedly suggested by the easels and canvases and pots of paint and clay sculptures on tall stools that disordered the room and the dozen spattered drop cloths that covered the flooring. It was an old canyon house up above the valley, made of rounded rock and rotting clapboard, needing a lot of work it was probably never going to get.

"I don't think the Sixteen/Eights are anything much to worry about—but don't go away unhappy. There might be a bit more to the story." He thought things over while he ripped open a twist-off beer. "Every club had an older adviser called an Apostle who was sent down from the Pledge of Honor folks. They were the adult version of us, a lot like the PromiseKeepers or the old Shepherding Movement, if you remember them. I think the big P of H was broken into what they called Belief Teams of a dozen or so, and each team had a leader called a Head Coach who reported to a higher group called a Roost that was run by an Umpire. Everybody's got to invent some kind of goofy hierarchy. Eventually you'd get up to the Synod and the National Director. It was all about family values and stuff that seemed okay to me at the time, but it got a lot weirder when I got some perspective on it. Keep your kids off dope. Keep your woman in her place. Stuff like that."

One of the other boys was watching him now. "Jesus, Kirk, I didn't know you were into that."

"Eat me, Don."

The skinny boy named Don sneered, "Bunch of chubby white boys who live with their moms and wear Star Trek hats, I'd'a thought."

"Little you know. A lot of them were jocks."

"Same difference."

Kirk Grosvenor sighed and shrugged.

"Was racism a part of it?" Jack Liffey asked.

He thought about it. "The topic didn't come up much, but—"

"Whoa!" one of the boys exclaimed. The TV station had lost its signal, and the big set displayed the streaming static that TV techies called grass. He changed channel and they saw an instant replay of the fireball from a circling helicopter near the same location. After the fireball collapsed, the gas station seemed to be settling in for a determined burn.

"I did hear some rumors. . . . We talked a lot about committing to the seven great virtues, and we read the Bible, and we made public pledges at rallies and handed out literature, stuff like that. But once in a while we'd hear about another group. It was called DEL, Defenders of the European Legacy, but I heard mention of Gideon's 300, too. It was supposed to be more activist, I mean *really* activist. But you know how rumors operate. If we couldn't even get the name straight, how could we know what they did? Maybe they didn't even exist."

"You never saw any sign of them yourself?"

He paused to think it over. "Truth is elusive, man. What do you know for sure?"

"I know it's not going to rain *up*."

The boy smiled. "Here's the best I can do. One day there was a guy talking about seeing an encampment of illegals over by Grimes Canyon. Some of the kids bitched about how dirty the Mexicans were up there, living in cardboard and black plastic, shitting in the hills and not paying rent." He laughed. "Johnny Griffin, he had a big moral thing about paying your rent. I think his dad's a slumlord. The hills are full of poor Mexican strawberry pickers, killing themselves for peanuts or hanging out at Home Depot for day labor. I suppose Johnny wanted them to tool big condos down in Malibu, commute up to the Home Depot in their Lexuses, pay their rent regular. I seem to remember our Apostle taking a special interest and asking exactly where the encampment was. Anyway, pretty soon there was a brush fire in Grimes Canyon and two Mexicans died. Who knows? It could have been a cooking fire, like the paper said."

"Oh, shit," the boy named Don burst out. "Cooking!" He jumped up and ran to the kitchen.

"So who was your Apostle?" Jack Liffey asked.

"His name was Perry Krasny. He was the assistant football coach at the high school, and he coached Pop Warner, too. Pretty sinister job, if he *was* the point man for the American Nazis, but he didn't really strike me that way."

There was a sizzling noise from the kitchen, and a puff of steam made its way around the corner.

"Here we go again," the third boy offered. "Spaghetti al dentifrice."

"Did Krasny ever talk about race?" Jack Liffey wondered.

"Probably a little. That was another lifetime ago for me, though, man. The big thing with Pledge of Honor was that you have choices; everybody can choose the good over the bad. You know what I mean?"

There was a clatter in the kitchen and the third boy groaned.

"I argued with him once. I said what about some poor guy in China who's never heard of Jesus, is he going to hell? And if he conceded that, what about the guy who's raised a Muslim or a Buddhist or something and he's only heard of Jesus once?" He screwed up his face thinking, then took a long pull off his beer. "Perry said everybody in the world gets a chance to believe in Jesus, and God sees to it that when the chance comes, that person has a real option to believe. So if he rejects Jesus, it's his fault. It seemed pretty lame to me, even then. I mean, weird coincidence that all these bright guys in India, given a real chance, turn Jesus down, and all the dimwits in Alabama accept Him."

"Bad news, dudes." Don appeared in the living room holding up a large serving fork that was poked into a solid mass of spaghetti the size of a soccer ball.

"Would you like some advice?" Jack Liffey offered.

"Oh, sure."

"Next time try putting a splash of oil in the water before you cook it, and after you drain it, run tap water over it for a few seconds. It'll wash off the starch and keep it from sticking."

"And set the timer, dude," Kirk said. "You could try that. Maybe that'd save the trips to Pizza Hut."

"What's that smell?"

Ornetta crinkled up her nose and Maeve sniffed the air, but by then it was so powerful there was nothing to do but make a face and pretend to retch. "That's *aw*-ful."

They peered around the corner near the projects and saw a big billow of jet-black smoke reaching out sideways, like the paw of a giant black cat. It looked like Mussa's Retreads had been raided and the old tires stacked into a barricade across Brooks and set alight in three or four spots. The barricade was just beginning to brew up with that dreadful pungency of old rubber.

The smoke got thick fast and two boys ran out of it smack into them, bowling Ornetta over. One stopped to apologize and help her up.

"Say, girl, you got a dollar I could borrow, just till I get home?" He danced from foot to foot, glowering at them. Maeve shuddered involuntarily.

"We got no money," Ornetta said with determination.

"Aw, hasta la vista, baby." He ran on, and Maeve came out of the anxious trance of immobility that had overcome her and pulled Ornetta back around the corner.

Ornetta seemed to have gained strength from standing off the boy. "I best get you home safe," she said to Maeve, a kind of overblown adult authority in her voice.

Maeve smiled but took her hand as if accepting the smaller girl's protection. "Please."

thirteen

Blood Sisters

It was still over 90 out, he was sure. His back ran with sweat and the crickets down the canyon were burring away so fast you couldn't hear individual *cricks*. He'd read somewhere there was a formula you could use to calculate the temperature, counting the chirps per minute and multiplying by something, then dividing by something else. But, as with so many handy tricks, he had forgotten it.

There was a lot of dark hillside below him in Fry's Arroyo, a side canyon off Simi; far behind him, low in the cleft of the arroyo, shone the bright lights of Simi Valley itself, like a peek into another world. A small plane circled over that world, seemingly on guard to make sure none of LA's troubles spilled into that happy enclave. Jack Liffey had hiked carefully out into a vacant lot on a weedy spur of the hill, where he had a view back toward the hillside houses.

Kirk Grosvenor had led him here on his motorcycle, pointed out the particular stucco ranch house, and then roared away on the out-sized Kawasaki. The building the boy had fingered was two houses west from where he clung now to a big sumac bush, and it looked bright and conventionally suburban. Still, if the house had been any closer to the big city, no schoolteacher could have afforded it. There was a lot of glass and a flat roof and a deck out over the canyon and, amazingly enough, three men on cheap patio chairs on the deck, sipping beer from cans.

"Certissimo," a voice barked above the general drone. At least that's what it had sounded like. He could hear the natter of their voices, but the still air must have been against him because he could not make out much of what they were saying, except in snatches. He would have to work himself closer.

"What are you gonna do, take hostages?"

He intended to work his way along a line of low bushes that marked the outer rim of the yard. Unfortunately he would have to crawl to keep his silhouette down, and that would pretty well write off his slacks. He grimaced and sank to his knees as he left the shelter of the big sumac. The dirt seemed fairly firm. He was near enough the steeper slope that he didn't like the thought of a chunk of land giving way. There was a smell of sage on the air, and astringent dust. He moved in as close as he could and looked around for a moment to orient himself. Far in the distance the V had widened slightly, and he registered the bright necklace of the freeway crossing what little he could see of the valley.

"Trust the niggers to burn down their side of town again. Every ten years."

"Bri, don't use that word in my home. For God's sake, we're not *racists.*"

There was a laugh. "Yeah, we just don't like Afro humans very much."

A bright light came on suddenly in the nearest house. Jack Liffey froze, then scuttled behind one of the squat bushes to minimize the glare washing over him. He heard a faint squeal and peeked through the foliage to see into a glass box where a man and woman had just spilled out of some interior room. They appeared to be wearing each other's underwear, the woman in striped boxers and the man chasing her around a sofa wearing panties and a black bra on backward. The men on the patio next door couldn't see into the room so no one bothered to pull the curtains.

"I buddied with some smokes in 'Nam. They should just have their own homeland so they can deal with all that victim shit in their own way."

The man in the bra had caught up to the woman. They wrestled and groped for a while, the woman playing keep-away with something small in her hand. It was hard not to watch, and hard not to let it send him off into thoughts of Marlena, playing similar games somewhere. He felt sick.

" 'Course, you know if they dropped a half million humans into Watts, the whole place would be prosperous as shit in five years."

Jack Liffey could see the three men on the deck fairly clearly now, faces lit by weak carriage lamps at the corners of the railing. One had a tidy salt-and-pepper beard and his shirt hung open in the heat. Another man was a few years older, huge as a mountain, with a buzz haircut like a marine recruit, resting his penny loafers, sockless, on a small redwood stool. The third man was only visible as a shoulder beyond the other two. A smallish German shepherd wandered up to the big man for a pat and ear scratch and then, disturbingly, took a step toward the railing and oriented his body toward where Jack Liffey crouched. He remembered how much trouble he'd had hearing them, the sounds of their conversation simply not emanating toward him, and he hoped his scent hung immobile on the air as well. The dog froze in a pointing posture, staring straight at him. He held his breath, but the beast seemed disinclined to do anything more.

"Sometimes I give up hope, man," the bearded man whickered. "The whole joint's just going backward. The papers and TV are all run by Jews. They can't say a bad word about the queers and foreigners. They think abortion is a great thing: *Kill* those babies. You know, I sit down to read a article in the paper, and after the first three words I swear I know exactly what it's going to say. I don't think any of those liberal jerk-offs ever had a new idea in their life."

The big man with the buzz cut emitted a sound only vaguely like a laugh. It seemed to Jack Liffey that the others treated him like the top dog and called him K, so he was probably Perry Krasny. "There's no reason to get downhearted, my friend. We've got clubs all over the country, kids turning to the Bible, taking the pledges. And they're recruiting other kids. All we have to do is offer some leadership and take them forward a step at a time."

"I guess you're closer to all that."

They droned on. The dog snapped once at what must have been a flying insect, but its head came back to stare fixedly toward Jack Liffey.

In the nearer house, the woman tipped herself forward and abruptly stood on her hands, and the man began to tug the boxers off her. Jack Liffey closed his eyes and tried not to listen too hard to the men on the deck as they bandied about their half-truths, quarter-truths, and no-truths about cultural purity and social breakdown across the hot evening. Driving up here, he hadn't known what he had in mind beyond identifying Krasny's house and maybe getting a peek at him, and now that he'd had his peek he had even less idea of what to do next.

Jack Liffey missed a few exchanges, and then Krasny started pontificating again. "Don't forget who's the good guys here. No matter what happened with the prob-*lem*. We didn't mean it, you know? It's not like we did something for personal gain. It was just an accident, the prob-*lem*. Now there's a little more we got to deal with."

"Aw, man. This is so *fucked up*."

"Don't use that language. My kids are right inside."

They spoke softly for a minute, and he couldn't make out what they said. In the nearer living room, the upside-down woman had spread her legs wide like a scissors and the man leaned forward to put his head between the blades. Jack Liffey lay flat on the dirt and stared out over the canyon, away from the houses, nausea making him feel wretched. He wondered how to get out of there without upsetting the dog or looking at the lovemaking again.

"Woo, that was some talking to," Maeve said.

"We be okay."

They lay in twin beds five feet apart in a dark hot stuffy bedroom, and it was far too early to go to sleep. "I'm glad *you* think so," Maeve said. "I don't have to go on living here."

They had tried to slip in the bedroom window after their escapade, but something had already roused the old women, who had worked each other into a complete tizz searching the house and the neighborhood for them. Ornetta and Maeve had stood side by side in the dining room for the tongue-lashing, and Maeve would have been sent home on the spot except that her father hadn't answered his telephone.

Then they'd all eaten in grim silence, baked chicken in some thick batter made to seem like fried, and some heady boiled leaves that Maeve had never had before. It hadn't been the moment to ask what they were. Then the girls had been sent to bed.

"I ain' sleepy."

"Me neither. You could tell a story."

There was quiet for a moment. "I got one about the bad time after the slave time. This from Ami and it don't got very much magic in it. You want to hear it?"

"Oh, yes," Maeve said eagerly.

"You know, this is after the Sybil War. Slave time be over, but Ami say those Robert E. Leegrees just kick they slaves out on the road after Mr. Lincoln say they free."

A siren wailed along their street in Oakwood. Ornetta touched the charm under her nightie but kept right on going.

"Peoples had to learn to live then by bein' smart," she said grimly.

Ornetta told of a man named Richmond and his terrible hunger after walking for many days toward the north without food, but Richmond had always been a trickster, even in slave time, and he saw his opportunity at a house where two other freed slaves had been put to work chopping wood. They told him the owner was a fair man and gave a good meal for a day's work, and his wife was already frying up a huge chicken. So Richmond hired on too, and chopped his cord of wood, and at dinner he told the family that he had the perfect way to divide up their fat hen.

" 'You is good folks in the heart to take us in. This first division be easy to compute. You the master and the head of this fine house and so the head belong to you for sure. Next, you the wife and always right next to the master, so you get the neck, right next to the head. And my two brothers here, they got a long way to go to shake the dust of slavery off they shoes, so they get the two feets to help them on they journey. And me, I'm just a poor ol' colored tramp, so I take the onliest part that's left.' And he grabbed it up and jumped out the window and ran."

Maeve laughed for a while, her belly heaving against the hard bed, and then she started crying a little, she wasn't sure why.

In the end, he had to peek into the house again. Who was it said there were four things you were a lot better without: love, curiosity, freckles, and doubt? Freckles seemed harmless, he thought. And he was too far away to see them anyway.

"I talked to our pal at Rosewood about him." The voices drifted across the night.

"It makes me nervous thinking there's a detective out there heading toward us like a missile."

"Uh-huh."

Jack Liffey's spine prickled, and his eyes came back to the deck where the men sat stewing in their malice, the dog a gunsight aimed straight at him. Rosewood was where his friend Art Castro worked, a big-time detective agency with a classy office in the Bradbury Building downtown, the kind of place where they loaded you up with expensive electronic toys to monitor corporate crime and sent you down to the minors if you didn't get results.

"He's not really a detective. Got no license or nothing. He just hunts for missing kids."

"Uh-huh. And we know some."

Too many pennies were dropping at once. Jack Liffey was focused on every word, but lying deep under that attention a wrath rose up in him. He wondered who in Rosewood would finger him for this bunch. There was too much history between himself and Art Castro to figure him for it. He tried to picture the other faces in that posh office suite, room by room, and which of them even knew him by name. That was one trouble with going up against people like this, he thought, Pledge of Honor probably had friends everywhere.

"I'm not a big fan of trying to scare people off. Even if you do, the old coon just hires somebody else. I think, if they're getting this serious about the prob-*lem*, we got to go to the root, do something about the old coons themselves."

"I'm not going into darktown while this shit storm's on."

"What could be a better time, Bri? Lots of cover. If his house burns down and somebody shoots him twenty times, it might have been anybody."

The dog chose that moment, as if stirred by the talk of shooting, to start to gnar softly.

"What is it, Rex?"

The dog came to the very edge of the deck, at its nearest point to where Jack Liffey crouched maybe thirty yards away. A steady growl emanated from the back of its throat now, eyes boring into the night. There was only a three-foot jump from the deck down to the hillside.

"Must be a skunk."

"Uh-*uh*. Rex alerts on bigger game."

He could hear the chairs scrape as the three men stood up, but his eyes were locked on the enraged and trembling dog as he squatted transfixed behind his bush, like a deer in the headlights.

"Ow." Maeve held out the needle and squeezed a drop of red-brown blood out of her index finger.

Ornetta took the needle without hesitation. She poked herself stoically and smiled at the blood that ran quickly down her brown finger. Then they pressed their fingers together.

"Always and forever, we be together, one for all, all for one."

Maeve repeated it word for word.

"Now we blood sisters."

They hugged, careful to keep their bleeding fingers away from their nightclothes.

"That makes Mr. Liffey my daddy too."

"And you can call him Dad, like me."

"I guess we best clear it with him first," Ornetta said, realistic in her new kinship. "And Nana your nana, too."

fourteen

Looking Down the Subway Tunnel

"**W**hat is it, Rex, a prowler?"

Even the crickets seemed to have stilled as all Jack Liffey's concentration focused on the angry dog eyes across far too little space.

"You strapped, K?"

"There's a thirty-ought with a night scope in that case."

It was much too late at night to be the meter reader. Jack Liffey knew he had to take off running very soon now, but there wasn't much to be said for trying to sprint back across the empty lot toward his car. The dog would have him in three bounds. He had a chance to get away if he giant-stepped recklessly down the alluvial hillside. Just possibly he could stay ahead of a dog that was fighting its own way down the steep loose turf. But then what?

Unfortunately then-what lasted too long.

"*Romp*, Rex!"

The dog was suddenly a blur of action. It hit the dirt below the deck smooth and fast. Jack Liffey had barely stood up and turned on his heel when the dog was on the far side of him, slewing up soil as it came around like a dirt bike.

"*Lash*, Rex!"

The beast froze a few inches from him, growling angrily and steadily.

Lash, he thought. He hoped to hell it meant Stop in dog.

"Brian, go inside and tell Kelly and the kids to go to her sister's."

He chanced a look back at the deck just as the bearded one handed off a rifle to go in the door. The rifle was taken by the quiet one, whom he'd only seen as a shoulder, and this one tugged up the bill of a baseball cap, came to the rail, and aimed the bolt-action rifle rather vaguely, a scope sight on top and a big infrared illuminator on the side. The big man with the buzz cut boosted himself over the railing to hop down to the dirt. He moved pretty nimbly for such a big man. Jack Liffey's mind thought up tales and discarded them as fast as they came. They would have his wallet in a few seconds anyway and know who he was.

He glanced down the hill, but it was steep and almost denuded of plant life as a fire precaution. It would be a hell of a roll and tumble, at least five hundred feet.

"Don't even think about it, Jack. It *is* Jack, isn't it? I'd have Rex meet you at the bottom and rip your ass off."

He noticed that the big man had a smell about him, as if he hadn't bathed in a while. Then the guy had his wallet.

"Well, indeed. Jack Liffey, as I live and breathe."

The drapes had been drawn in the nearby house, but the athletic couple were still visible as heads poked between the curtains, watching the drama outside. Krasny gave them a wave suggesting that everything was under control, and the gap in the curtains slammed shut.

"You probably noticed that you don't train an attack dog to the obvious words. Somebody with a big voice might get them to do the wrong thing. Probably not, because they're good about knowing who the good guy is, but no point risking it. If I were to say the right word, this dog would eat you for supper."

"Heil Hitler?" Jack Liffey suggested.

Krasny emitted that unpleasant sound again, roughly like a laugh. "Not a very smart guess, but then a smart guess might have got you hurt."

"Hey, K." It was the bearded one, calling from the patio deck. "You better come deal with Kelly, okay?"

Krasny rolled his eyes. "Come out here and watch this guy."

They traded places, the bearded one a lot less nimble going over the railing, and Jack Liffey tried to size him up. If he remembered right, he'd seemed less enthusiastic about the white-power crusade, or had he just been more plaintive about it?

"Don't do nothing there, guy. I know the magic word for the dog too."

"I'm not going anywhere."

Jack Liffey studied the frown on the bearded man's face and began to talk as fast as he could. He expounded rapidly on the multicultural roots of rock-and-roll: Scottish ballads mutating into bluegrass up in the Appalachians, and slave drumming and gospel laments evolving into the blues down in the delta, and then meeting head-on in river towns like Memphis to turn into something magic and new. "Listen to Chuck Berry, man, you can still hear the country beat in him. You want to undo all that hybrid vigor?"

Krasny was back, leaning over the wood railing, and Jack Liffey's heart fell. "Come on up here, fellow. I like Chuck Berry too. And Bill Alexander. You can really hear those country rhythms in him."

The bearded man gave Jack Liffey's arm a powerful tug, and with the dog crouched only a foot or two away they made their way awkwardly onto the patio deck.

"Aw, shit," the one with the rifle said. This was the first good look Jack Liffey had had at him. Something seemed to be wrong with his eyes, and the baseball cap had a logo that said DISREGARD PREVIOUS HAT. He was staring at his foot, which he lifted off something. "I skooshed a snail. What the ugh's a snail doing up here?"

"Looking to eat my mint, probably," Krasny said.

"This snail sucks," the man complained morosely. He propped the rifle on the railing, sat on a plastic bucket chair, and began scraping his sole with a penknife. "Skooshies," he said to himself, and shuddered.

"Have a beer." Krasny shoved a beer bottle in Jack Liffey's hand. He was tempted, because it wasn't really the moment to explain how he wasn't in a drinking phase of his life, but he set the bottle down on a glass table.

"Not a good enough brand for you?"

"I'm not drinking, thanks."

"Then sit. Bri, would you go make sure Kelly's actually out of here?"

The bearded man went into the house.

"Hey there, Jack, what do you have when a hundred liberals are buried up to their neck in sand?"

Jack Liffey said nothing.

"Can't guess? Okay: not enough sand." He gave his approximation of a laugh, a kind of deliberate bray that did not seem to have much to do with humor.

"You're not very funny."

"Of course I'm funny. I'm the funniest man in North America, if I say so. And I'm the guy who's going to make it safe for white sissies like you to go on enjoying your life."

He wasn't enjoying his life all that much as it was, Jack Liffey thought, but he wasn't going to play straight man. Krasny eyed a chair and passed close to Jack Liffey, his huge presence pressing him back a few inches like the bow wave of a steamship; then he sat and became rooted. "Go on, sit."

Jack Liffey sat in another plastic chair.

"So. Maybe there was a time for cultures to mix and learn from one another, but it isn't working any longer. All you got to do is look around. I tell you, Jack, go down to some Korean minimart in the middle of Watts, with the glass security cage inside and the insulting graffiti about gooks on the outside, and see if you can find out what these great Asian and African civilizations are learning from each other."

He had decided that arguing was a bad idea, but despite himself, he replied. "You're talking about people living in poverty. I've seen people mix fine when they all had jobs."

"Lost your job, did you, to some smart gook?"

Krasny was quick, Jack Liffey thought, and observant. Of course, what had in fact taken his job was the imperative to maximize profits, working itself out as merger mania and a runaway shop, all of which had been implemented by very white, very European men. But this time he managed to stay silent.

Perry Krasny suddenly looked at Jack Liffey with an almost wistful stoicism. "All your life, the rim of civilization has been patrolled by men like me with guns to keep out the barbarians. Cops and soldiers and warriors and even ordinary security guards. First it was the Russians and Chinese and North Vietnamese, and now it's self-degraded thugs with colored skin. Let us not be hypocritical. My ring of defense makes possible your fine humanist fantasies of what the world is like. Men like me are your sacrifice to your self-image."

The one called Brian came back out the sliding glass door and closed it. There were no more chairs, so he waited at parade rest. "She's gone."

"Great. And what none of you liberal pantywaists ever manage to understand is that the dirty work is nowhere near over. Any people that lets their country be wrecked deserves what they get. If you open your eyes and look around, you will see that we are the only thing standing between white people and a flood of filth. I may even lose this fight some day, and all the you-rang-ee-tangs and Mexicans will end up overrunning this country, attended by all you liberal sissies. Who knows? Even if you can give me mathematical proof that the white race is going to lose, I am still going to do my best right now to prevent it."

"And you're going to kill a lot of ordinary people like me along the way." He eyed the one called Brian but could see no doubt in his eyes.

Krasny grinned. "We got a saying, you know: Kill the body and the head dies."

They had kicked the twin beds closer together so they could giggle and talk in the dark. It was still far too early to go to sleep. Now that they were blood sisters, Maeve had told Ornetta about her stepdad Bradley hitting her. The memory was starting to soften up and recede, along with her outrage, so she didn't play it up very much.

Ornetta went silent for a while and Maeve thought she might have fallen asleep. "Sis?"

"Jus' deep in my head." There was another long pause, filled with some tension Maeve didn't understand. "My momma was a princess in New York City," she said finally, her voice happy, but something hollow echoing under the happiness sent Maeve rigid with attention.

"We was staying in this big palace with lots of rooms and all these princes come to talk to Mama, like in the old days when the king daughter so beautiful. And they one prince is special for her, he protect Mama and live next door. He got big gold chains and laugh a lot. Mens bring him food in boxes and other mens stand around like old-time genies, they arms folded, to protect him.

"I had my own room, too, and lots of dolls and things. But Mama got sick and I asked the magic to make her better but it wasn't working so Grandpa Ban had to come get me. That's where I got my magic bottle, gives me wishes. You wanna see?"

She was clutching the neck of her cotton nightie, where she seemed to go so often when she needed reassurance.

"Uh-huh."

Ornetta wriggled right up to the gap and fished a necklace string into sight. Maeve didn't think of herself as particularly wise in the ways of the world, but she did know a crack vial when she saw one.

She hopped quickly across the intervening space to dive under the thin quilt with Ornetta and hug her. "Oh, sweet little sister, I'll never let anyone hurt you, I swear to *God* I won't." And Maeve burst out crying.

While they conferred among themselves, he worked out that the bearded one was named Brian and the one with the cap was Doug, still worrying about the mess on his shoe, scraping at it from time to time. Krasny and the bearded one whispered together for a while longer, obviously trying to figure out what to do with their captive.

Jack Liffey looked for ways of escape, but the dog squatted at his feet, glaring up attentively at his throat—a kind of sinister version of His Master's Voice—and the rifle was well out of reach on the far side of Doug.

"Listen to me," Krasny said to his friends. "I am put on the earth to enjoy myself when I can and do my duty when I must. If I were perfect I'd be Jesus, not His poor servant. I am an extra force of nature, it is true, but my sweetest fruit is my gentle nature." He threw his head back and gave out his approximation of a laugh and then abruptly turned serious. "We have the future of the whole Christian nation in our minds at every moment of our lives, and that justifies us in anything we have done or feel we must do. You both know that."

"If you're going to kill me anyway," Jack Liffey said, "at least tell me what happened to Amilcar and Sherry."

They all eyed him as if he had just farted in church.

"That's none of your business," Brian snapped, which told him all he needed to know. Doug frowned and studied his shoe all the harder.

"Ever stand up front in those old subways in New York?" Krasny asked. He settled back into his creaking plastic chair. "The ones that let you see out to the tracks? You could watch the future rushing at you faster than you could do anything about it, the driver in the booth right next to you winking out of existence and coming back as you pass bare lightbulbs on the tunnel wall, and leaving you wondering if he was in charge at all. That blackness just up ahead—maybe there was nothing but a flat wall painted black waiting for you. It's not a time you want to be smeared with snake oil. You want the truth when you're looking down the big black subway tunnel. But do you really want the truth now, Jack Liffey?"

He watched the man press his palms together in front of him like a Hindu mystic. Jack Liffey had to admit he found something energizing in the man's utter confidence and all his off-center vitality, but it left a bad taste, as if a kind of promiscuous sense of charity had seduced him into complicity with evil.

"Do you want the truth?"

"I think the truth is a lot more complicated than any of us ever imagine," Jack Liffey said, "and it's a good idea to let it happen in its own way rather than trying to force it." It was the best he could do.

He was tempted to say something insulting before he acted, but it would have been stupid to take even the slightest risk of alerting them. He jumped up out of the chair and pushed off the decking all in one motion, away from the dog, diving straight over the railing with a hideous plummeting-elevator drop in the pit of his stomach.

"Chew, Rex! *Chew*!" he heard behind him. He fell a lot farther than he wanted and hit the dirt at an odd angle and slid for a bit, disoriented in the darkness, but he shoved himself off the slope with both hands and by some miracle, windmilling in space, managed to right himself, hit the slope with one foot and get himself into a gi-ant-step rhythm. He let one foot dig deep into the soft dirt as it came down, then kicked off to fall another thirty feet or so and land with the other.

Chew, he thought with a chill. He might have guessed that one.

fifteen

Rest in Peace

Each long plunge sent his stomach up through his throat, left foot kicking off into the darkness, then ramming itself down into the silt; right foot hurled out in trust that the slope was still there as he giant-stepped into darkness. He prayed that nothing would catch at his ankle during the descent. His worrying Other insisted on picturing himself catching a foot and lurching forward in a swan dive into the abyss.

Just after his dive, he'd heard the dog come after him with a thump and a scrabbling sound, presumably four legs working hard in the soft dirt. The sound seemed to be gaining fast.

Ahead of him about a hundred yards below he could faintly see a line of dense brush, but there was almost no vegetation up on the slope where his feet dug in. The animal got ever closer behind him and a growl started up. He hoped the dog would have the decency to wait until he hit bottom to bite him. *Chew*!

Jack Liffey wrenched off his jacket in mid-stride. It had been a smallish shepherd, at least there was that. He wrapped the jacket hastily over his forearm as the dog closed. At what he judged was the last possible moment, he flung his arm around behind himself and went into a feet-first slide on his flank. The fiend was right there, bearing down. Jack Liffey's padded forearm whipped into the dog's jaws, and he grabbed for the animal's collar with his other hand. He got his fingers around the leather and held the dog's jaw hard against him as the two of them skidded crazily down the grade, locked in a death embrace.

The dog worked its teeth against the padding, growling in renewed frenzy as it discovered its entrapment, all four legs backpedaling against the slide. It was incredible how strong a small animal could be.

"Lash!" he shouted, but it did no good.

One of the fangs was coming through the matted cloth, and it hurt like hell. Jack Liffey managed to wrench his body around and slam the dog over himself to the opposite side. The dog's body hit heavily, the furious chewing interrupted for only an instant before the dog's legs were digging for purchase again. Jack Liffey found that opposing these mad surges of dog energy was exhausting him.

"I got a night scope, mister! Don't you hurt that dog!"

"Call it off!" he shouted up the slope.

"Not a chance."

His jacket was beginning to give up the fight, and it wasn't going to be long before his forearm was raw meat. Jack Liffey got flat onto his back in the slide and then dug his heels. The instant his heels caught, momentum took him upright, lifting him and the dog off the hillside. He felt his back straining under the weight of the animal. Rex must have weighed in at fifty pounds.

Loco, forgive me, Jack Liffey thought.

He transformed all that momentum into a body spin like an Olympic discus thrower and flung the dog straight out from the hill. There was a sharp pain as the angular momentum ripped the dog's jaw off his forearm. A plaintive howl rose into the night and then a gunshot sent him giant-stepping downward again into the darkness.

"*You bastard!*"

In a few seconds the howl choked off abruptly far down in the ravine and two more shots cracked. He thought he heard the sizzle of a round passing near his ear.

The shots got him kicking off recklessly, and this time he stumbled and began to windmill again, which might have been what saved his life. He landed hard on his chest and slid another twenty feet, the air knocked completely out of him so his insides went solid and he could not breathe. He came to a stop and lay in agony for a long time with his nose in the dirt, fighting lungs that did not seem to work. The shooting had stopped, but the lack of air was beginning to panic him.

A breath trickled into him finally, then a shallow exhale, and he eked another small breath, as something inside began to loosen up. Maybe he was going to get to stick around for this life after all. Gradually he became aware of his surroundings: There were no voices calling after him anymore, no more gunshots. He guessed they were regrouping, sending a car down to wherever the ravine would empty him out. Little by little, he found he could expand his lungs. He hoped someone had called the police over the gunshots, but maybe they were a nightly occurrence out in this farthest rim of suburbia, all the would-be Daniel Boones potshotting coyotes and jackrabbits off their decks.

He scrambled down the last few yards into cover in the bottom of the ravine, wedging in among water willows, mule fat, and yerba santa, where he settled to his knees and tried to get his bearings. He parted the leaves cautiously. Back up the hill he could see a spill of light from the deck, where one man was silhouetted against the sky like a tiny tin figure. The figure appeared to be scanning back and forth slowly with the rifle. He knew he had better stay well down in the brush, because his image would stand out like a giraffe at noon in that night scope. These days, you could buy the damn things from gun catalogs for a few hundred dollars.

He brushed himself down and found that his thin shirt hadn't been torn in the ragged descent, testament to the looseness of the silt on the hillside. Remarkably there was only a skin abrasion, where the dog's fangs had been torn away, and one little puncture.

There was a faint scent of damp off the ground, though in high summer it could only have come from lawn runoff. There would be no running streams up here. He felt with his hand, and the sandy bottom of the ravine seemed dry enough.

What would Daniel Boone do in this predicament? he wondered. Make his way back up the hillside, treading in his own moccasin tracks? Whistle up a faithful Indian companion? There were damn few real options. If he followed the canyon down, he figured he would run smack into one of the Gideon's 300 sent to outflank him. And up was worse. The night was dark, but his eye followed the ravine up and he could see how the vegetation thinned out progressively until it gave up completely many yards below a drainage pipe at the high road. That was just about where he had parked, he thought, but if he tried to go that way he would be completely exposed for the most perilous part of the climb. If he settled in for the night, they'd eventually send someone after him. And the longer he waited, the worse it would get.

Down was easier, he thought, so down it was. He got up off his knees and started picking his way discreetly through the brush, trying not to sound like a moose beating the undergrowth. It wasn't steep down here, but underfoot there were tippy flat rocks, matted vegetation, and loose gravel, all invisible, so he planted each foot carefully before shifting his weight. Here and there, the land dropped away a foot or so in a little terrace and he clung to the branches of the brushy willow to lower himself.

He checked the deck up the hill and saw the figure still on watch. There was a suggestion now from the man's posture, a hand to the ear, a cock of the head, that indicated he was consulting a cell phone tucked up to his ear. As Jack Liffey returned to his descent, the aroma of sage grew stronger on the warm air and he realized he could hear faint traffic sounds, probably from the Simi Freeway far out in the valley. The Ronald Reagan Freeway. There was even, oddly, a smell of frying hamburger on the faint warm wind.

What little light there was caught on a white plastic pipe emerging from the hill at chest level. It wasn't much bigger than his forearm and it trickled water. He heard it as much as saw it. As he passed the outlet, he could tell that the matted organic matter underfoot was damp. He hoped nothing nasty was coming out of the pipe, but only the runoff from late night lawn watering. A bit of mud clung to his shoe and the going got squishy for a while, but it hardened up again quickly.

About fifty yards ahead, the ravine fanned out wide and ended at a road embankment as if dammed there. A big culvert pipe passed under the road. Anyone up on the embankment would have been clearly outlined against the lights of the city far out in the valley, and there was no one. So far so good. If he could crawl through the culvert, he might just pass into some domain where there was more than one route downward.

Every hair on his body stood abruptly to attention. An animal squeal *right there* had torn the quiet, coinciding precisely with something soft under his foot, something that yanked away and then hissed angrily at him. As his heart thundered, his mind fastened on the dog he had hurled out into space, but that squeal had nothing to do with a dog, not even the vengeful spirit of a dog. Whatever it was waddled away into the brush, leaving a glimpse of white fur, a stripe—and then, unmistakably, he knew what he had stepped on. A smell billowed over him like rotten fruit, like death, like a chemical plant gone up in flames—in fact, like nothing else on earth. He had been skunked.

His legs, his right leg in particular, had been sprayed point-blank and that sweet caustic smell, which he had never minded much as long as it was faint and distant, off in the brush along the highway as his car roared past, was now so strong it made him ill with revulsion.

He sat down and started to take his pants off but thought better of it. Down in civilization he would be better off stinking of skunk than running around in his underwear. And by now it was on his skin too, so he was going to stink for the foreseeable future. He was a walking beacon for a quarter mile around to anyone with a nose. He leaned back to get his own nose as far as possible from his legs and retched into the dirt. Fortunately, he hadn't eaten in a long time and it was only dry heaves.

Just as he stood up, a dark van came fast around a spur of hillside, the kind of sudden ominous digression you met in a nightmare, and squealed to a stop directly above the culvert. That dark rectangle sat there now, completely out of place, a poisoned shape against the rounded innocent slopes. He heard the far door open, and then saw a figure in a cap come around to stare uphill. The figure carried something in each hand, and a bright flashlight began to probe and flit. Jack Liffey ducked deep into the recesses of a mule-fat bush, just as the man must have caught wind of him.

"Aw, Jesus H. Christ," Doug complained, into the hot pungent night.

"And then Robin went back to her bedroom to get the birthday cake with the sixteen candles on it, and she saw that her big poodle had eaten about half of it. Oh, yeah, I forgot to tell you she'd baked the magic powder she got from the rabbit into the cake."

This was the third time Maeve had been forced to loop back through her improvised story. Storytelling wasn't anywhere near as easy as Ornetta made it seem, but the girl was being very patient. She had turned on her side in the bed and seemed to be rapt. She listened without interrupting for almost ten minutes.

"And so—poof—he wasn't a poodle anymore, he was a handsome prince with a big chin and long curly hair, and he was grinning at her and promising to carry her away because of all the kind things she'd done for him earlier." She knew she hadn't told it very well, but Ornetta smiled.

They heard noises in the house and listened intently. They were worried; the older women seemed to have aged another ten years over the day, first worrying about the riots, then fretting about the girls, in addition to carrying all their unspoken worries about Bancroft Davis, who was staying by himself across town now and had a heart condition. It was not the best night to be in need of medical help from the outside world.

"Maybe I could have your daddy as a kind of backup daddy?" Ornetta suggested, as if dropping her expectations a notch.

"I'm sure." Maeve wondered how she herself would have responded to so much loss, if it would have left her with the feeling that she needed a backup for every relative. A grandma, a just-in-case grandma, maybe a third-stringer. "I'll tell him we're already sisters."

She looked at the tiny spot on her finger, where she had pricked it to mingle her blood with the younger girl's.

"I wish there was some easier way to be blood sisters," Maeve said. "It still stings."

"I guess it gotta hurt," Ornetta said in a small voice. She seemed to know.

With his getaway blocked at the embankment, Jack Liffey had retreated a safe distance up the ravine. For the moment, Doug seemed content to wait, as far from the skunk smell as possible. Now and then he flashed the beam of his powerful flashlight idly up the canyon, with side trips probing the slopes.

The man up on the deck had disappeared, ominously, so there were now two more on the loose somewhere. Jack Liffey wondered if one or both were working their way down through the canyon foliage. He listened but could hear only crickets and faint traffic and the buzz of a light plane far out over the valley. Then he heard a gunshot, close below him, and his whole body convulsed in reflex.

Doug had both arms straight out, and he appeared to be aiming a big pistol, cop fashion, alongside the flashlight. The man's arms ratcheted up a few degrees and he fired again, then lifted and fired again, apparently firing blindly at likely bushes. There wasn't much chance of getting hit, but Jack Liffey hugged the ground to make as small a target as possible. There was one zinging ricochet off rock not far away, and after eight shots the pistol fell silent and the flashlight went out.

These guys were really nuts, Jack Liffey thought. He stared hard. It seemed the man was dialing up a cell phone.

His ear caught a strange sound far up the hill, a *foomp* like the slam of a big airtight door. He squirreled around in a squat and focused on the row of houses up there. Nobody on deck. Before long there was a glow at the very top of the ravine, near the drainpipe, throbbing to light up the weeds at the edge of a vacant lot. The glow pulsed yellow like a Boy Scout campfire off in the woods. He heard a car start up somewhere in the direction of the luminescence, every sound proposing a direct personal threat. A chill tapped at his neck as paranoia took hold and he snapped around, but Doug still stood on the road, talking now on his cell phone.

The sound of the car engine above dipped lower in strain, as if working hard against resistance, and then a large shape made its way slowly into the vacant lot: a car shape with glowing windows. It was hard for him to believe his eyes. In terrible slow motion, a car with a fire brewing up inside it was rolling across the sloped lot. It looked like a second car was pushing it. The car tilted down abruptly where the lot ended, hung for an instant and then pitched off into space. It was a white car with darker fenders on one side. *It was his Concord.*

The car didn't fall far before its front bumper caught on the dirt and threw it sideways, to tumble side over side with an enraged momentum, tossing off sparks. The roof hit, then a big hop. The crashing and banging of each impact filled the night with gathering discord. He could picture a huge *Looney Tunes* fireball heading straight for him like a living creature, eating up everything in its path. He looked around hastily, but all he could do was shelter flat in a small outcropping of rock. He went down on his stomach, keeping his neck wrenched up to watch, mesmerized by the terrible downward crash and somersault that was coming his way. He had always assumed that real cars going over real cliffs did not explode the way they invariably did in films—an effect that was undoubtedly touched off by a half stick of dynamite strapped to a gallon bottle of gasoline—but his car was already on fire. What would happen if the gas tank ruptured on one of its impacts? He tried to remember the last time he'd filled up.

All this ran through his mind in a flash, and then the crashing doom was very close. He clasped his arms over his head and felt a shock in the earth, far too close, heard a horrible rasp of metal rending, and then felt the breeze of the poor dying Concord passing directly over him. He sat up quickly and noticed that Doug and the van had skedaddled.

What was left of the Concord tumbled side over side one more full revolution and then hit roof first with a dull final crump against the culvert, trembled a little in a death throe, and fell back into the shallow basin below the road. It sat in suspense for a few moments, shining nobly from whithin, and then fire licked upward from the torn rear quarter: not an explosion, but a steady increase until flames shot forty or fifty feet in the air, lighting up the hillside. He saw one sad torn door lying short of the burning hulk, a door he had spent some time hunting down in find-it-yourself junk yards. There were probably a few other random pieces of Wisconsin engineering up and down the ravine.

Rest in peace, my old friend, he thought sadly.

Maeve could tell by the smaller girl's breathing that she had fallen off to sleep. They were only a few inches apart in the bed, and she could feel the girl's heat. It was unbearably distressing for her to imagine Ornetta lost in that big threatening world of New York, so she imagined her instead sitting cross-legged and bright-eyed in a green park, recounting for even smaller girls the tale she had just told Maeve, of Abba-Zabba and the Thieves. She wondered what it was that gave some people such resilience that they remained kind and cheerful, while so many others, exposed to the same abuse and loss, turned mean.

That was what it was, she thought—why she was drawn to Ornetta so much more than to Mary Beth. There was so much to learn from Ornetta, who took into her heart what she had to from the big mess around her, transformed it into something magical, and endured the rest with courage and grace.

Then she remembered something her dad had told her once, a flash of gruff wisdom from his own father, he had said. She had always retained the words, even the tone of voice he had used, and now she knew just what the words meant. She had been asking him idly about how you decided the really big things in life whenever you came to one of those crossroads. He had spoken in a slightly different voice, probably a mannerism of his own father's that he attached unconsciously to the words. *Always pick the path that leads to where you can see farther,* he had said.

sixteen

Wonder Woman

The glare from his burning car had lit up the small bowl of hills like a stage with the players about to enter, and luckily enough they had indeed come hurrying in from the wings. A couple of good Samaritans in an old Jaguar had stopped within minutes of the crash to see if anyone was lying hurt near the wreck. Not long after that a pumper and a fire rescue truck had wailed up, with a half dozen firemen jumping out to drench the burning car and the brush around it with two small hoses. They were soon joined by a big Highway Patrol cruiser and a sheriff's car. Two more sedans parked off the road, and before long a whole crowd was combing the roadside where the ravine fanned out into a small floodplain near the road. He didn't see any of the men of Gideon's 300.

Jack Liffey considered playing the wounded driver and staggering out of the brush to let them whisk him away in an ambulance. But there would have been too many questions to answer, and the people in the house up the hill would have simply denied everything. So he stayed in a crouch behind a big bush, with emergency radios crackling on the hot dry air and crisp nearby voices calling out for wounded survivors. One radio was so clear he could make out every word. A dispatcher was urging the firemen to hurry up so they could get the trucks back on call—everybody else was down in LA, lending a hand with a hundred separate storefront fires. Apparently the rioting was beginning to rival the 1992 uprising.

Voices called out, fussed about the skunk smell on the air, queried each other, joked awkwardly; then a phalanx of volunteers responded in concert to the deputy's instructions and started a slow uphill sweep. Jack Liffey crept back to a much denser clump of shrubbery.

He burrowed into a small sumac, where a freshly fractured bough looked like it had taken a shot from his car, and noticed a glint of metal on the ground, a shiny oblong. He felt a pang when he recognized the flat paddle lying there as the recessed door handle of his car. It had ripped away clean. He bent down, picked up the token, and tucked it into his shirt pocket, more sentimental about the old car than he had realized. After all, he excused himself, the old Concord had given its life so that he might live.

As he heard the search draw near him, Jack Liffey crashed about a bit and came out of the sumac. "Nothing in there," he announced matter-of-factly, "except a dead skunk. *Damn.*"

A square-jawed man in a sheriff's hat looked a little startled, then sniffed him out.

"Sorry if I drifted into your bailiwick," Jack Liffey said. "I'll try over to the side there."

"You do that, friend. *Well* to the side."

Then he was up the embankment and walking down the road as if heading for one of the parked cars. There was no sign of the enemy. He turned a bend and saw it was only a mile or so down to the first lights of civilization. He picked up the pace, still a little worried that one of Krasny's boys might drive up behind at any moment, and realized just how weary the night had left him. Fear and tension did that to you. With a sudden sharp stab, thoughts of Marlena reappeared. He hadn't thought about her for hours.

The image of her with another man dropped on him with a vengeance and immediately hollowed out his sense of well-being at his narrow escape. He came to a dead stop for a moment, feeling sick to his stomach again, and then pushed himself on. He could feel the last of his elation collapsing, and he did what he could with it, throwing his head back and reciting aloud what he recalled of Yeats's "The Second Coming," the only poem he had ever memorized.

> ". . . And mere anarchy is loosed upon the world,
> The blood-dimmed tide is loosed,
> And everywhere the ceremony of innocence is drowned."

The dirt alongside the road turned into a paved sidewalk as civilization drew nearer, but the gloom wouldn't leave him. It wasn't really her affair that ate at him. He could and would get past that if Marlena came back. *If.*

The shock of loss seemed to have changed utterly how he felt about her—stunning him like the high-amperage jolt off a power tool. It demolished in one instant all of his ambivalence, to leave his own cravings stumbling around in a haze of tenderness for her big promiscuous heart. He had an overpowering urge to make it all work out, but he was powerless. It was not up to him.

He glanced around at the hillside against the velvety moonless sky, feeling as lost and helpless as a newborn. It was the defined horizons that were gone, Jack Liffey thought, the sense that he existed at the center of a small, secure, comprehensible world with love in it. When that was gone, all you had left was a kind of agitation, a desperation to find something solid. He walked with his eyes closed for a moment, lurching when one foot went off the sidewalk.

He yawned uncontrollably and realized how deeply exhausted he had become; his thoughts were nearly incoherent. He passed the first outlying houses of a subdivision that crowded up to a concrete block wall. The wall ran ahead to a big, bright, empty cross street. The windows of the houses were all dark and brooding. He could barely keep his eyes open.

At low points in his life, driving through unaccustomed towns or along unfamiliar streets, he had often imagined himself penniless and homeless and thought, *There*, that would be a good place to crash for the night, a refuge where he could store up whatever discarded food he could gather from Dumpsters and live for a few months: protected from the elements, out of sight, unlikely to impinge on other lives and draw notice. He felt the tug of such a place now, a hollow between a bus shelter and the block wall, protected by some overgrown ivy and shin-high wild geraniums. The summer night air was still blood hot and his resistance to the call of sleep melted away.

Jack Liffey slipped behind the bus shelter and lowered himself slowly into the ivy, crunching and crackling. His horizon collapsed to little more than a ragged line of geraniums surrounding him, and then even that tiny world winked out.

"Girls, rise an' shine for breakfas'. Sleepyheads don't catch no trains."

Maeve opened her eyes to wonder what trains Ornetta's aunt was talking about, but then she decided it was just an expression.

"Skip the train. We can catch a jet plane a little later on," she whispered, and Ornetta giggled.

Maeve and Ornetta talked for a while, recounting their dreams.

"Little gals, let's get our bottoms wigglin'."

"We up, Aunt."

They got out of bed and dressed. The tongue-lashing of the night before seemed to have evaporated as completely as their dreams, and the whole bustling household was bright and amiable for breakfast. Maeve was pleased. In most of the families she had known, there would have been a good half hour of harrumphing and recrimination in the morning, and an apology of some kind would have been expected from the kids.

"Your daddy doesn't answer his phone, honey, and we have to get home to Bancroft while we can. Curfew starts again at noon. What do you want to do?"

"I can just take the bus home." She was not about to suggest her other home, with her mother and Brad.

Ornetta's grandmother smiled mildly. "I really don't think there are going to be any buses running today. And I couldn't let you go off by yourself. I'd never forgive myself if something happened to such a sweet girl."

"I'll come with you then. Dad probably got up early to do something about his job. He usually does find the people he looks for, you know. He's really good at it."

"That's good to know. I guess you'd better come home with us, then."

He dreamt of space aliens creeping up on him with big sparkly ray guns, filling him with dread, and then awoke with the sun catching him from just over the houses, low in the southeast. He was sore all over, and it took him a moment to shake the vivid, busy guilt-ridden dreams and remember where he was. *Skunk,* he thought. Why hadn't he dreamt of skunk? The smell was still overpowering. *Marlena.* That was overpowering too.

There was a Quicki-mart across the street, and it was lucky he carried a spare twenty loose in his pocket for emergencies. He bought every a roll of paper towels and every six-ounce can of tomato juice they had in the cooler from a reluctant olive-skinned clerk who stood back at arms' length to take his money. Behind the store he opened the little cans, one after another, and rubbed the juice into his trousers and legs. He'd read about bathing dogs in tomato juice to neutralize the skunk smell, and it seemed to be working. Luckily they were charcoal-colored slacks, and the residue didn't show too badly once he wiped himself down with the paper towels. It made him look like a wino, but it did take care of most of the stench, leaving him smelling more like spaghetti Bolognese.

Back outside, he saw that his bus bench had been taken over by a raggedy woman wearing too many layers of clothing and tending a shopping cart chock-full of random stuff. He was wary of striking up a conversation, but she smiled pleasantly when he sat down and asked him if that bus went to Idaho.

"I really doubt it," he said. Of course, just about every bus line in the country connected ultimately with every other one. That was the theory he was operating on, anyway, though getting to the West side might not turn out to be much easier than Idaho. He'd have to ask the driver how many changes it would entail.

"No skin off," the woman said agreeably. "They don't like me there anyhow."

"Where are you trying to go?"

"Do you hear?" she asked suddenly, cocking her head.

He listened, but there didn't seem to be anything unusual on the air, just distant traffic noise from the freeway and a few birds twittering. "What?"

"That buzz."

He looked for power lines or anything that might be responsible for a buzz. He couldn't see anything and he couldn't hear it.

"That's the sound of people changing their minds," she explained.

"Ah." He nodded. Actually, it was the sound of schizophrenia, he thought sadly. How diabolically clever the country had been to close down the asylums and turn all the voice-hearers and tinfoil-hat wearers out onto the streets with referrals to local outpatient clinics, and then just not build the local clinics. What a great con trick, a real swindle on the weakest among us, he thought. And, as usual, in the richest country on earth, no one seemed particularly interested in rectifying a problem that only affected those who didn't vote. On the plus side, he decided, if you absolutely had to find a plus side, it was a kind of gift of event-filled freedom to people who were well equipped to turn it into a fabulous personal narrative.

"They land up there every night," she said breathlessly, nodding to the very hills where he had landed the night before. He didn't really want to know who *they* were.

"Genny, hon, listen to this!" Aunt Taffeta fiddled with the knob of the old tube radio on the kitchen table, but she'd lost the station.

"What was it?"

"Turn on the TV, quick. They done took away that Ab-dullah—you know, the baseball man—in a amble-ance."

Genesee Thigpen went alert suddenly where she sat. "I already told Ban we were on the way. I hope it's not something bad."

He was the sole passenger on the MTA bus. At first he had sat halfway back, but he'd found his mind going into overdrive writing a letter to Marlena. It had been a letter full of self-recrimination and pleas for another chance, touching on every single occasion he could recall in which he had not attended tenaciously enough to her wishes. Since he couldn't actually write the letter down, the exact text plagued him like a cold sore taunting his tongue, and he went over and over the wording until he decided he had to do something else with that mental energy or he would go nuts and start hearing people changing their minds.

He had then moved forward to the seat nearest the driver, diagonally across the aisle, facing the big PLEASE REFRAIN FROM TALKING TO DRIVER WHILE BUS IS IN MOTION sign, which they had both been ignoring for a while now. She was short but very strong-looking and wore a British bush jacket with all the pockets. When he'd mentioned coming down out of Simi, something about her reaction had suggested she didn't like the place much, and they'd struck up a conversation that had taken itself off into the realm of racists and homophobes.

"Look, there's no point being coy here," she said, when she seemed to decide she could trust him. "I'm gay. I've got pretty strong feelings about any place where the words *family values* really mean a bunch of mental defectives want to beat me senseless."

He laughed. "You look like you can hold your own."

"How do you think I got this way? I take tae kwon do. When the Sex Nazis come to my door, I'm going to take at least one of them with me."

"You ever hear of Gideon's 300? Pledge of Honor?"

"Naw. I don't take much interest in what those people call theirselves."

"These guys don't like you much and they don't like blacks," he said. "Last night they blew up my car. And today they're promising to kill an African American who's a friend of mine."

It hadn't taken him long, once his doleful self-absorption had wound down a bit, to recall the threat to Bancroft Davis. He realized he had to warn the old man and, if possible, get him away from the Brighton Street house where the Krasny legions could put their hands on him all too easily. He'd tried to phone from the first bus stop and got the same peculiar honking tone he'd heard after the '94 earthquake when everyone in the eastern United States had phoned LA to see how their friends and relatives were doing and had jammed the circuits for days. He wasn't too worried about connecting up with Maeve, she'd be okay in Venice, but Bancroft Davis was an old man who was all by himself in a small house while a handful of gun-toting fanatics were planning to take him out. For some reason, his head bobbed a little as he suffered a vivid sense memory of his flaming car thudding down.

"You serious?"

"I need to get into LA to warn the man."

"You may not get much past Van Nuys on the bus this morning. I don't think anything's running into LA. It's like 'ninety-two. The freeway's open, but only because it's an interstate. They say the cops got all the off-ramps blocked so you got to go right on through to Orange County or more."

That might just keep Gideon's 300 out of town too, he thought, but he couldn't count on it. It was a big town, and everybody had a secret shortcut somewhere.

"Got any suggestions? I've got to get there."

"We could commandeer the bus and crash the barricades, but I don't really recommend it."

"It's a thought."

She ground to a stop at the curb just past a busy intersection. An old man on the bus bench shook his head, and she shrugged and started up again. "Do you have any idea how bored I get? Even the flakes that get on and torment me break down to the same half-dozen types, over and over. I could use some standing up for what's right. You're for real, huh?"

"I know it sounds strange." He decided to take a flier. "The guy I'm talking about is named Bancroft Davis. He was a well-known civil rights leader."

"I don't know the name, but I'm going to take a tiny chance on you." She pulled the bus over to the curb at a fast-food shop and yanked the brake. "Come on."

She went straight to a pay phone. "Babs, this is Toni. You always liked *Wonder Woman*. Well, I got your chance for you at last."

* * *

"Have you tried the cops?" Babs asked him.

Jack Liffey shook his head. "First off, who's to say they'd believe me? Second, they don't have anybody extra to spare right now to guard a single old man."

Babs had been waiting for the bus at Sepulveda and Victory, parked in the lot of a coffee shop in a rusty little Geo Metro. She offered an absolutely astonishing resemblance to Veronica Lake, tall and willowy with long platinum hair. It was ironic, he thought, that of the roommates, Antonia was about five-three and drove an MTA bus, and Barbara was at least five-ten and had to jackknife herself into a Geo Metro. She turned out to be a junior high English teacher. She had heard of Bancroft and was gung-ho to help.

"You're probably right about the cops being preoccupied. The reason I'm off today is they shut all the city schools. With the busing, even up here a lot of our kids come from the curfew zone."

"Curfew zone?"

"You been out of touch, I'll bet. The borders are the 10 freeway on the north, the 405 on the west and south, and the 710 in the east."

"That's a big area to shut down. That's the whole middle of the basin."

"Uh-huh."

"Why did things suddenly turn so much worse?"

"You *have* been out of touch. Abdullah Ibrahim died this morning."

"Oh, Jesus. Not another visit from the cops?"

"An ambulance was called to his home to get him. That's all anyone knows so far."

"Is there looting yet?"

"According to the radio, the curfew is just preemptive. But I think it's worse."

"Can we get into the curfew area at all?" He might have to rethink his mercy mission if a full-bore riot was on.

"The town's not really shut up tight yet. It'll take awhile to sink in, but the freeways are locked up."

"Laurel Canyon? Beverly Glen?"

"I bet they're both backed up solid." She smiled. "But I know a route. Let's *do* this thing."

"You're Wonder Woman," he said. "I'm just Tonto."

"Now *that's* a mixed metaphor." She backed out of the slot in the parking lot with a jerk of the clutch.

"Actually, it isn't a metaphor at all," he said, "but who am I to contradict an English teacher?"

"You're even literate. Where on earth did Toni find you?"

"At the bus stop, of course."

She smiled. "Of course. Let's *ride,* Tonto."

seventeen

Nearby Ruckus

"**E**ver been over on this route, Tonto?"

"I think I prefer Jack," he told her. She had wrenched the little car through a number of inexpert maneuvers above Ventura Boulevard until they ended up on a street called Woodcliff, and the Metro was now winding up the Santa Monica Mountains, still on the Valley side, past plain-looking tract houses, the more expensive cliff-hangers thumbing their noses from farther up.

"And I'm Babs, but I really am into the Wonder Woman thing. I've collected the comics and memorabilia for years."

He had a lot on his mind and he wasn't really in a chatty mood. He looked at his watch. The crystal was shattered and the hands had stopped somewhere in the early A.M. He tried to remember how it had got that way, and all he could recall was hitting the dirt pretty hard just before his car tumbled past overhead. It was only a Timex, but he had a feeling that the fates were stripping away piecemeal everything he possessed. Soon he would be as naked, pink, and propertyless as a newborn, sitting out there squalling on the highway just as an acid rain started up.

"This road goes up to Mulholland, and then you jog over a bit and find Roscomare to take you down into Bel Air. I used to do a lot of subbing, and if I had to get over the hill at rush hour, this would often work better than anything else."

"Everyone in town's got a secret route or two," he said.

She ground the gears whenever she had to downshift for the curves. "I guess LA's that kind of place," she said.

"What time is it?"

"Almost noon," she said.

She dropped two gears going around a tight turn and his head jogged hard when second took hold, but he still decided not to offer to take the controls. He glanced at the watch again, a reflex. It was still broken.

"There are problems with the early Wonder Woman," Babs said suddenly, apropos of nothing. "But she was strong and smart and self-sufficient, and she stood up for women."

"Is that a problem?"

"No, no, no, not that. But she did have some pretty dainty friends. Etta Candy was her best girlfriend. She was addicted to eating sweets all the time and saying things like *woo-woo* a lot."

He thought about it. "Woo-woo. What an innocent era."

She shrugged. "Hold on. In the fifties this creepy Freudian psychologist Dr. Wertham came along and launched a national crusade against Wonder Woman. She was a castrating woman, he said. Unnatural. Obviously a man-hating lesbian. He went after Batman and Robin too; they were obviously queers. The result was the horrible Comics Code. Diana Prince, which is Wonder Woman's real name, had to surrender her Amazon powers and run a dress boutique, if you can believe it. Thank God for the women's movement. They brought the real Wonder Woman back in the seventies."

"It was a pretty bad time, all that Cold War hysteria to be just like the neighbors," he said.

"No kidding."

"Every time I hear somebody getting nostalgic about the fifties, I think of what it must have been like to be black or a political dissident."

"Or a woman," she added. "Think of all those poor actresses who had to play ditzoids their whole careers. Needless to say, lesbians didn't even exist."

Speaking of the Cold War, he noticed the top of an old air raid siren over the hill ahead. The Metro putt-putted over the top at Mulholland and they were on the LA side of the hills now, passing the siren on its pole, sad brown paint peeling off its little conical hat. The old sirens hadn't been fired up for twenty or thirty years; they just waited there, dead and forgotten, all over the city. He'd grown up with the ones near his San Pedro school detonating with a rising scream at precisely 10 A.M. on the last Friday of every month. And then there were the teachers unexpectedly yelling "Drop!" into submissive classrooms. People talked about the trauma of all that atomic fear, but nobody he knew had taken it very seriously. How often could kids get worked up about adults crying "Wolf!"?

"Did you have drop drills?"

"I'm too young. And I was back east, where they used to call it Duck and Cover: put your head between your legs and kiss your ass good-bye."

He chuckled. "The Cold War was pretty funny, given enough perspective. I remember when the Cincinnati Reds had to change their name to the Redlegs. I wonder why people were so damned *frightened* of things that were different. Still are. This country is about as rich and powerful as it can get. What on earth do they think is going to go wrong if some people somewhere worship Allah or two women live together?"

"Thanks for that one. I don't know either."

Coming down the south flank of the mountains, there were a few turns where they had a good view out over the city. Three or four massive vertical plumes of black smoke rose into mushrooms like votive offerings, a familiar sight by now.

He was going to need a car, so he had her drive him to his friend Chris Johnson's place in West Hollywood, where he knew there was an old VW up on blocks. As soon as Johnson's parole officer had let him off the hook for his phone-hacking conviction, Chris had bought a T-1 line and launched an Internet nursery business called green-thumb.com, whereupon he'd stored his old car and taken to driving around in a big beat-up Ford three-quarter ton.

On the way up the cracked walk to Chris's door, they could hear the popping of distant gunfire and a number of sirens heading off on missions. As they waited, neither one mentioned the commotion, as if they'd lived for years in Beirut.

"Hi, Chris. This is Babs."

They were both a little stunned by the room. Where Jack Liffey remembered a welter of electronics and computer monitors, there were now hundreds of little plastic pots with houseplants in them. The air smelled like wet mulch.

"Pleased to meet you," he said.

"You always seem to live your work," Jack Liffey said. "What does Dot think of all this?"

"You should see her place. She has the tropicals. Most of the business is drop-ship, which means other people do the storage and shipping for us, but I like to keep my hand in with some of the local deliveries." He sniffed. "Nice pants, dude. Want some parmesan?"

"I had a run-in with a big tomato."

"Uh-huh."

"What's this one called?" Jack Liffey pointed to a row of what looked like frozen green flames, about a foot tall.

"That's sansevieria, snake plant. It's actually a succulent, and it'll survive almost any sort of neglect."

"I know wild plants out on the chaparral, like sagebrush and creosote bush and buckwheat. Knowing houseplants is a little too much like cooking quiche."

"Just not a houseplant kinda guy."

"I need to make a phone call rather badly. Down into South Central. Is there any way you can get me through that strange busy signal?"

"So you want me to violate my parole and hack into the phone system so you can share smoochies with Maeve?"

"Something like that."

Johnson frowned at him. "Unfortunately I can't. The circuits got overloaded early this morning and they all went blooey. *Blooey:*

That's a technical term in the phone biz, Jack. The cell networks are down too. I'd like to help you, but you just can't comb a hairy ball smooth. That's another technical expression."

"If anyone can get technical, you can."

Chris Johnson expressed his regrets at the demise of the Concord, and they trooped out to the backyard where a big rounded hump under a tarp sat beside the driveway, up on four concrete blocks. The rest of the yard was jammed with more potted plants, some of them under a gauzy net that cut down the sun. "You're welcome to take Mr. Volks on approval, but you'll have to put him back together. I had a guy drain the gas and pull the carb and plugs and battery when I stored it. I know the theory of how it goes together, but I don't work on cars. You're always in some uncomfortable position and you need some tool you don't have."

"I'm not sure I could do it," Jack Liffey said. He turned to Babs. "Know anything about working on cars?"

"You kidding?" she said.

"Just hoped."

"I know VWs from the outside," she said. "I mean, I can tell you the year. My family had a string of them."

"That'll be useful if we have to go on *Jeopardy!*" They had assembled around the car, and he lifted the tarp like a coroner trying to establish the cause of death.

" 'Sixty-two," she said, right away.

"How can you tell?"

"Tailights are bigger than the tiny little oval ones, but smaller than the later fat ones. Door handles still have the big square button instead of the trigger. The 'sixty-three had a crease in the engine cover for a bigger engine. This is still a twelve hundred engine. They made so few changes every year that it doesn't take much to date a Beetle."

"You're going to have to put up with no fuel gauge," Chris Johnson said. "This one still has the big lever to switch over to the reserve tank. It's got about fifty thousand miles on the engine."

"That's not bad, if I remember right," Babs said. "About half its life expectancy."

"Cheap to rebuild," Chris Johnson said.

"I'll get under it and get dirty," Jack Liffey said, "if you two will hand me the parts and give me moral support."

All of a sudden, Babs turned and stared hard at Chris Johnson for some reason. "You have the most amazing yellow-gold aura. I know it's not cool to say it, but I can see these things."

Neither of the men had any idea how to respond to that.

"The brightest aura I've ever seen."

"What about mine?" Jack Liffey asked, to ease Johnson's embarrassment.

She cocked her head at him, tucking her tongue into the corner of her mouth, and studied him for a moment. "Pretty weak, I'm afraid. A bit blue. I think your soul is wearing out."

"I probably need my hundred-thousand-mile rebuild."

"Must be."

He rolled up his sleeves. "Let's put this puppy together."

Genesee leaned in and loosened her husband's top shirt button, supporting herself on the walker, and Bancroft huffed and puffed on the sofa and motioned the girls back to give him a little room.

"Would you like some water?" Ornetta asked.

He nodded with his lips tight. Ornetta hurried away toward the kitchen and Maeve saw the old man and woman exchange a look that meant, Let's keep it light and not worry her.

"It's his heart, isn't it?" Maeve said, very softly.

"Shhh."

Bancroft Davis took a tiny pill out of a little bottle and put it under his tongue.

"He'll be okay, honey. Why don't you go. . . ." But she couldn't think of something to tell Maeve to go do.

"I won't say anything," Maeve whispered.

The woman nodded. "It's too much excitement going on."

Ornetta came back with a tall glass of water, and her grandfather drank some of it and pretended it was just what he needed. He smiled, as if relaxing, but Maeve could see the tension in the way he held his chest. Ornetta seemed to sense something too.

"I seen all the weeds taking over my magic garden, Nanny. Can we go fix it up? I promise we stay in the yard."

Maeve could see the woman considering and then reluctantly opt for the lesser evil. "But just in the back, okay? *Promise.* And you come straight in if you hear any ruckus nearby. You hear, girl?"

"Yes'm. We seen plenty enough trouble already."

And they had. Bancroft may have seen some of it on TV, but they'd actually passed through the thick of it. Driving east from Venice, they'd passed a big grocery store called Buddha Market that was being thoroughly looted. It was on the flank of the Baldwin Hills, just as Slauson descended into the West Bank of Crenshaw, an area that was slightly better off than the flats farther east.

Only one lane of traffic had been crawling past the market because an MTA bus lay on its side in the street with every window broken out, so they had a good long look at what was going on. People had been spilling out the shattered doors of the market and fanning out in all directions, carrying boxes and bags or pushing shopping carts heaped with goods. It was like watching ants rescue eggs from an anthill that was being flooded. And the market *was* being flooded for some reason. A wet mush oozed out the doors, apparently made up of paper goods and vegetables and other lumps carried along by muddy water.

Farther on, a small video store had been emptied out already and the sidewalks sparkled with broken glass. The shell of a burned-out police car rested near the curb. As if the vehicle hadn't already suffered enough, a circle of men were peeing on it while a young man wearing a green bandanna over his face slowly beat the underside to death with a street-side trash can. Genesee Thigpen had driven grimly on toward home, her hands stiff on the wheel, not saying a word.

Groups of people had stood around everywhere, seemingly waiting for something. Throughout the entire trip, Genesee and her passengers had seen only one other police car, parked discreetly near a closed-up strip mall, with a video camera sticking out the window.

"This my garden," Ornetta said when they got outside, and then, softly, "It's his heart, huh?"

"I think so," she said. "But it looks like he'll be okay." She wondered if being indefinite about it dodged the moral dilemma at fibbing to a sister. It was the kind of thing her father worried about a lot, and she was beginning to see that things weren't always black-and-white, just as he insisted.

Ornetta beckoned and Maeve joined her at a lean-to roof off the side of the house where an old wheelbarrow was stored, loaded up with a number of gardening tools. They heard the slow *bop-bop-bop* of a semiautomatic weapon somewhere, but they exchanged a glance that managed to exclude the sound from Genesee's instructions about nearby ruckus.

"Give me a hand, Maevie."

They each took a handle and tugged the wheelbarrow out of its shed. Together they pushed it across the bumpy lawn to the flower-bed, which had become choked with weeds. "These my snappy dragons. I tell you 'bout the day the snappy dragons had to guard the king's Easter eggs?"

Please please don't make any final decisions until we talk again, he wrote on the pad. He added some more, mostly self-recrimination, anything he could think of from the mea culpa letter he had churned over in his head, but soon he broke off and left the pad in the center of the kitchen table.

He had got the old VW going without much trouble and insisted on leaving Babs behind with Chris, though she wanted to come along to help him. Oddly, the two seemed to have taken a shine to each other. Chris turned out to be a collector of old Wonder Woman comics.

Mar Vista was outside the curfew zone, so he hadn't had any trouble getting home. The instant he'd come in the door, Loco had started going bananas out in back; eventually Jack Liffey took some dog food out and tried to feed him. Mostly Loco just stiffened his front legs, hunched back on his rear legs, and barked up angrily at him, undoubtedly accusing him of neglect or worse. Too late, he noticed a second burrowed-out escape route by the fence. Loco gave him one last tongue-lashing, scrabbled through the tunnel like Steve McQueen making the Great Escape, and headed off down the alley at flank speed in that strange half-sideways coyote lope. He didn't look back. Evidently he had held off the getaway until he had a witness, out of some canine spite. Another loss, Jack Liffey thought, but he just didn't have the energy to go after the dog. Loco would either come home to eat or he would not.

Back in the house, he suddenly realized that Marlena's Chihuahua was gone too, presumably now at her new love nest, which was just as well. If the rabid little rat dog had started going gaga, as was its wont, he might have stored it in the microwave as he had fantasized so often.

He changed his pants, picked up his .45 automatic from the hollowed-out *Oxford Companion to American Literature* where he stored it, and then went back to the kitchen and grabbed a hunk of cheese out of the fridge and chewed on it to discover just how hungry he was.

He tried to call Bancroft Davis again, but the attempt was about as effective as talking into the toaster. The phone didn't even buzz back at him. It was remarkable, he thought, how dependent everyone had become on the magic of sending the human voice miles and miles over wires. With the phones down, getting a simple message of warning ten miles across the city was an ordeal.

As he'd guessed, where Washington Boulevard passed under the 405 into the curfew zone, the underpass was blocked with yellow sawhorses. They were taking the curfew seriously. A number of cars were lined up to plead their case with a couple of bored cops. Mostly the cops were turning people away, but once in a while in the queue ahead of him, they would swing away a sawhorse and let someone pass. It was only mid-afternoon, so he guessed they were letting people with the right address go home.

When he worked his way to the front he dug out his driver's license. It still listed his residence as the condo in Culver City, and for the first time he realized he'd probably be back in it for real pretty soon. You can go home again, he thought. You may have to.

"Going home for the night?" the cop asked.

"Uh-huh."

"Any guns in the car?"

Jack Liffey laughed. He hoped his sudden shiver hadn't shown. It was hard to keep his eyes away from the glove box. "You must be kidding."

"We got reports from previously reliable sources."

"Reports?"

"About white vigilantes, thinking this is a pretty good opportunity to hide in the bushes and notch up a few Nee-gro scalps."

It was hard to read the man's attitude.

"Is that a suggestion?"

"Oh, no, sir. Of course not."

Jack Liffey was thinking, Gideon's 300.

"Have a good evening, sir. Sunset is at seven-thirty-five. Don't be caught outside after that. You *will* be arrested."

"I'll stay indoors with my sniper rifle."

"That's the ticket. Be discreet."

eighteen

Honorary Niggah

Jack Liffey saw a guy in checked pants sitting along Slauson with one of those glass crack pipes in flagrant use, puffing, then grinning up at any traffic that passed, like a child acting out. There wasn't much traffic, but where it bunched up at a bottleneck to creep past a toppled bus, it almost seemed a normal volume. Traffic also slowed to gawk at a burnt-out police car. Too, there were more intimate signs that something was amiss: at red lights, cars wouldn't stop parallel, but one or the other would lag back; no one seemed to want to make eye contact. And for the most part the flow stayed well away from the curbs to avoid the broken glass spilling into the streets. The last of the sun glittered orange off this snowfall of glass in his rearview, and he guessed he had about forty-five minutes of light left.

He had the windows down against the oppressive heat, and he could hear automatic gunfire rattling away not too far from him. For some reason, he didn't think it was aimed at anything, just fired aloft out of emotional abandon, like New Year's Eve in the Middle East. But he had no real reason for feeling that way.

Idling at a light, he could hear a lot more gunfire, farther away, overlapping and counterpointing, making a kind of running sound track to the evening, but the VW engine was so loud it drowned out most of the battle sounds when he started up again. A whole row of storefronts had identical tidy BLACK OWNED signs in the windows, and he wondered if that might not strike a roving band of looters as suspiciously corporate. A sudden chill overtook him, and he downshifted and floored the balky old VW when he caught sight of a big teenager in sweats heading fast for him, waving a baseball bat. The hurled bat clanked off the engine cover. He figured he'd just missed becoming an item on the evening news.

He saw a big ladder truck parked diagonally by a freshly burned out fried-fish storefront and the firemen were standing around, pointing at a number of smoldering wooden studs and talking them over, as if some might be more interesting than others. A couple of cop cars watched over the firefighters like mother hens. Up here on the flank of the Baldwin Hills, it was still largely the land of those with jobs and futures. He'd read that Baldwin Hills–Crenshaw was the largest middle-class black community in America. But his expedition soon took him down into the plains of despair, South LA proper, and the difference was stark. A lot more of the storefronts had been abandoned, boarded up for years, and the nail salons and music shops gave way to storefront churches with hand-lettered signs: MOUNT HEBRON FULL LIVING GOSPEL MISSIONARY CHURCH.

A minimall had been trashed and looted, the metal grilles ripped open as if by a giant, and drawn here and the flat there were no longer attendant police vehicles. People were no longer waiting around on the street corners for trouble either; they were running, either toward it or away. At the limits of his vision there was a lot of rapid movement, as if he were driving through a big track-and-field meet. Three boys raced straight across his bow and disappeared between houses. A lone young man sprinted through a small park carrying a big, clumsy cardboard box in front of him, contents unknown. A motley pack of dogs of all sizes trotted along the sidewalk, a big German shepherd eyeing him like an angry cousin of the dog he had killed in Simi: Rex; he remembered the name. One white mutt skulking back in the pack might even have been Loco, but if he'd got this far already, Jack Liffey figured he must have taken a taxi.

All of a sudden he noticed that the traffic had thinned to nothing, and he began to feel terribly conspicuous on Slauson. At the first opportunity, he zigged south a few blocks to 60th Street, which ran parallel, and headed straight toward the old man's neighborhood. Even with the window open, the old VW was like an oven, and he wrenched the wind wing around as far as it would go to direct moving air on him.

His SOS mission was beginning to seem a pretty bad idea, and he wondered what good a warning would do in any case. He couldn't picture Bancroft Davis going to the mattresses, crouching there at his front window with a long rifle ready for bushwhackers. But delivering the warning was an unequivocal duty, he knew that much, *and* it kept him from thinking about Marlena.

He found himself obsessively complying with all the laws of the road, though there was virtually no chance of getting a traffic ticket. It felt as if he were honoring a pact with a very grouchy god: *I will do nothing whatever wrong and you will ignore me.* The VW puttered along at 25 mph and made a full shift down to first at every stop sign.

He held up at one corner when he caught sight of a blur to his left, and the blur became a low-rider racing along the cross street, a dark Pontiac from the late fifties, the windows so blacked out it might have been driverless. He heard the old automatic transmission throb a gear change as the car accelerated across the intersection. Then he heard and finally saw what must have occasioned the flight.

Loud banda music thumped away its polkalike beat, the bass notes hammering up into his chest, and a fancy purple truck with huge knobby tires and desert lights came into sight, giving chase to the Pontiac. Two Latinos stood in the bed, gripping the light bar and aiming handguns over the cab. They seemed to be firing their revolvers methodically at the Pontiac on all the heavier beats of the music. Jack Liffey crouched low in his seat, as if that might protect him. The chase rounded a corner two blocks on, and the dull woofer beats and gunshots trailed them for a bit, like something unpleasant left on the air. The strange pursuit stirred some memory, maybe from a film, but he couldn't place it.

Streetlights were winking and coming on, glowing spots in the still bright evening, as he rounded the corner at Brighton and saw the twin row of skinny fan palms stretching away to the south. He was two blocks north of the Davis house and he pulled to the curb, killed the engine, and scrunched down in the seat to look things over. The only other car on Brighton was a beige 1962 Comet a half block away. He knew no one was in it because it was upside down, like a bug waving its legs at the sky, and the roof was crushed flat— another reminder that all was not well in South LA.

Farther east a fat column of very black smoke rose angrily like the funnel of a tornado, something very big and toxic ablaze. The main drag of Vermont was only two blocks east of him. All the doors on Brighton were shut, all the windows shuttered or curtained or dark. He had half hoped to see sandbagged gun emplacements protecting the neighborhood, manned by the Rolling 60s Crips, but there was nothing.

There was a heavy thumping on the air and then he saw it, a helicopter coming over low. It was either TV or police, and it had a big dark sphere suspended between the skids, like a grasshopper trying to loot something valuable. For an instant he saw a dull red glow off the sphere and could only guess that it was some kind of infrared surveillance equipment. That was the LAPD's signature, all right, too much technology and too little contact. What could they possibly do from up there, drop warning leaflets? Launch air strikes on looters!

Suddenly he saw fiery green dashes rising lazily to the helicopter and the machine tipped up to show its belly and scooted away to the east. Surprisingly easygoing, the line of green flashes tilted east to follow the chopper, as if it just wanted to tap the machine on the shoulder to remind it of something but couldn't seem to catch up. The last time he had seen something like that he had been on leave in Saigon and had got caught up by accident in the Tet offensive. He could not imagine how someone in South Central had come upon tracer ammunition, but that green color was a signature of the AK-47.

He wondered again—now that he was here—what good it was going to do to barge into Bancroft Davis's house and offer up a strange alarum from outer space. "Some white men in a racist group called Gideon's 300, or maybe they're called the Defenders of the European Legacy—anyway, they may be driving over here from Simi Valley in the midst of this riot to try to kill you." Davis would probably just shrug it off, or at most he would be vigilant for a few hours and then go to sleep. Would they come at all? Jack Liffey wondered. The trek would be just as hard for them as it had been for him, maybe even worse.

He could wait in the house alongside Davis, of course, furniture against the windows to seal them inside like Davy Crockett and Sam Houston in the Alamo, armed with his single .45 automatic pistol, as Krasny's boys sneaked up on them from all sides with rifles, Molotov cocktails, rocket grenades, and bazookas. Who would notice a single house torched suspiciously that night?

On the other hand, he thought suddenly, he could use the only real edge he had. They would never expect somebody to set an ambush for them out on the street. Three doors up the block from the Davis house and across Brighton, there was a vacant lot, probably an old burn-down that no one had bothered to rebuild. The city had a policy now of tearing down abandoned structures before they could become crack houses, so the whole of South LA had a scattering of abandoned weedy lots like this one.

He could see that the curb ramped down in front of the lot where a driveway had once been, but he decided to wait where he was until the street got a bit darker. He hunkered down below the seatback as a band of young men, maybe twenty strong, trotted past ahead of him toward Vermont. One boy waved a purple Lakers banner, but a couple of the others seemed to be carrying rifles and they definitely weren't the rooting section.

He didn't think he had ever before gotten himself into a situation quite as ludicrous as this: a white man in an old VW with Rustoleum red fenders parked in the heart of a full-bore riot in a black area to defend a black man from other white men who were—perhaps—sneaking up on the neighborhood. It was like zebras trying to slip into the middle of a high school prom to stage a duel. In a book, you wouldn't believe it. That was the difference, he thought: Fiction had a meaning and life didn't. And because it didn't, it never worried a whit about plausibility. It could be every bit as absurd as it wanted to be, just as outlandish and meaningless. An incident jumped up out of the muddle, no reason really, and the light of history flashed on it for a moment and then it was gone.

Randomness, my old friend, he thought. If that mob of kids had followed the Lakers banner down the cross street just twenty feet behind him, instead of the street ahead of him, they would probably have noticed him and trashed his car, with him in it, and whatever he might have represented as Bancroft Davis's savior would have evaporated in that simple accident of route. The same fate could strike Gideon's 300 too, of course, the whole gang of them squeezed into the back of a dark van heading his way, bustling and restless in there like circus clowns, and the van could blow a tire right in front of a mob looting a sporting goods store, and a dozen hunting rifles could fill the van with holes in a simple excess of enthusiasm.

When the blow was truly aimed at you, he thought, there was nothing much that could come between you and the pain. He guessed the point was to find a way to be at peace with that. And suddenly he was thinking of Marlena again.

The sense of loss flooded back in, just when he'd started feeling he belonged to the world again. Things still existed out there but he was no longer part of them, cast out of the fraternity of the ordinary and the happy. The last time that had happened, losing his job and family, he had gone on a binge of coke and booze for almost a year. It wasn't quite that simple, of course. The job had gone first, and it was mostly the binge that had cost him his wife and family, but the point was, he knew better now. There was nothing to be gained by a retreat into blotto. He'd eaten the apple of knowledge, or the apple of something or other—maybe just shame. The escape was worse than the fate, and you had no choice but to take your loss neat. *Marlena.* He loathed self-pity and what it did to him inside, but he hadn't found the way to clamber up out of it yet.

Two men carrying a sofa dashed back from where the mob of boys had gone, and he saw how much darker the night had become. About half the streetlights had been shot out, and color was fading out of the world to leave mostly shapes and shadows. Another helicopter was circling, flicking its searchlight around on the ground like a hiker looking for a lost trail. As the reddish smudge faded out of the western sky, here and there he could see faint light inside a few houses, leaking around blinds or curtains. The neighborhood was inhabited after all.

He didn't turn on his headlights as he started the car and putted noisily to the vacant lot, then swung around quickly and backed up into the weedy quarter acre. His head bobbed as the car jounced across uneven ground and crunched through rubbish. He stopped just deep enough into the lot so he could still see the Davis house three doors down, killed the engine, and yanked at the handle to pop the trunk in front. Chris had folded up the old tarp and thrown it in for him. He got the tarp out and spread it over the back half of the car, jiggering it so he could still get in the door and leave his window clear for air.

He figured he would now be invisible, with the tarp blocking any illumination that might backlight him through the rear windows. He retrieved his .45 from the glove box and wedged it under his thigh where he could get to it quickly and settled in to watch the house. It was full dark now, and he could see the faintest yellow glow spilling from the front and side windows.

Three teenage girls with cornrowed hair sauntered casually up the road as if the city wasn't burning all around them. They carried lumpy shopping bags.

"You a caution, Bea."

"Mama gon' bust my booty for this excursion."

They moved on, leaving an odd sense of normality on the air that lasted until a deep explosion went off somewhere not very far away, near enough that he could actually feel a shock wave as a faint puff on his cheek. A Molotov cocktail, or maybe just cooking gas, the vapors slowly diffusing out into the air in some confined space until they reached just the right ratio of combustible gas to oxygen, the flashpoint. He could sense how disturbed he was inside, under the enforced calm. It was the result of so much dream-state threat, like the hangover of an earthquake—what should be stable and certain in the world around him no longer so. A car in a dream become a bright plastic toy tractor, carrying him unstoppably toward a cliff. His bedroom walls developing ragged holes to reveal *out there* a bright alien world. A water tap turning itself on and off. Awareness that his own existence had become as tenuous as the daydreams.

He slid down until the back of his neck rested on the hot plastic seatback. The angst of the last two days had left him exhausted, all the way down to the bone, but still strangely wired. His eyes had adjusted completely to the night out there and he was satisfied he had the catbird seat. Nothing was stirring at Bancroft Davis's house or anywhere else in the neighborhood. Overhead, pinpricks of light circled, and the sound of gunfire and sirens continued, but all faraway for the moment, almost consoling.

He awoke with something hard against his forehead, his heart thudding. *Shit.*

"Yo, Arnold. What's your bidness here?"

Jack Liffey didn't do anything for a moment. His consciousness gathered toward a central redoubt from a number of outlying posts, like Keystone Kops retreating in disorder into a very small space. It didn't take him long at all to figure he'd fallen asleep at the switch, inexcusably dreaming he was awake, and now there was something, probably a pistol, against his forehead. Luckily the accent and diction did not suggest Gideon's 300.

His heart thumping away erratically, he turned his head gradually. A few inches away he saw a 9mm Glock, a weapon made largely of plastic, which accounted for the fact that it hadn't been cold against his skin. Holding the pistol was the guy with the teardrop tattoo and all the earrings. He remembered the name: BigLenin. The Rolling 60s Crips.

"Boo-yah," the young man said, the formulaic mimic of a shotgun blast. "It so damn easy to smoke a cave boy like you this night. One-eight-seven and the pig be busy elsewheres."

One-eight-seven was cop talk for homicide. The young man wore one of those tight head covers, silky black, with a loose flap over the nape of the neck, like something for the Foreign Legion. It was a pretty good sign of the gulf between the communities, Jack Liffey thought, that he didn't know what it was called, he had never seen one in a store, nor did he know what store he would go to if he wanted to buy one.

"I'm here to guard Bancroft Davis. You're right about the dangers of the night. Some Klansmen are on their way here to kill Mr. Davis."

"You just trippin'."

"Same guys who burned the cross on his lawn. I know you remember that."

"Big," someone called, "it's five-oh on the way."

A siren swelled and then diminished almost immediately.

"Peace out. They not comin' into the land of the hard tonight."

Jack Liffey decided to take a chance. "I could use your help guarding him."

"We got better shit to take care of, Arnold." He smiled, without much humor in it. "I recently acquired a fine DVD machine, and there a whole lot of movies out there for me."

"Hey, this man fought all his life for civil rights, down in Mississippi. Against fat white sheriffs."

BigLenin looked to one of his friends, as if seeking corroboration.

"Word is born," somebody said. "The man was down, back in the Martin Luther King time."

"Well, I can't see no crackers making it over here tonight in they rusty ol' pickups."

"I did," Jack Liffey corrected him.

A finger came out and nearly touched his nose. "Then you better watch the man's back, Arnold, and don' be goin' to sleep out here. We hold you responsible, since you got nothin' better to do. You strapped?"

"An old forty-five. You want to offer something better?"

"Yo, Road Dog, lessee the MAC."

"Aw, Big—"

"Stay true, Road. Plenty more where that."

All he could see of the second man was an arm, light coffee color with tattoos all over it. The arm handed something angrily to BigLenin, who dropped it in Jack Liffey's lap. It was a little Ingram MAC 10, like some ugly square toy, not much bigger than his pistol, looking as if it had been made out of old beer cans in some rural province of China. It was dented and scraped and had seen a lot of abuse. He could tell by the weight when he picked it up that it was loaded; a gray plastic magazine stuck well out of the handle. If he remembered right, it held thirty-two 9mm rounds.

"You ever tested this?" He had the feeling it would blow up in his hand if he tried to use it.

"Gimme the jammy."

BigLenin grabbed the submachine gun out of his hands, held it casually overhead, and with one roaring squeeze sent five or six rounds straight up. The barrel only stuck an inch out of the receiver, so the noise was earsplitting. For an instant, Jack Liffey worried about the police, and then he realized that this was get-out-of-jail-free night, the law having retreated to other parts.

"It be tested." He tossed it back into Jack Liffey's lap, still warm. "You get Mr. Bancroft Davis through the night, Arnold, and maybe you a honorary niggah."

nineteen

Boogers

The pack of feral dogs strutted down Brighton at cruising speed with outriding scouts glancing warily left and right. He wondered if it was the same pack he had seen earlier. If it was, it was gaining constituents, a good fifty strong now. They seemed proud and confident, as if this very night their species had finally reached critical mass and they were on their way to supplant humans as the rulers of South Central. The biggest dogs, the rottweilers and shepherd mixes, held to the front of the big ragged wedge like an officer corps.

One dog out at the edge moved faster than the others. Jack Liffey barely believed his eyes when he looked close. He had seen three-legged dogs before, usually tripodding along in some hamlet where he had stopped for gas, unfortunate beasts who had been wounded in some accident. He watched intently as this black terrier, with its tail up like a question mark, bobbed around awkwardly in a wide half circle and then bobbed back, and sure enough, against nature and physics, it was a two-legged dog. Only the left front and right rear legs remained, and the animal obviously had to keep up a good head of steam to stay upright. It sprang along faster than the others, circling and panting heavily, a living rollerblade.

One of the pack leaders barked once in Jack Liffey's direction, a casual warning, and he was happy to be inside a car where he could lock the door and roll up the windows if he had to. They did not seem to sniff him out, though, probably because the air was alive with the tang of fire, feathery wisps of ash drifting here and there on a faint erratic breeze. The pack went on past, with the two-legged dog circling around at the rear, almost toppling as it leaned, and then bounding hard into catch-up mode. There was some sort of moral about brute determination there, he thought.

The smoke was building up like a dreamy fog on the air, haloing the few streetlights that had not been shot out. He wondered what was burning, though it was probably just the usual furniture and liquor stores, schools, and post offices. Untrimmed palm trees went up like torches if you could get a flame up into the thatch.

He guessed it was only about eleven, but he was still having a hell of a time staying awake, waging an almost unwinnable war against the lead weights suspended from his eyelids. If only he could nap for a few minutes. In frustration, he slapped his cheek. The blow was harder than he'd intended, and his ear rang. *Brilliant,* he thought in annoyance. Liffey vs. Liffey, stopped by the ref, TKO in one. Then he recalled there was no such thing as a TKO anymore. The people who ruled boxing had done away with the distinction, and it just went into the books as a normal knockout now. Then he was bent over watching a prizefight far below him, tiers of seats all around filled with cheering fans. It seemed a bit like a movie he'd seen somewhere before . . . and then he awoke with a start as a door slammed.

Not again, he thought. But there was no one at the car window this time, and his mind could take its time coming into focus. Down the road, he saw Bancroft Davis in a flannel robe leaning against his wife in their driveway, as they stumbled urgently toward their Mercury. Shaking his head to clear it, he almost went to help them when he noticed dim faces in the front window of the house, which threw him into confusion. One was their little granddaughter Ornetta, but he figured he had to be fast asleep still because the second face in the window looked exactly like Maeve's. He felt a chill—but surely, he thought, they were over in Oakwood. They wouldn't have come back into the heart of the riot.

The old couple got into their big car, and still Jack Liffey hadn't moved. The car ground once and quickly kicked over, and as it backed out, he realized he was really and truly awake. Where were the two of them off to on a night like this? The old man had looked pretty unstable, and he remembered how shaky Genesee had always been, pushing a walker ahead of her. It had to be something damned urgent to force them out into this deadly night, of all nights, and to leave the children behind.

The Merc left at a good clip. The girls' faces were gone from the front window, and he wondered if they had been a hallucination. It was possible. A number of images he'd seen in his dream still hung with him: a dog glaring at him, a woman with her hair on fire. Before he could make up his mind to go over to the house and investigate, he saw a dark van drifting slowly down Brighton without headlights, and a shudder of alarm worked its way across his shoulders. His hand found the little spray gun BigLenin had given him, and a finger went into the trigger guard. His thumb felt out the tinny little safety and snicked it off. He hadn't done much to help so far, but now might be his chance. As long as he didn't use the MAC-10 to blow away a neighbor out on patrol or local kids scavenging for loot.

He was almost positive he had seen that van before, blocking his escape from the Simi ravine. Dark and featureless, like a messenger from some far more evil world, it rolled deliberately past him, making almost no noise, and hesitated just where it shouldn't, in front of the Davis house. He came out of the VW, his heart racing, as a wine bottle wrapped in a flaming rag arched high toward the house, then another. He took off toward the van as the first Molotov burst against the clapboard siding of the bungalow and flared orange. And then Jack Liffey was flat on his face. Someone had body-blocked him hard from the side. The MAC–10 was no longer in his hand and a knee dug very hard into the small of his back. He felt his arm wrenched up behind him.

"Be cool there, Mr. Rootietoot."

He knew the voice. A horrible sickness clenched the pit of his stomach, and he pictured Perry Krasny behind him, the shoulders of a Brahma bull and all that weight. No wonder they'd come down the block so slowly. The big man must have been reconnoitering Brighton on foot, a flanking patrol, some sort of Ranger training.

"The old people aren't in the house," Jack Liffey said quickly. "There's only kids in there."

"Uh-huh, sure. Forgot the milk for the morning coffee, did they?"

"They drove away in a hurry just a minute ago. I think he was sick."

"We'll just wait around and see what comes running out then."

"*God damn*"— Jack Liffey wriggled and fought, but the man's weight was far too much for him—"there're *kids* in there!"

Through weed stubble he could just see the front of the house start to flame up.

Maeve and Ornetta had tugged on their clothes after they'd stirred awake to the clatters and bangs of the aftermath of the heart attack. They had emerged to help Genesee get Bancroft Davis up out of bed and into a bathrobe, but she had ordered them to stay in the house and used some superhuman reserve of strength to support her husband down the porch and toward the car.

Ornetta clung to Maeve's hand and breathed hard, close to sobbing. Maeve clasped the smaller girl against her to comfort her just as they heard the breaking glass and a kind of *whoomp* sound, like nothing either of them had ever heard. An orange glow flickered through the front curtain. It took only one peek to know what it was. "Let's get out!" Ornetta shrieked.

They ran into the bedroom and Ornetta grabbed a big metal loop that stuck out of the wall beside the window. She tugged hard but had to wave to Maeve for help, and the two of them heaved together until it gave all at once, like a cork coming out of a bottle. The sash was already up and Ornetta pushed hard on the ornate burglar bars with both hands. They swung open with a rusty creak like an old gate and both girls climbed out into the darkness, right past the wheelbarrow and garden tools.

"They must be after your granddad," Maeve said.

"Then his heart go and save his life."

They crawled to a hurricane fence on the side of the yard, just past a spindly little tree, where Ornetta put her back to the chain link and shoved hard with her legs to push the bottom of the fence out and up a foot. Maeve thought of the loose fence slats in Venice and wondered if Ornetta had found an escape route from every home she had ever known.

"Roll under, Maevie, and hold it for me."

She wriggled underneath and held the chain link up with both hands while Ornetta rolled through herself into the neighbor's yard. They dusted themselves off and sneaked around the dark house to a hedge that divided back from front yard. Ornetta knelt and pushed herself into the hedge.

"Dirty old boogers," Ornetta exclaimed softly.

Maeve wriggled in with her to look through the leaves and she could see a dark panel van out front with its sliding door open. The pulsing firelight was growing now, lighting up the van, and they could see a man kneeling inside wearing a black ski mask and aiming what looked like an army rifle at the house.

"I bet they're waiting for him to come out," Maeve whispered.

Something was moving in the vacant lot across the street, too, just at the edge of the long shadow cast by the van, but they couldn't quite see what was there. Maeve looked hard, and it was like demons churning in the dark, one of them rising up out of a thick puddle on the ground.

"If it's little kids, we won't shoot 'em coming out. We're not monsters, Jacko."

Jack Liffey felt a wave of intense hatred. That anyone would make *that* the gauge of virtue—not shooting children fleeing a fire.

He could see that the bungalow had caught fire now, flames licking up the siding and over the front eave. He had to believe the girls had escaped out the back. Thinking anything else was insupportable, unbearable. There were no sirens heading their way, and he doubted the fire department had any units to spare. For this night, smaller fires were going to burn until they ran out of fuel.

"Doesn't it strike you that none of this has anything to do with advancing the white race?"

"*Au contraire*, Liffey. I know where we started out, and I know where things got complicated. There's been a mistake, fuckin'-A right, but we all have to accept the consequences of what we do and finish them out. Even if they don't look much like they did when we started."

"Sure, I see that." To keep him talking.

The noise of a helicopter swelled overhead; it seemed to be circling. The fire had attracted that much attention, at least. The man didn't seem concerned, and when Jack Liffey twisted his neck around for a glimpse, he saw that Krasny was wearing a ski mask. Even the flesh that showed through the cutouts had been blacked with burnt cork. Being caught on TV wasn't going to worry Krasny very much. The license plates were undoubtedly off the van, too. He held a .38 snub-nose revolver in his free hand. Nothing fancy or high tech but perfectly adequate for putting a hole in you.

"So what happened? Did Amilcar give you some lip?"

"Not me, Brian. We were done up like this to put a little scare in the miscegenators, but the guy yanks Bri's mask off and gets a good look, and then tops it by saying something foul about what he sees. Showing off for his girl. Leave it to a mouthy nigger to push his bad luck. Bri lost it and his pistol went off, and then poor Doug reacted and chopped them both down. What could a man do?"

"Yeah, the uppity ones are the worst."

The weight intensified briefly, and he winced. A bright light came on from the helicopter and swept over the ground.

"I wonder what they think they're going to do with that big searchlight?" Perry Krasny said cheerfully. He sounded like he didn't have a care in the world. "Maybe fly in a big magnifying glass and burn us up like ants?"

"Where are the bodies?"

"What's it to you?"

"I always wondered what I'd do if I accidentally killed somebody. Bury the body in the hills? Cut it up and send it down the drain?"

He heard a snigger. "They're in Rose Hills, with all the other dead meat. Nobody's ever there at night. We dug down another couple feet and tucked 'em under a coffin waiting to go down. Can't you just see the cops trying to find a couple extra bodies in a cemetery? Oops, not that one!"

"Clever of you."

"No shit."

The shaft of light found them for an instant, turning the world into glare, and then skidding off a bit; it wobbled around them as the helicopter circled.

A new shadow blocked his view of the fire. "Nobody's coming out of there, K. Let's beat it."

"You a Christian?" Krasny asked Jack Liffey.

"Not much."

"Make what peace you can. You're gonna get to know the big answers real soon now. Best pray to your humanist vapors." Jack Liffey's arm was released and the pressure was suddenly gone from the small of his back. His heart thudding, he rolled onto his back and saw the hooded Krasny standing over him, aiming the pistol.

"You don't have to do this."

"Sure we do." The pistol jumped. Jack Liffey felt a searing pain, like a sword through his shoulder, and shouted out. Then forcing his eyes open in the face of the terrible burning pain, he saw the pistol tracking toward his heart. The two men were silhouetted against the smoky brightness as the searchlight found them again, and he wondered if this was the last thing he would ever see, if the final image really did burn onto your retina. Not now, he thought, not yet. *I want to find out how it comes out.*

The light kicked up a notch and Jack Liffey sat up. He didn't want it to happen lying down.

"This is for the dog, you fuck."

Perry Krasny aimed his .38 straight for the heart and fired. There was no white tunnel, no kindly uncle waiting for him. In a burst of incredible pain, the world went right out.

Maeve shrieked and fainted. At that moment, the light from the helicopter had finally resolved what she was seeing across the street. She had made out a big man in a mask standing directly over her father, and then the big man had fired a pistol right into his chest. Ornetta held her tight, but with all the other noise she didn't think the men had heard the outburst. She watched as two masked men sprinted back to their van and slammed inside.

Ornetta saw that the front of her house next door was engulfed by fire and a corner of her mind mourned for her dolls and books and especially an old silver pin from her mom, but she was happy Ban and Nana had got away.

"We'll get you boogers one day," she promised the receding van.

She was just about to look away, back to the empty lot, when she saw a big Chevy pull out of a driveway with no lights and block the van's path. The tires of the van squealed and smoked, as it tried to back away from the Chevy. Then she saw something that she didn't understand very well until much later.

Little green fires made a line from the sidewalk toward the van, first one line and then a second. It was all accompanied by a terrible cracking noise, she wasn't sure what, like a powerful lawn mower chewing over an endless pile of twigs. The truck stopped moving as the tires deflated. She saw the silhouettes of men on the sidewalk with their legs spread, four of them. They had guns that were spitting red now instead of green.

The sound was definitely a hammering of gunfire, going on and on, and she could see a lot of damage happening to the van. Windows were blowing out and metal was tearing open and the van was lurching and jumping. Two more shapes moved into the street, holding rifles down at the waist and firing away without stopping.

The helicopter with the light circled back around but a lot higher. In the weak light she could see it was the Rolling 60s up there at the corner, at least a dozen of them, and every last one was firing some kind of weapon point-blank into the van.

"Got you, you old boogers," Ornetta said aloud.

twenty

Somebody Cared

Maeve wept in big convulsive sobs as she lay in a heap up against her father's bloody shoulder. Ornetta had to tug her own leg free from where Maeve's sharp knee had pinned it to the ground. Horrible dark blood was running down the man's shoulder, threatening to drip onto Ornetta. She was petrified that this man was going to be dead before she even got to make him her daddy. She begged her genie to come save him, but his face looked terribly chalky white.

She heard a big pop and looked back at her house. The fire seemed to be dying down after charring the front pretty badly. Two helicopters were still circling overhead without making any attempt to intervene, and the one with the searchlight was concentrating on the torn-up black van at the corner. The men who'd shot at it were gone. The light went off all of a sudden and its helicopter scooted away.

Please, please, please, genie, she thought. Save this man.

Maeve heard Ornetta wail and realized she had better get some control over herself to take charge of things. She took several deep breaths to try to calm herself, then pushed herself up on her arms. She couldn't help herself, she had to look with dread at her father's face as she grasped Ornetta's hand hard. She found it impossible to conceive a universe in which her father was only some inert object—she almost pictured a casket, a cemetery, but her mind shied away quickly—instead of someone she could always watch as he went out into the world and bumped against it, someone to be consulted and listened to. The thought of her father set off a whole spray of images: him bending over with mock gravity to help her with an algebra problem, sawing a plank across two doors and wiping off the sweat with the back of his hand, hugging Marlena outside the motel at Sequoia and sticking up a V behind her head as Maeve took their picture.

Jack Liffey's face abruptly quivered in some kind of tic, as if he'd been stuck with a pin.

"Maevie!" Ornetta shrieked.

Maeve immediately put her hand against his neck. She tried to put it where she'd seen in movies and right away she felt a pulse thumping away inside, going pretty fast in a kind of hoppity beat.

"Oh, God, Ornetta, he's alive!"

They hugged each other, and then Maeve noticed the place on his shoulder where thick blood was seeping out like pudding. She had two Kleenexes in her pocket, and she wadded them up and pressed them against the wound.

"Ornetta, give me that belt off your skirt."

Together the girls cinched a tourniquet tight over the shoulder to hold the ball of tissue down, and then they knotted the ends up the best they could.

All of a sudden Maeve noticed a small hole and scorch mark on the pocket of his shirt. She felt a chill. She remembered watching the big man shoot him almost point-blank in the chest and visualized a much worse wound hidden under there. She investigated gently with a finger in the hole and felt something odd. She reached into the pocket and found a big hunk of metal.

"What's this?"

It was a shiny chrome rectangle with rounded corners, maybe two inches by four, and it was bent hard in the middle, as if somebody had tried to fold it over, with a big dimple pushed into the bend. It looked like there was a skooshed-up bullet stuck down in the dimple. She pulled back his shirt to see a bad purple bruise under the shirt pocket. His chest looked like it had been hit with a hammer and pushed in a little, but the skin wasn't broken.

Wing flaps came out of nowhere and both girls jumped and cried out. A large black bird passed right over them and settled onto the open door of a VW that sat nearby. The big crow was so black they could barely make out its shape, and it watched them with glowing disdainful eyes. Go away, Maeve thought. It's not time.

"I think he's in shock. We've got to put his legs up."

Maeve looked around and found a discarded plastic paint bucket, which she retrieved and rooted at his feet. Using both arms, she lifted one of his feet to rest the heel on the bucket, but when she lifted the second leg the first one fell off. Ornetta was throwing rocks at the bird, which squawked at her once as a stone bounded off the car's roof and then flapped away.

"Black birds is bad news."

Maeve enlisted Ornetta to hold both of her father's legs together on the bucket while she tugged her dad's leather belt out of his belt loops and strapped his legs together loosely.

"We need to get him to a doctor," Maeve said.

"They a car right there." Ornetta pointed to the VW she'd just hit with a rock.

"I can't drive it. I'm sure it's a stick." She stared mournfully at the VW, wishing she'd been braver about driving lessons, but the responsibility of guiding all that noisy machinery around amid other noisy machinery had always frightened her, and she'd put off learning every time her dad offered.

She wondered where his old car was and the thought stirred a recent memory, a scrap of memory: the piece of metal she'd just found. Her eye went to it, discarded in the weeds by her dad's hips. It looked just like one of the door handles of the old Concord. Funny how you could recognize something like that, even when it was mangled and far out of place. She could tell her mind wasn't working very well, fastening on something as stupid as that.

Maeve scooted around on the ground and lifted her father's head gently into her lap. The weeds around her smelled of urine and rotting garbage, and the air was full of the smell of smoke. Grief took her for a moment. She used her blouse to wipe the sweat off his forehead and then clung hard to him.

"You'll be okay, Dad. Ornetta and me'll take care of you. I promise."

She thought back, one by one, to all the bad things she'd ever thought about him and tried to undo every one of them so the gods would be on his side. There weren't all that many bad thoughts, she hedged, just in case Somebody was listening. But she couldn't deny that there were a few.

He had a temper, and it snapped out once in a while, but his flashes of anger passed quickly, and they were almost never at her. In fact, they were often at somebody hurting her. *Actually*, she offered up to whoever might be listening, *my daddy is a pretty good man*. That set her weeping for a while until she noticed with a chill that Ornetta was gone.

"Ornetta!"

Before she could jump up to go find her, she saw Ornetta coming across the street with a wheelbarrow. It was too big and heavy for the little girl but she was managing somehow and she trundled it right up into the vacant lot. The wheelbarrow contained two old-style metal roller skates, some clothesline, scissors, and a bottle of water.

"We can try," Maeve said, divining the idea immediately and wiping away her tears.

Ornetta had apparently figured out that two girls their size would not get very far if they had to lift a wheelbarrow with a grown man in it. They tucked roller skates under the rear skids and lashed them on with clothesline.

Then it was a real challenge of geometry and strength to get her father up and into the body of the wheelbarrow. Finally, they did it by pushing the barrow over on its side, tying his torso to the bed of the wheelbarrow and then both of them leaning back with all their weight to tip it upright. One skate had slipped in the process and they had to retie it. Maeve tucked an old rag under her dad's head for a pillow.

"How'd you think of this?" Maeve asked, somewhat in awe.

"The magic tell me," Ornetta said proudly, and clapped her hand to her chest. Immediately she screamed and dropped straight down on her bottom, as if all the strength had gone out of her legs.

"What's the matter?" Maeve's emotions, already on edge, soared up into panic immediately.

"It gone!" She fumbled around in her shirt, evidently hunting for her magic bottle. "Oh, *no!*"

Maeve knelt to hug her. "It'll be all right."

"No, no, we in bad trouble now."

Maeve knew how much the girl relied on her sense of the magical and the comfort of her amulet, but they didn't have time to hunt it down. She wondered if Ornetta would be able to carry on without it. She'd push the wheelbarrow by herself if she had to.

"Oh, we lost. We doom." Ornetta was shaking her head back and forth, her eyes clamped shut.

Then Maeve had a brainstorm. "Ornetta! Look at me."

The little girl stilled and opened her frightened eyes.

"You haven't had the magic bottle since we got dressed so fast. You got us out the window without it. You got us under the fence. And you thought up the wheelbarrow by yourself. You don't need the magic bottle anymore."

The little girl's hand still went uncertainly to her chest.

"You can make your own magic now."

It took a moment for the idea to sink in, and then another minute's arguing and reassuring before Ornetta smiled shyly and got hesitantly to her feet. "I *try.*"

Maeve was so proud of her she wanted to hug her and abandon herself to weeping all over again, but they didn't have any time to waste.

To keep Jack Liffey's legs elevated, they made a big loop with clothesline and slung it around their necks. Then they lifted his ankles into the loop and adjusted the rope until his legs remained at half mast.

"We do our best."

Each of them took one rubber handgrip. They pushed as hard as they could. The wheelbarrow ran pretty rough across the weedy field, balking and fighting as they grunted and shoved. There was a tendency to circle left because Maeve was taller and stronger than Ornetta, but when they got onto the sidewalk and the skates settled on smooth concrete, the wheelbarrow just took off with a raucous clattering and Maeve began to think that the whole crazy enterprise might just work. Once they got the thing moving it wasn't hard at all to keep it going.

"Where's a hospital?" Maeve asked.

"Drew-King that way," Ornetta pointed southeast.

"How far?"

Ornetta thought for a moment. "I don't know. Some miles, I think."

"Then we better get a move on," Maeve said, but her heart sank. She had hoped it was only a few blocks. She stared out into the threatening darkness, and the enormity of the task crashed against her like a wave. She hoped somebody would see them along the way and take pity on them.

Over the first few blocks, their world, which had been very small while they were focused on getting Jack Liffey into the wheelbarrow, enlarged enormously to include noises and dangers that were all around them in the darkness. Not far away, they could hear the roar of a lot of people and the crash of breaking glass. Metal rang against metal. Gunfire rattled. The crowd noise swelled and ebbed, like waves on an urban beach. The girls eyed one another but neither felt like commenting on what they heard.

Before long they had given up the sidewalk and were pushing the wheelbarrow in the street, near the curb, to avoid the ups and downs of the sloped driveways. It didn't seem there was going to be any traffic to worry about on Brighton, anyway. The old metal-wheel skates made a regular rattle and a loud *rat-a-tat* across cracks.

"I need a rest," Ornetta said, after several blocks.

"Sure. This is hard work."

They let the wheelbarrow roll to a stop and allowed Jack Liffey's legs to drop so they could unhook and rest. Maeve felt the pulse in his neck again. It seemed pretty fast and his skin was still clammy. The night was so dry and warm it was frightening to feel his skin cold like that. Maeve tried not to think too much about the dangers out there. Mostly she'd been trying to focus her mind on the thirty feet in front of the wheelbarrow.

She could see how frail Ornetta was, bent forward to catch her breath, but she pushed away the feeling that the whole project was hopeless. She longed for one of the girl's stories, but Ornetta needed her breath for the effort.

The unseen crowd roared, and the sounds of destruction seemed to reach a crescendo.

"We better go," Maeve said.

Ornetta nodded. "Wish we had Mr. Genie to help."

They lifted Jack Liffey's legs back into the loop of clothesline that dangled from their necks. It took a good push to get the wheelbarrow going again, as if he had gotten heavier in the wait.

Maeve grunted with the effort and tried to think of something besides her fears. "This looks like a nice neighborhood."

They had just crossed 80th Street, and the old houses here were much bigger, all the lawns green and manicured. It looked like a picture in a magazine of some prosperous town back east.

"Rich folks live here. Maybe you and your daddy could come live here, near me."

"I'd love that," Maeve said. "But we're not rich."

"Let's swap who we is," Ornetta said, on some inspiration. "I be white and you be black."

"Use your magic," Maeve said. "Let's both be something new, maybe blue polka-dot."

Ornetta laughed softly, but a near burst of gunfire made her flinch. There was a sharp scream somewhere, which broke off abruptly, and then maniacal laughter. A block ahead they could see a man pacing on a roof with a big rifle. They decided to turn the next corner to move east, away from the man with the gun. They turned south again along Budlong, just a block from the big thoroughfare of Vermont that they were trying hard to avoid. The mob sound was fading behind them, but from time to time they heard the whoosh of a vehicle racing along Vermont, or the sound of something breaking, or the thud of some heavy object hitting another heavy object.

A half dozen dogs ambled toward them down the middle of Budlong. A big yellow one like a police dog had his tail straight up in the air, and Ornetta stamped a foot. "Shoo, you dogs!"

Maeve experienced a terrifying daydream of the dogs attacking them suddenly, as if the animals sensed that the normal order had been lifted for the night and the city left up for grabs. In her head, she saw the animals racing straight at them, jaws open to bite, but in real life the dogs just sniffed at them and one growled deep in its throat. The animals steered clear of where the girls rattled along with their odd burden.

Soon the girls had passed out of the ritzier area of Vermont Heights back into a neighborhood of small bungalows. One little turreted Spanish stucco house was on fire, blue flames licking out the tiny windows that spiraled up a turret, but nobody was there to fight it.

Two blocks ahead of them they saw something going on out in the street, and before long they could make out a barricade across Budlong. The road was blocked by three cars, a toppled Dumpster, a tangle of palm fronds, and some smoking trash cans. It looked like people with rifles were crouched behind the barricade to defend their neighborhood. There was even a flag of some sort, tacked together out of colored cloth. The girls talked it over and concluded they had better slide over to Vermont to avoid the barricade.

"Those peoples skitzing and I don't want no part of 'em."

"Good idea."

They turned east and approached Vermont cautiously, staying near the curb. It was a lot brighter and busier than the residential streets. They rested a moment at the corner to inspect the wide boulevard, and in the distance up to the north, they saw some of the crowd that they had been hearing. A solid mass of people had spread out into the roadway, like an army trying to besiege a fortress but caught in a bottleneck. Closer by, looters in ones and twos climbed out of broken storefronts and hurried away with their prizes.

They were blacks and Latinos of all ages, intent on their own pursuits, mostly laden with boxes and shopping carts and avoiding eye contact with one another. So much lawless activity frightened Maeve deeply, but she made herself concentrate on her immediate surroundings. Her father needed her to be strong now.

"Recess over, sister."

The girls pushed the wheelbarrow along the curbside lane of the wide avenue, swinging out a little whenever they met a spill of broken glass or a mound of debris. Most of the shops had been grated over or covered with plywood that said AFRICAN AMERICAN, but even some of these had been ripped open and people came out of the gaps and hurried off with unlikely loads. Two young men stepped over a broken-out window frame, carrying between them an old-fashioned brass cash register with the cash amounts on little flags. An old woman in a flowered housecoat scudded along furtively close to the buildings with a floor lamp in each hand. A little boy dragged along two red wagons piled with canned goods, shedding a can here and there when one of the wagons bounced. Once in a while, a car rocketed past, its lights out.

One thin woman dragging a big sealed carton snapped at them, telling them to get on home, but nobody else seemed to notice that two young girls were pushing an unconscious man down Vermont Avenue in a wheelbarrow. Three boys wearing green bandannas raced out of a gap between buildings and turned down the sidewalk toward them, their hands full of candy bars. They glanced in passing at Jack Liffey.

Across Vermont ahead of them, Cheung's Used Cars was alight with burning vehicles. Somebody had torched every single car in the lot, and something out in the middle was blazing brightest, so glary that it was hard to look at, flames licking up into the colored pennants overhead. Maeve wondered if cars really exploded the way they were always doing in the movies, and Ornetta must have had the same thought because they hurried to get past.

"Your arms hurting?" Maeve asked.

The girls stopped to rest in front of a storefront with a hand-lettered sign saying THE UPPER ROOM C.O.G.I.C. There was a lopsided cross drawn on the white-painted window, with raylike lines meant to suggest a glow. On the shop next door the same hand had drawn a crude piecrust with similar rays coming out of it and the words

BEAN PIES. She imagined a pie full of long green beans, but she couldn't believe that was what the sign referred to. She was so scared she thought of banging on one of the doors to ask for refuge, but she knew they had to get her father to the hospital.

"We gettin' stronger," Ornetta said bravely.

Maeve stooped to pick up a Baby Ruth a looter must have dropped, the wrapper unbroken.

She bent it in half, back and forth until it broke, and they shared. Maeve thought it tasted delicious, so sweet it made her teeth hurt. She wondered if, for the rest of her life, every time she saw a Baby Ruth she would recall this night.

A car engine revved and a station wagon with a window smashed in swung back and forth recklessly down Vermont. The way it was swerving, the driver had to be drunk, wrenching the steering wheel back and forth. The recklessness intensified the sick feeling in Maeve's stomach, the way heedless craziness always did, and then she felt a stab of real fear as her mind worked out the geometry of the next couple of swerves and she pictured the car careening right into them.

Ornetta waved her arms and shouted at the driver. Maeve got in front of the wheelbarrow and held out her palms as if to deflect the car with her body as a last resort. The swerves became so violent and screechy that it was a wonder the car didn't roll over. Maeve was paralyzed on the spot and couldn't even close her eyes as the car bore down, roaring as if stuck in a lower gear. At the last instant the big station wagon swung its tail again, dragged sideways noisily a few feet, and then angled away from them. Just as it turned away, something sailed out the window toward them, struck, and skidded near their feet. The explosions began almost at once, and both girls screamed and threw their arms around one another.

The banging went on and on, assaulting their ears, and they both let all the terror pour out of them in a loosed flood of wailing.

Maeve began to recover first. "Hush, hush," she kept saying as she clung to Ornetta. "It was only firecrackers."

Maeve was ashamed of herself, but she was shaking with convulsions now and she had to sit down on the curb and try to breathe deep. Ornetta kicked angrily at the dead string of firecrackers.

When the panic finally started to wind down, Maeve noticed that her father's head was rolling back and forth on the lip of the wheelbarrow. The sight was like a shot of oxygen. She hurried to him and knelt to hold his head still.

"Daddy, don't worry. We're getting you to a doctor. We'll be there soon. I promise." She looked around wildly for any kind of help at all, but the street was deserted, utterly empty.

"Oh, Ornetta, he needs help!"

Ornetta was already up, tucking her neck into the rope. A feeling of hopelessness was back, but there was nothing to do but keep going. She joined Ornetta and they leaned hard into the wheelbarrow. It seemed glued in place and it took a strong push and grunt to get it started forward again. She'd almost forgotten how loud the the roller skates were. The clatter echoed in the empty street.

Soon they heard another sound over the rattle of the skates. It was a throaty rumble, like a big airplane flying very low toward them. The girls glanced at each other.

"What's that?"

They couldn't see anything in any direction, and then Maeve realized that she felt the noise in her feet as much as hearing it. Finally Ornetta pointed excitedly down Vermont. They hadn't seen anything sooner because there were only little slit headlights. As the first of the monstrous vehicles sped closer, they could see there were more like it behind, a military convoy of some kind heading toward them. They looked a little like tanks, olive green with sloped sides and big black tires. There were lumps and projections all over the strange cars and big olive backpacks hung off most of the bumps. Two soldiers in visored helmets and puffy jackets rode on the top of the first vehicle, their rifles gripped tightly. Without even slowing, the armored car blew right by them through the intersection where the light was blinking red.

The ground trembled as the next one approached and they could see just how fast it was going. One of the soldiers glanced curiously at them, and Maeve waved for help, but the soldiers made no response and the vehicle flashed past. Three more of them were coming on, spaced out by half a block, and each one had two men riding on top, neither of whom even looked at them. As the next one approached, the girls yelled and jumped up and down, and a soldier noticed and called something down a hatch. Then he looked back and shrugged as the vehicle went by. On the last one, a really young soldier flashed them a V-sign and grinned, and then the convoy was receding north on Vermont, showing tiny slitted taillights.

"Motherfuckers," Ornetta said softly.

The curse shocked Maeve. It was the only curse she'd ever heard Ornetta use, and the word seemed too old and too crude for her, too far from the world of magic amulets. "I can't *believe* they just left us here."

"Hey, girls!" A woman's head poked out the window of an apartment above the shops. It was a large black woman in a slip, clutching a sandwich. "What you young ladies doing out there?"

"We got to get her daddy to the hospital. He hurt *real* bad."

"Aw, honey. You two in a bad way. Wilson, c'm'ere."

A thin old man in a T-shirt stuck his head out beside her.

"Those girls got them a hurt man in that thing, say her daddy he need a doctor."

"Can you drive us?" Ornetta pleaded.

"We ain't got no car. It broke down for good last month." The man and woman talked to each other, too low for the girls to hear down on the street. "You wait there," the woman called down. "Lemme get dressed. Ain't a fit night for girl or beast to be out alone."

For the first time in hours Maeve's spirit lifted a little, and she felt warm tears of gratitude rolling down her cheeks. Somebody cared.

twenty-one

The Wheelbarrow Girls

They emerged from a featureless door between the boarded-up shops, the woman first. She wore a leather jacket despite the warmth of the night and went straight to Jack Liffey and felt his neck.

She was a big woman, but her weight didn't make her seem fat. Her size, and the confidence she projected from within, made her seem to Maeve like a perfectly natural part of the whole scene, even an inevitable part, a landmark. "He need a doctor, all right, but I think he'll make it," she declared after a moment. "Now, you girls move aside. Wilson gonna push that thing."

"We can get to Chester's house and get his truck," the man named Wilson offered. He was wiry and thin and his hair was graying, but he looked strong.

"I'm Mrs. Leta Lee," the woman explained, as the man hooked himself up with the rope that held up Jack Liffey's legs without asking any questions. "That's Wilson Lee. What's your names?"

"I'm Maeve Liffey. This is my father, Jack."

"I'm Ornetta."

Wilson hefted the wheelbarrow rather than pushing it on its skates. His arms were stringy but very strong, and you could see each long muscle tensing a little under the skin as he pushed. The reprieve from all that clattering noise was a mixed blessing because it meant they could hear the rattle of gunfire from all around.

"You two must be pretty strong. How far you come?"

"Sixty-two and Brighton," Ornetta said.

"I declare! You gonna be famous."

Wilson turned hard left in the road and set out diagonally across the avenue, and they followed. "We best get off Vermont," he said. "There plenty more army coming."

They left Vermont to head east on 87th Street past a row of boarded-up stores.

"Say on the TV the National Guard's comin' to seize this part of town, street by street. Don't say who from."

"We can help push," Ornetta insisted.

"Wilson strong, honey. He be working in a rubber factory twenty-seven years."

They heard and felt another rumble behind them, exactly like the convoy of armored cars. The sound seemed to race north on Vermont, and Leta Lee did her best to ignore it.

"Wilson was vice president of the union," she said. "That lowdown-dog company threw him on the street after twenty-seven years of work and didn't give him *nothing*. They shut down and move the whole thing to China."

"My daddy was laid off too," Maeve said. "He couldn't find another job."

"Is that the truth? Wilson had him some troubles that way, hisself."

"It doesn't put no food on the table to be complainin'," the man said. "I get my Social Security in a couple years."

The man looked down at his burden. "Where your daddy work?" Jack Liffey hadn't moved in a long time, and Maeve was afraid to look at him too closely.

"He used to be a technical writer in an aerospace company, but when he couldn't get another job he became a detective," Maeve said proudly. "He says he isn't really a detective, he just finds missing children. His last job was looking for Amilcar Davis. That's Ornetta's uncle."

"He find him?"

"We don't know," Ornetta said. "Ami, he disappear with his girl-friend in Claremont. Didn' you hear?"

"I might of, hon. I'm not sure."

A low-riding Buick rumbled around the corner ahead, the head-lights flashing once as it drifted toward them. Maeve felt a chill of fear. As the big, dark car neared, she could just see a young man's face inside. He had rings in his ear and a blue bandanna on his head.

"What's your bidness in this 'hood?"

"We gettin' this man to the hospital," Leta Lee said with im-mense authority. "He hurt bad. You gentlemen could give us a ride, get you a reputation for years to come."

"Save that shit, Mama. Check it out, we don' be transportin' no peckerwood nowhere."

"It's the right thing to do, son," Wilson Lee said.

"Get yo' bitch ass out of here, old man."

The car accelerated away, hands coming out both sides to flash their strange gang finger signs as the car turned down an alley.

"Kids got awful mean somehow," Leta Lee observed.

"Some of 'em," her husband agreed. "We know plenty of good kids. Honor they mothers and stay in school to be somebody."

"Yeah, we do."

"Leta, look at this." His voice had gained a new edge, and his neck was craned to look behind. The whole street behind was filled with a pack of dogs, little dogs, big dogs, and very big dogs, just standing at attention watching them. There were so many animals that they spilled up onto the sidewalks. It almost looked like a con-scious maneuver, soldier dogs flanking out to the sides to keep the humans from doubling back.

"I ain' never seen nothing like that before," Leta said.

"We seen some of them back on Budlong," Ornetta said. "Maybe they followin' us."

"There's lots more now," Maeve said.

"Let's jus' walk," Wilson said, a guarded worry in his voice. He set the wheelbarrow down to readjust his grip and lifted again with a lit-tle grunt, and for the first time Maeve could tell it was a strain for him.

"You can just push it along on the skates like we did," she said.

"This way quicker," he said, moving faster than before. "You girls get up front of me. And somebody tell me what them dogs doing."

"They're not doin' nothing," Leta said. "Just lookin'." But there was a catch in her voice right at the end. A moment later, she added, "Some of 'em walkin' slow now."

Maeve glanced back. The dogs in the middle of the street were pacing forward deliberately. One tiny dog ran out of the pack and stood to the side, yipping like a cheerleader. The gunfire had retreated into the far distance and the tiny dog's complaint went on and on.

"Don't like this much," Leta said. "They all be comin' now."

The one yelper stopped abruptly, and then the only thing they could hear behind was an eerie sandpapering, dozens of paws padding along the asphalt. Leta Lee turned back and put her arms on her hips and stamped her foot.

"Shoo, you dogs! Git!"

A few of the smaller dogs in front hesitated, but the pack flowed around them, advancing relentlessly. Leta caught up and pressed the girls ahead of the wheelbarrow. Maeve walked backward a few paces. The streetlights were broken here, and in the gloom the dog pack looked like a big lumpy blanket gliding a foot above the ground, taking the shape of the curbs and the piles of rubbish that it flowed over. She remembered her awful daydream of a dog attack and hoped she wasn't responsible for its coming true.

The pack held to a kind of seething, stewing progress, dogs at the sides trotting forward a little faster than their kin and then holding up and merging back in. One funny-looking dog out at the edge moved along fast with a peculiar pogo-stick hopping.

"Still comin', Wils."

"Uh-huh. Le's turn the corner there. We see if they maybe go on straight."

They turned south on Hoover, both of the girls backing up apprehensively ahead of the wheelbarrow. They weren't far up the street when they saw the first dogs come around behind them. There didn't seem any question where the dogs were headed. Now and then there was a little yip or a growl on the air, but mostly they were deadly quiet, stalking, offering only the pattering-rain sound of their paws on the street. The pack flowed around onto Hoover like a military column, those on the outside picking up the pace to keep up. Maeve saw the bounding dog at the margin of the pack again. She thought it was missing a leg.

"Maybe we should try to get in one of these houses," Maeve suggested.

"We're close to Chester's," Wilson said. "Your daddy need help real soon. I don't think we got time to hunker down."

He didn't mention it, but Maeve could see that her father had gone a whole lot paler, almost as if he'd been spray-painted white.

"Leta, y'all brung your little piece?"

"Uh-huh."

"Get ready to give it to me."

"I don't know if I could use it. You ain' never used it neither."

"No problem."

A low growling began to spread through the pack, rolling like waves from side to side. When Maeve glanced again, the dogs were a lot closer to them, only a few seconds' hard run behind Wilson Lee. Some of the dogs in front were snapping their jaws. It was like mousetraps going off. Maeve had never seen dogs do that before.

"I don' know 'bout this, Wils."

The growl changed pitch to a snarling sound and built up steadily until it seemed almost like a single angry rasp from a single giant dog. Some sort of climax seemed to be at hand. There was a lot more jaw-snapping now, as if the pack was passing through a swarm of flies.

Maeve noticed that Ornetta's eyes had grown big. She took her hand and gripped it hard. "Use your magic wish."

"Turn in that alley, *now*," Wilson Lee commanded.

You could almost touch dirty brick buildings on both sides. The pavement was half eroded away and the surface of the alley was weedy and full of trash. The girls turned into the alley first, then the woman, and finally Wilson Lee, the wheelbarrow bouncing a little on uneven paving. He set it down about thirty feet up the alley, then took a little silver pistol from Leta and stepped quickly back to the alley entrance. He spread his legs, doing his best to block the whole space, and his wife went to stand right behind him. The girls huddled together by the wheelbarrow and then hugged each other across it while Maeve kept one hand on her father's shoulder.

The midsize dogs in the front of the pack came around toward the alley like an implacable military column. They advanced on Wilson Lee, snarling, but unaccountably paused a few feet away from him as more dogs flowed up behind them.

"Dogs, it's me and you," he said.

Wilson Lee fired the pistol into the ground ahead of the dogs. As small as the little pistol was, it sounded terribly loud, the shot crashing and echoing off brick, but the front dogs didn't do any more than break off their snarl for a few seconds, then start up again. Maeve felt herself shaking with fright, tears rolling down her cheeks.

"Dogs shoo now," Ornetta said in a small voice. "I magic-order you."

It didn't seem to be working. Maeve looked up at a louder snarling, and she could see a wave of animals building up beyond Wilson and Leta, barking and jumping in some kind of primeval frenzy, forcing the dogs in front forward whether they wanted to advance or not. She saw the head and neck of a shepherd, snapping its black muzzle and a rottweiler emitted a continuous howling. There was even a furious white mongrel that looked a lot like her dad's Loco, but she knew it couldn't be. Little pit bulls were burrowing through the bigger dogs, yapping to get at the humans. There was even the strange bounding dog that she remembered, held tight to one side by the press of the pack.

She saw Wilson aim the little pistol straight at the biggest dog and she closed her eyes. Two horrible shots rang out in the brick space and then a yowl of pain. She had to look. The big rottweiler lay in front of the pack thrashing its legs, and the other dogs set on their wounded comrade instantly, tearing and feeding like cannibals. The sound of the feeding frenzy became so savage that it filled her consciousness. Only this horror existed on the whole earth.

Something in her insisted that these animals had never been pets. She couldn't believe a tame animal would ever become so bloodthirsty. They were demon dogs; they had burst straight out the gates of some hell hidden beneath the streets of the city.

Wilson fired again and again.

"You girls run!" he shouted, as he and Leta linked arms to block the alley. But there was no way the girls could comply. They were both limp as old rags, shaking uncontrollably as they gripped hands across the wheelbarrow.

Then there was a fierce honking and a car engine gunning. Maeve looked up to see, beyond their defenders, a big Chevy Suburban with its bright lights full on drive right into the dog pack. A dog squealed, hit, and the pack parted a little. The car kept honking its horn and bullying itself into the dog sea with little spurts of acceleration. A black man almost as old as Wilson stuck his head out and shouted at the dogs at the top of his lungs. The dogs turned angrily to bark at him and some of them leapt up at the car window. Others got their heads down and stretched their forelegs to snarl and threaten. The Suburban skittered forward and back unpredictably, still honking and gunning its engine.

"You got that wheelbarrow man in there?" the man shouted.

"We sure do," Wilson replied.

"Well, back up, man. Give me room!"

Leta Lee grabbed up both sobbing girls with superhuman strength, and Wilson hefted the wheelbarrow and pushed it forward to where the alley widened into a parking lot. The Suburban's engine roared and it humped up into the alley to fill the whole space. It roared again as it came forward, scraping a bumper along one wall, and finally it stopped with its swing door just clear of the building. A woman inside threw the door open. They could hear a frenzy of dogs barking and leaping at the back of the vehicle, but none of them seemed brave enough to dash underneath.

"Get him in here. We been looking *all over* t'other side of Vermont."

"How you know?" Leta asked, as she and Wilson fought the knots that tied Jack Liffey to the wheelbarrow.

"The girls and they wheelbarrow be on the TV."

A colorful panel truck came roaring down the alley ahead of them, striped red, green, black. It stopped a few feet away, and a big bearded man in an African cap stepped out just as Wilson wrestled Jack Liffey out of his wheelbarrow. The dogs seemed to be barking harder, as if working up their nerve.

"That the wheelbarrow man?" the newcomer called.

"Uh-huh. He need a hospital so clear the damn road."

"Salaam. We'll get you all there."

A pit bull finally shot under the Suburban and emerged toward Wilson Lee, who was preparing to lift Jack Liffey. The dog barked maniacally as it charged in a blur of little legs, but Leta Lee caught the animal with a full kick that sent it keening a long way into the parking lot. They moved Jack Liffey into the back of the Suburban as gently as they could. Just before clambering in, Ornetta waved shyly to the other vehicle. "That the Mwalimu man," Ornetta said. "I been at his Umoja place with Ami."

They wedged Jack Liffey feet first into the long bench seat at the back, and Maeve and Leta knelt against him to hold him there.

"You all buckle up or hang on. This alley's rough."

The door slammed and the Suburban bounced hard over ruts as Maeve rested her face against her father's legs. All of a sudden she was trembling all over like some machine gone out of control. Her mind relaxed its terrible vigilance and everything just poured out of her. She wasn't sure how long she rode that way, sobbing and shaking. Before long the ride smoothed out, and her knees began to hurt on the floor.

"Sit up, hon. It's okay now."

She lifted herself onto a corner of the seat, still shuddering, and settled beside her father's feet. Leta Lee stayed on the floor, holding Jack Liffey. There was no other place to sit. Maeve pressed her head against the window to try to stop the trembling.

"Not long now, folks," the driver said. "You girls truly somethin', you know?"

"'Course we are," Ornetta said. "We got magic."

"Some brave girls," Wilson Lee said, looking back at Maeve over the short middle seat. Maeve could see his wife reach behind herself without looking to put her hand on his arm. The woman's eyes were fixed on Jack Liffey.

"You a brave strong man, Wilson," Leta Lee said proudly.

He laughed softly. "You know the onliest thing I was thinkin', lookin' at those dogs and near peeing myself? I couldn't stop thinkin' of Buckwheat rolling his eyes and saying, 'Feets, don't *fail* me now.' "

"You the man." The driver laughed and reached back blindly with a flat hand and they shared a high five.

The big van drove fast along a wide empty street, following the striped panel truck that seemed to be escorting them, and as the drive went on and on, Maeve's distraction cleared enough to realize she and Ornetta would never have gotten this far, not in a million years. Two girls pushing a heavy wheelbarrow: It had been crazy to think they could do it alone. She wanted to say something, thanks or praise or just a burst of relief, but her whole body was wobbly and weak and she couldn't get her voice to work.

They came to a roadblock where the wide street went under the 105 freeway. There were rows of blue sawhorses, then big gray jail buses, and one police car after another with policemen standing everywhere. The Umoja truck was already there, the driver arguing with a California highway patrolman. He must have said the right thing, because a police car pulled out of the blockade to open a space for them, and Mwalimu waved and pointed them on into the gap just as a patrolman jumped onto his motorcycle. The motorcycle cop headed off with lights and siren going as their new escort.

"Ain't this jim-dandy," the driver said.

They turned onto 120th Street following an arrow sign that said HOSPITAL, and Maeve saw a dilapidated group of buildings like an abandoned school, all boarded up and grown over with chest-high weeds. A high chain-link fence sealed it all in; it looked like it had been closed up for years. There was a beat-up mural on the wall, and a big sign on the central building said LOS ANGELES DESTINY CENTER. Maeve thought of her father and felt herself make a little noise; it might have been a laugh. She filed the sight away in her head: a real hundred-point oddity. He would love seeing DESTINY when he got better. She didn't really want to look at him just then, though, or feel that clammy skin.

The hospital complex was so large they started to see it far in the distance. The wail of the motorcycle's siren shut down as it passed the bright red EMERGENCY sign, but if the point was to avoid attracting attention, it didn't work. Trucks with big TV dishes sticking up and TV channel logos on their sides were parked all along the road. The Suburban pulled up to the glass doors of the emergency room, but as soon as the side door came open, men with cameras came running from every direction.

"It's the wheelbarrow girls!"

"It's them!"

"Hey, girls, look over here!"

twenty-two

Doing the Right Thing Is Never a Mystery

It wasn't too long before Jack Liffey was ambulatory—as hospital types insist on calling it when you can walk under your own steam. The first thing he did was ambulate his way to a linen closet and steal a second gown to put on back-to-front over the first one to cover his bare, chilly ass. He could appreciate the desire for quick access to your body in a hospital, but since nobody was checking out his ass for anything in particular, he figured his dignity took precedence.

Then he ambulated right up the fire escape to find Bancroft Davis, who he'd discovered was flat on his back in a room almost directly above his own, recovering from a heart attack that he'd suffered on the climactic night of what was being called, variously, the Ab-Ib Disturbances, the Ab-Ib Uprising, or just the Ab-Ib Riot, depending on your perspective on law and order.

The first day Jack Liffey had gone up the stairs, Bancroft Davis had been sleeping, and the second day he'd been out for tests, but on the third day Jack Liffey finally found the old man, conscious and smiling weakly up at him. They both had time on their hands, and he knew he could plague Bancroft Davis to his heart's content with questions about life on the front lines of the civil rights crusade.

"I'll deny I said it, but it's true: I was a quarter inch from getting a gun, those days. The only thing that probably stopped me was it was about as easy for a black man to get a pistol in Mississippi as buy himself a nuclear warhead. There's one white woman just now let out of federal prison for supplying self-defense to some brothers way back then."

A young nurse leaned in, noticed Jack Liffey, and frowned. "Not visiting hours," she suggested.

"I'm not a visitor," Jack Liffey said, "I'm a noted cardiac surgeon."

That puzzled her, because he wore hospital gowns and had his arm in a black sling, but for some reason she withdrew.

"I thought they gave all of you nonviolence classes."

"I had the classes, but we don't all live up when the sheets and rifles come out."

"Fair enough."

"You know, the dean of all that nonviolence is right here in LA, Rev. James Lawson at Holman Methodist. He'd read Gandhi as a young man, and then he'd been to India, and he taught Martin about nonviolence, and Martin had him teach us. Lawson was the coolest, calmest, most peaceful man I've ever met."

An older nurse with fiery red hair peeked in. "You again? Mr. Davis is supposed to have complete bed rest."

"Give me five minutes."

"Two. Just this once." She ducked out.

Two weeks earlier, Davis had been reluctant to talk to Jack Liffey about those days, like a war veteran nursing his stoic memories deep in some private place, but he had loosened up for some reason—maybe the brush with death.

"One demonstration, I put my body in front of a white SNCC worker the Klanners had singled out to beat on, and they started beating on me too. We both went down and got in the fetal position the way we were taught, and we were getting kicked pretty bad when Lawson ambled over and started talking to the Klanners—just boys really, but *big* boys—about their cars. Their *cars*: how much extra horsepower they got out of using hot cams! They were so startled they began talking to him like human beings, and we got up and went on with the march. Man, he was something. Cool as a cucumber."

"Like your granddaughter."

He beamed. "And *your* girl, Maeve. The wheelbarrow girls." He chuckled. "Somebody ought to go and get that wheelbarrow and make a shrine out of it."

"It's yours to enshrine. It came from your backyard."

"I don't know how those little girls got you all the way to eighty-seventh and Vermont."

"I looked on a map," Jack Liffey said. "It's almost two miles. Of course, they had another six miles to go to get here. When I get out I'm gonna look up the folks that helped."

"I heard there were a half dozen cars driving around looking for you, but mostly over on the other side of Vermont where the helicopter camera lost you. Nobody official helped."

"Nobody official helped," Jack Liffey agreed. "That's why I want to thank the unofficials."

"You do that. But you know what I learned from Jim Lawson?"

"That's exactly what I want to hear from you."

He smiled. "Doing the right thing is never a mystery. You never have to explain to people why you're doing it—even your enemies. You just do it, and they know."

The door opened, and the redheaded nurse came back. "I'm afraid you'll have to return to your place now. Whether you're a famous surgeon or not."

Jack Liffey took Davis's leathery dry hand and squeezed it once. He hadn't told him what he knew about Amilcar and Sherry yet, and he didn't look forward to it. He had told the police; they were checking burial dates at Rose Hills, trying to decide which graves to dig up. And he had told Genesee Thigpen; it was she who had asked him to wait until after Bancroft recovered from the balloon angioplasty that was scheduled to open up his coronary arteries.

"Have your procedure and get better," Jack Liffey said. "We'll talk some more."

"Please. Then you can tell me the truth about Amilcar."

"Everything I know," Jack Liffey promised, staying as expressionless as he could.

* * *

That afternoon, Chris Johnson came to visit with a radiant-looking Babs in a long gypsy dress. They were holding hands, and Jack Liffey had a hard time not noticing.

"We got the VW back," Chris announced. "They traced it to me, since you neglected to change the registration in the few hours you had it. It used to have a good stereo and a rear seat and a battery, but other than that it's pretty much okay. You still want it?"

"Yeah, I'll pay you what it was worth when it was whole. When I can."

"No hurry, man."

For a while, they made delighted noises about his new permanent nickname, the Wheelbarrow Man, a name he had already heard several hundred times too many.

"So," Jack Liffey said. He pointed to where they were still holding hands. "I thought you were . . . uh. . . ."

"You noticed," Chris Johnson said dryly.

"I hit both ways, and Toni and I weren't working out," Babs explained. "Thanks to you, Chris and I fell in love."

"And you and Dot?" Jack Liffey asked him.

"Things change, man. What can I say?"

Poor Dot, he thought, with her house full of potted plants for her ex-lover's web site. Poor Toni, alone on her MTA bus, undone by her own good deed. But a lot of human sympathy seemed to have drained out of him for the moment. If he could lose Marlena so abruptly, everybody would just have to fend for themselves.

"It's an uncertain world," Jack Liffey said resignedly.

"You can bank on it."

And he still had Marlena to deal with. Someone on the phone had announced that Marlena was coming up to see him "with a friend." He put on a real shirt and motored the head of the bed up to a right angle. He wished it could be Maeve instead, but her mother had discovered all, including the escapade in Fontana, and had grounded her for four or five years without possibility of parole. Maeve called him every day, however, and he'd had a pretty good first-hand account of her wheelbarrow trip, plus giggled previews of a few new oddities she was saving up for him.

She had also told him about the metal oblong from his pocket, and they had laughed about the loyal old Concord saving his life, the door handle turning a deadly bullet into two broken ribs. Actually, as he told her, it was the second time the car had saved him from the fanatics of Gideon's 300—who, it turned out, had expired themselves in a hail of gunfire generally attributed to the Rolling 60s Crips. He wished he still had the door handle as a souvenir, but it had gone the way of all mementos of chaotic days. What was that Chinese curse? *May you live in eventful times.*

He knew how lucky he was, to be alive still and to have Maeve as a daughter.

This, he thought, was the first detective job he'd ever had that had actually taught him a positive moral lesson, instead of battering his ethics to the ground with a club. Even if he'd learned the lesson second-hand, from Maeve's phone calls. It was simple, really: If you truly need help, go to the poorest of the poor. They don't think twice.

He thought of the Reverend Lawson: *You never have to explain to people why you're doing the right thing. They know.* It seemed to be part of the same lesson, but he couldn't quite put it together.

The door came open a little, and Marlena peeked cautiously into the room. "Jackie, you decent?"

"Many people have wondered," he said, but he wasn't actually feeling very witty. The instant he saw the rich brown skin of her wonderful face, he wanted her desperately.

"Maybe it's not a good time, but I want you to meet my friend Willis Eversharp. Willis, Jack."

They eyed each other. He was too young by maybe a decade and too handsome, with one of those chiseled faces that Marlena watched on soap operas. The man stuck out his hand and Jack Liffey thought, What the hell, and took it.

"I'm pleased to meet you," the visitor said. It almost seemed he was about to add *Sir.*

"Willis." It was all he could muster, his heart sinking slowly in the west.

"We found Loco, Jackie. He come home with his tail between his legs and dug right back under the fence again, looking pretty sheepish. No telling what he done."

"If he's one of the dogs who ganged up on Maeve," Jack Liffey said, "his ass is toast."

"I don't know how to find out."

"Me neither. He's part coyote, and he's always had a pretty big disloyal streak." He realized what he'd just said and winced. "I didn't mean anything."

"That's okay."

"Willis, could you give us a couple minutes? I won't make this painful."

The man bobbed his head. "I'll be right here, hon." He nodded to Jack Liffey and went out the door, trying to make as little noise as possible, and Jack Liffey decided her new beau might not be such a bad sort.

"You happy, Mar?"

"I'm very happy, Jack. Him and me always like to do everything together—you know, church and lots of other stuff."

Some of the "other stuff" didn't bear thinking about. Implicit in what she said was the fact that there were a lot of things Jack Liffey had never done with her, and attending that fundamentalist millenarian church was certainly one of them. They did everything but hurl snakes. "Tell me one thing—and I want you to swear on Jesus. He didn't give you that black eye a couple weeks ago."

"Honest, Jackie, I swear on my holy faith." She raised one hand and put the other over her heart. Actually, over her breast, he thought, but he tried not to think about that. "It really was a stupid accident. Willis is very sweet with me."

He shut his eyes and nodded. "Okay. I'll just say this once. I still love you very much, Marlena, and I miss you, and I want you as a friend and a lover both, and if I knew how, I'd fight to the death to get you back, but if you're sure about this and you're happy and you need this guy, I give you both my blessing."

"Oh, Jackie, *thank you.* That's so sweet." She bent and hugged him, and the smell of her had him on the edge of tears.

"You'd better go now."

He was still pretty shaken and depressed an hour later when Genesee Thigpen came in with Ornetta.

"I've got to talk some things over with Bancroft," she explained. "Ornetta would love to sit with you for a while, Mr. Liffey."

"I'd love to have her."

The girl came shyly to the bed and felt his forehead with a small gentle palm. "You warm," she observed happily.

"I sure hope so." He remembered he'd been in shock the last time she had seen him.

"We owe you some money," the woman said.

"Don't worry about that now. *Please.*"

"Okay, but we remember our debts and we pay them." She rested a hand briefly on Ornetta's shoulder. "I'll be back shortly."

"Uh-huh. It okay, Nana."

The woman left and Ornetta boosted herself into the stiff visitor chair. She got right to the point. "When we was together, Maeve promised you could be my sort-of daddy. Maeve and me blood sisters. We touched blood." She showed a finger, but there was nothing to see.

Jack Liffey smiled. "How about uncle?"

The girl seemed to relax all at once. She gave a short laugh. "Uncle Jack. Uh-huh, uh-huh."

"You remember the first time we met?" he asked. "You were sitting in the front yard, and you told me about the revolt of the rhinestone animals."

She beamed.

"Nice story," he said simply.

"Do you know about the mean ol' dogs?" the girl offered. "And the magic wheelbarrow?"